KT-163-747

Praise for Richard Crompton

'A compulsive whodunnit set in Kenya, where tribal politics can get you killed' Ian Rankin on *The Honey Guide*

'[Crompton] has done something near-miraculous and made the figure of the incorruptible loner-detective fresh again'
Daily Telegraph

'A smashing debut, as fleet-footed as the warrior himself. It will make you long for the next instalment'
Financial Times on *The Honey Guide*

'Crompton writes with ease about traditional customs and the impact on Kenya of globalisation, creating a vivid portrait of a country struggling to come to terms with modernity'
Joan Smith, *Sunday Times*

'One of the most gifted crime writers of his generation'
Shots Magazine

'What really elevates the book is Crompton's experience as a journalist. He is able to bring depth to the story by examining the difference between the law and justice, not just in everyday Kenyan life, but in international politics and in the way that globalism has not just brought wealth to the poorer countries but also suffering' CrimeFictionLover.com

NIGHT RUNNERS

Richard Crompton is a former journalist for the BBC and other broadcasters, who lived for many years in East Africa. Richard won the *Daily Telegraph* Short Story Award in 2010. He lives in New York with his wife and young family.

richardcrompton.com

Also by Richard Crompton

The Honey Guide
Hell's Gate

NIGHT RUNNERS

RICHARD CROMPTON

First published in Great Britain in 2018
by Weidenfeld & Nicolson
an imprint of The Orion Publishing Group Ltd
Carmelite House, 50 Victoria Embankment
London EC4Y 0DZ

An Hachette UK Company

1 3 5 7 9 10 8 6 4 2

All the characters in this book are fictitious, and any resemblance
to actual persons, living or dead, is purely coincidental.

A CIP catalogue record for this book is
available from the British Library.

ISBN (Hardback) 978 0 297 60913 1
ISBN (Export Trade Paperback) 978 0 297 60914 8
ISBN (eBook) 978 0 297 60915 5

Typeset by Input Data Services Ltd, Somerset

Printed and bound Great Britain by Clays Ltd, Elcograf S.p.A.

www.orionbooks.co.uk

For Katya

CLOSE SHAVE FOR BOMET NIGHT RUNNER AS VILLAGERS NAB HIM IN THE ACT

Against the backdrop of government rejecting a bid to have their nocturnal antics recognised as legitimate recreational activities by the sports ministry, a night runner was last Wednesday caught in the act nude by villagers in Borabu area, Bomet County.

The 38-year-old man, only identified as Nyangure, survived death by a whisker after locals unleashed terror on him, accusing him of engaging in an ungodly activity closely associated with witchcraft.

The Standard, *Kenya, 27 February 2017*

1

If the raindrop goes up, she'll tell him. If it goes down, she won't.

She rides this route every day. Unlike the others – the busy ones, the hurries – she does not board the first number 36 that comes along. She loyally waits for GOD KNOWS, even if it's raining.

She clutches her ten shillings. The other *matatus* put up the price when it rains. Demand is higher. People don't want to walk. They don't want to reach their destination with their shoes caked in mud. But GOD KNOWS charges ten bob, rain or shine. It's one of the reasons she loves this one.

She also loves the *kondo's* friendly smile. She's at an awkward age: still a child, but apparently, in the eyes of many, almost a woman. Some of the *kondos* don't hesitate to remind her of this. They lean out of their doorways, eyes red and clothes stinking of *bhangi*, leering at her, crotch-grabbing, cat-calling. —*Sasa*, baby. Where you headed? I got a ride for you.

The conductor on GOD KNOWS is not like the other *kondos*. He's older. He's not a wannabe gangster. More like a grandfather. When the *matatu* skids to a halt, he doesn't throw the door open and shove the passengers inside, harrying and mocking the laggards. He actually says *good morning*. He's a gentleman.

And the driver. He doesn't attempt to weave his fourteen-seater through traffic like a rat through trash. He actually stops at junctions. Waits for pedestrians to pass. Lets other road users in. He queues to disgorge his passengers at the stand, rather than screeching to a halt in the middle lane of moving traffic and have his *kondo* chuck them out.

Nairobi is not a patient city. You have a place to be; you need to get there. In her case, it's school. Some mornings, she's painfully aware of time creeping past as GOD KNOWS gets stuck behind another donkey cart, instead of blasting it out of the way. She knows that BEYONCE or ARSENAL or TERMINATOR would have got her there by now, and she'll be in trouble if she's late for school one more time this week. But still she remains loyal.

And so does one other passenger. He is the only one who shakes his head at the other *matatus* until GOD KNOWS comes along. She hardly noticed him at first. Just another guy on his morning commute. Brown trousers tucked into gumboots. Baggy, oversized sweater, holes in the sleeves, but clean. A peaked cap. He could be a gardener, off to the suburbs, or an errand-runner in the city. He barely warranted a second look, and indeed she didn't cast one until, stuck on one particularly boring section of the Jogoo Road, she happened to feel his gaze upon her and turned. His eyes had flickered and slid to the window, as though they had merely rested on her for a moment in the course of idly wandering. But she knew he had been watching her.

Not watching her like the boys did. Or like the old men – though he was certainly old, older than her father, even. He was watching the way a kite watches, perched high up on a wire. She was part of the scene, she was in it; he watched the scene, therefore he watched her. She did not feel affronted. She was not being leered at – her presence was simply being registered. And that, strangely, she found comforting.

Perhaps it was because he was Maasai. They were known for being strange, those plain-dwellers. They lived by different rules. They looked at city streets and saw game-studded vistas; skies which no rooftops or towers could constrain. The watchful eyes were like the looped earlobes which hung low along his jawline, the mark of his kind. He was a warrior. Even in gumboots and a sweater, he could be no other.

She had been looking for someone to tell her secret to, and after a few days she had begun to wonder if it mightn't be him. He shares her loyalty to GOD KNOWS: that is the first mark in his favour. Secondly, the *matatu* crew appear to know him, and trust him, although they don't acknowledge it openly. The *kondo* greets the Maasai like any other as he palms his coins and ushers him aboard. But there is a look that passes between them each day – a blink – that speaks of an understanding. And because she trusts GOD KNOWS, she begins to think she might trust this stranger.

And it has to be a stranger. Too many here know her. Her school, her family. Word gets around. The only way to keep a secret is to carry it yourself. But the weight of the burden is becoming too much to bear.

There's one more reason she feels she might be able to trust this Maasai. It goes against everything she's heard, everything she's been taught. It's a rule ingrained in this city; a mantra mothers teach their children. *Don't tease dogs. Don't play in traffic. Don't trust the police.*

For he is a policeman. Despite his tatty clothing, she is sure of that. She had spotted his handcuffs, clipped to his belt at the small of his back, when he sat. He pulled his sweater down quickly enough, but she had noticed. She was not surprised. The Maasai ears and spindly frame didn't fit with the few policemen she saw regularly, batons twirling lazily, moustaches twitching contemptuously, pot-bellied and prowling for any infraction that might allow them to impose a 'fine'. No, he was not one of those. But his watchful eyes were policeman's eyes, all the same.

If he does not look like other policemen, perhaps he is not like other policemen. Perhaps he is an outsider, like her. Perhaps he will understand.

Today it is raining. The *matatu* is full: unlike others, GOD KNOWS sticks strictly to the 14 PAX MAX ordinance stencilled along its side. Even so, the passengers steam and heave against each other as the vehicle inches along the greasy streets.

The Maasai policeman is there, two rows ahead, just behind the driver. She can see the back of his shaved head, looped ears wobbling every time the *matatu* hits a pothole. Next to him, a mama with a round-eyed, woollen-hatted twin drooling over each shoulder. Between her and the door is the *kondo*, standing hunched, neck and head bowed against the ceiling. His shoulders glisten through his shirt: half his job is outside, in the wet, and only when he has filled the vehicle can he pull himself in and slide the door behind him.

On the next rows, some schoolchildren – not from her school – a smartly dressed young man, and a woman with a basket of trussed chickens, which cluck and flutter in her lap. An office girl applies lipstick with a steady, practised hand, despite the jolts, and pouts into her small mirror. On her own row, the back row, a fat man who winces with every shudder and lurch, and a Somali man of uncertain years with a black robe and a splendid henna-red beard, smiling, apparently, at nothing. Between the two men, trying primly to hold her legs away from both, a tiny middle-aged woman clutching a well-worn Bible that overflows with notes in cramped, spidery letters.

Although she's pressed up against the window by the fat man, she does not mind. She likes looking at the shapes made by the mist. Colours emerge and die. Mundane things like billboards and shopfronts become blazes and flares of light. People walking past are elongated and ethereal.

On top of it all, the rain makes tracks. Droplets flicker their way from left to right, descending when the vehicle slows, and rising when it moves once more. Like ants, they follow much the same path, hesitating sometimes, sometimes striking out in a new direction.

She decides to let a droplet make the decision for her. She chooses one and places her finger against the cold glass nearby. If the droplet passes above her fingertip, she resolves, she will speak to the policeman today. If it passes below, she will remain silent.

Horns blaring ahead. The *matatu* slows. The droplet begins to fall.

Figures passing outside the windows seem to speed up. Around her, the passengers stir. In Nairobi, it pays to be sensitive to the rhythm of things. And somehow, the rhythm has changed. The Somali, she notices, has stopped smiling. The fat man looks as uncomfortable as ever. The middle-aged woman opens her Bible. The mama, occupied with her babies, is oblivious. The back of the Maasai's head reveals nothing.

Something more than the usual city hubbub can be heard outside. Distant voices.

The chicken lady rises. She asks the *kondo* to let her off. He protests that it's not her stop yet. Stay dry. We'll be moving again soon.

She clucks like one of her stock. The conductor relents and slides the door open. Such is her impatience to exit that the basket of trussed birds bangs against one of the schoolboys. She jumps out, glances forward, puts the basket up onto her head and splashes rapidly in the opposite direction.

With the door open, the voices are louder, closer. There is no mistaking it: it is the sound of trouble. Voices of anger and voices of fear. The passers-by are passing by in only one direction now: the same direction the chicken lady went. Away.

The boy who'd been hit by the basket nudges his friend.

They get out too. Picking up on the unspoken warnings, so do the Bible woman and the Somali. The fat man hesitates, torn between his desire to stay seated and dry, and to protect his considerable skin. After a moment, he chooses the latter. He looks down at the girl beside him as he hauls himself up. His look seems to question why she is remaining, but he says nothing.

Now there is just the *kondo*, the driver, the Maasai, and her. And just at the same moment that a break in the raincloud sends a watery glow of gold to illuminate her window, there is the sound of engines revving, and the *matatu* jumps into gear and starts to move.

All this time, her finger has remained upon the glass. The raindrop, which had been similarly stalled, trembles and jerks into life. With an impulsive leap, it flies above where her finger-tip rests, and when the *matatu* brakes sharply, it shakes free of the pane, disappearing altogether.

That's it then. She must speak to him. She smiles, and flattens her palm against the window to wipe away the mist.

She moves her hand away to reveal a scene of carnage. A man's body lies in the road, prone, head bloodied. A cart has been tipped on its side. Another man, holding a bin lid as a shield, crouches behind it.

A dark shape grows: someone running towards the *matatu*, heading straight for her window. He runs lopsidedly, the weight of the rock held aloft in his hand unbalancing him. He releases it.

She feels herself enveloped in softness, and knows it is the Maasai's woollen pullover. There is a muffled explosion and she hears thousands of tiny objects impact around her like gravel.

With a movement swift and strong, arms elevate her, and she is borne. She hears the grinding of the door as it slides open and senses the air change as her rescuer leaps out, suspended for one long, ecstatic second in the air – before movement vertical is transformed to movement horizontal, and she hears his feet pounding the ground beneath.

Then, once again, up – and she feels something cold under her. The pullover pulls away. She is sitting on a high window ledge. Reluctantly her hands move away from him and grasp the grille.

—Stay here, he urges.

She nods.

He turns, and runs back to the stricken *matatu*. She sees now that it has drawn up hard against a barricade of sorts, made from oil drums and metal poles. The man with the bloody head has risen, and is staggering away.

Meanwhile other members of the gang have been laying into the *matatu* like jackals falling upon a corpse. The windscreen has been transformed into a sagging net with a hole punched into its middle. Within, a figure just recognisable as the driver. He is struggling with his seatbelt. From the darkened interior, his eyes flash with fear.

Every time the Maasai attempts to get close, he is met with a jackal's snarl. A long, curved *panga* blade is waved. The corpse is being stripped. Something with wires – the radio, perhaps – is the subject of some bickering, and eventually wrested from one man's hands, the winner scurrying away to melt into the background throb of bodies.

One of those bodies thrusts forward. He is cradling something white in his arms. The white thing flashes and flushes pink, as the liquid within sloshes. He holds the opaque petrol can aloft, like a trophy. A cheer goes up. Everyone loves a bonfire.

A lot of people seem to be screaming, but in fact it is just the driver. His visceral bellow bounces inside the *matatu* and rings from the buildings around it. The scream only pauses as he gulps in air, perhaps aware that each lungful could be his last.

The jackals, smelling danger – and petrol – back away from

the vehicle's gaping ribs. The Maasai seizes his chance. He plunges within. A dance is performed without, the can shaking wildly, spewing liquid that pours down the windows in rivulets like the rain which had been there just a few minutes before.

Coming out of the door like coming up for air, the *kondo*. He sprints to the side of the road and immediately slithers down into a drainage ditch, plunges his hands into the filthy water and scoops it over his head. No sign of the Maasai or the driver, who is not screaming any more. It is not clear whether this is a good or a bad thing.

The Maasai emerges, just as another slew of petrol is thrown over the door. He spits and reaches down. The driver's head is red with blood. The Maasai drags him from the vehicle; the driver's heels dumbly clatter onto the ground as they clear the doorway. The Maasai drags him to the building where she sits. Looking down from her windowsill she can see the driver's face and scalp are covered with hundreds of tiny scratches. Minuscule pieces of glass stud his skin like tiny jewels. His eyes are a sliver of white. She hears him faintly groan.

The ringleader of the mob, having exhausted his petrol can, lets it tumble to the ground. From his pocket he produces a plastic lighter. He smiles and gives it a little shake.

—Kenyan made, he says. —Only works half the time. What do you think, Maasai? Want to take the risk?

—Don't be stupid, says Mollel. —You've made your point.

—Oh no, says the ringleader. —I don't think I have. You see, my friends and I run this route. No one passes through here without insurance. And your friend here would not pay up. Now, that's very foolish. You see, the insurance we provide is fully comprehensive. Accident, theft . . . and fire.

He presses the lighter with his thumb. The wheel grinds. A spark. A flame. He smiles. —How about that? It worked.

He approaches the *matatu*, then gives an arms-length flick, and ducks away as the vehicle *whooms* into flame. Even from where she is sitting, she can feel the heat. —Don't come any closer, Maasai, he continues. —You've got as much petrol on you as that thing. You don't want to end up the same way.

—If I go up, says the Maasai, so do you. He points down at the rainbow trail of petrol in the mud. It connects the two of them. —You're confident that you didn't splash yourself?

A flicker of doubt passes over the ringleader's face. —You're under arrest, says the Maasai.

She does not know what makes her look down at that very moment, but she is glad she does. About to pass almost directly beneath her, another man is creeping forward. She just has time to glimpse a stocky frame, a neatly clipped haircut and beard, and a slick leather jacket. But more important than that, she sees the gun in his right hand.

For a moment she wonders if she will ever find her voice – after all, she has failed to speak to the Maasai all this time. But then the scream comes. —Look out!

The Maasai springs forward. He knocks the ringleader to the ground. The lighter grinds but no flame comes. Thank goodness for Kenyan quality. The man with the gun lands his boot on the ringleader's wrist. Together, he and the Maasai haul the ringleader to his feet. The man with the gun slips it back into his belt, and swaps it for a set of cuffs, which he deftly places around the ringleader's wrists.

And then, in the chaos of the fire being put out, and the wounded taken away, the barricades being dismantled and the gang members rounded up, she realises: the Maasai is gone. She knows immediately that he's done his job here, and won't be riding her route any more. And still, she has not spoken to him.

2

There are a million different stories about how the world was made, where the stars came from, the origins of the animals, of the people, of love, of death. But there is only one Maasinta. For the Maasai, everything starts with Maasinta.

Maasinta was the first Maasai. He was everything a Maasai should be: tall, strong and handsome. He was as gentle as the wisps of mist that cling to the mountainside at dawn, and he was as fierce as a mother buffalo guarding her calf.

It was Maasinta to whom Ngai, the creator, gifted cattle. From that day, all cattle have belonged to the Maasai.

Maasinta had many sons; his second son by his first wife was Lelian. The descendants of Lelian are called Ol-Moleliani, or Mollel, for short.

Maasinta revered his first wife, the mother of Lelian, but he truly loved his second. The first wife was housed in a hut on the right-hand side of Maasinta's. The offspring from this union became known as the *Odo Mongi*, the right-hand moiety.

The cattle of the right hand are red. They are lean, and spirited, and snort when there is danger. They have been known to charge at lions. The *Odo Mongi* are proud, and fierce, and consider themselves the guardians of the Maa way of life.

For all that, in old age Maasinta would turn left more frequently than right. The *Orok Kiteng*, the left-hand moiety, are descendants of Maasinta's second wife. Their mother was young, and plump, and welcoming. Maasinta bequeathed to her sons the black cattle, which are docile and fat. They yield good calves, and good milk, and good meat. They are fine creatures but they are stupid, and often taken, even by wild dogs.

Every clan and every village has its *Odo Mongi* and its *Orok Kiteng*. They are two halves of the same body. Inseparable. When there are decisions to be made, about whether to pack up the houses and move to better pasture; or how to deal with a thief; or whether to make peace or wage war against another clan, the sagest voices are those of the *Orok Kiteng*.

But when it comes to fighting, the *Odo Mongi* will be at the front.

The *Odo Mongi* have taken on the role of custodians of their father's realm. Perhaps it is because they know they are the lesser-loved that they strive all the harder to please him. When there is a question of tradition, the *Orok Kiteng* defer to their brothers.

When an *Odo Mongi* marries an *Orok Kiteng*, it is the father's name and moiety that is taken. Hence Mollel. But a calf sired by a red bull and black cow may be red, or black, or mottled. No one would dream of blaming the calf for that, or trying to make them be something different. And yet an *Odo Mongi* boy cannot be mottled. No nuance for him. He is expected to react, not reflect; to instigate, not investigate. Each of the two moieties tempers and complements the other. The two impulses exist side by side. They are not supposed to reside in the same person.

But it happens. Mollel was one such mottled calf. He grew up with his *Odo Mongi* father largely absent; his mother was *Orok Kiteng*. She left her son in no doubt that she blamed *Odo Mongi* traits for her husband's betrayal. Pride, Mollel learned, is both essential and shameful; impulsiveness is admirable, but dangerous. He grew up scorned by his peers for his caution, and when he tried to prove them wrong, he was scolded by his mother for the bruises earned by his bravery. He was constantly second-guessing how he should behave, and his hesitancy hung like a banner proclaiming his dilemma.

His brother showed no such ambiguity. Lendeva, three years younger, was a full-throated and unashamed *Odo Mongi*, recognised instantly as such by the junior warriors who adopted him as a kind of mascot for their age-caste, even while they deliberated about whether to accept Mollel, now of age, into their ranks.

But he was accepted, and found, in the rigorous training to become a warrior, a certain peace. The warrior's world is one of rules and ritual. There are no shades of grey.

What there is, is a lot of waiting around. A lot of doing nothing. Warriors are the masters of doing nothing – perhaps because their intermittent moments of action are so intense and pure, it would be a shame to spoil them by packing activity into the rest of the time. Warriors enjoy lolling on the short grass between the *bomas*, pleating each other's hair, carving a figure from horn, singing softly and watching the boys do the boys' work of herding and the women and girls do their work of milking and cooking and everything else.

But when they need to – when an elephant, smelling cooking, decides to break through the mud wall of a family's hut at night; or the dogs catch a whiff of a leopard that needs to be chased off; or when some rival warriors from an itinerant clan come smilingly for your sisters – why then, it is spears ready, clubs raised, and more often than not, it is only a show of strength that is needed.

Police work is not so different. Slack time – and there is a lot of it – is spent polishing boots or cleaning a gun, rather than braiding hair and sharpening daggers. If things get really slow, there is always paperwork to be tackled, usually on faded carbon forms in white, pink and yellow triplicate; two fingers picking at sticky typewriter keys.

It is a rare policeman who goes looking for trouble. Most keep their head down and wait for trouble to find them. It usually does. Those moments – those heart-pounding, dry-mouthed moments of stress, excitement and terror – can come from nowhere. That alone makes the form-filling and the boot-polishing worth savouring. You never relish boredom so much as when you've laid your life on the line.

What is lacking from the routine of an ordinary *polisi* on the beat is deliberation. He goes where he is told and he does what is called *the necessary*. And that's enough for most officers. Perhaps a side hustle here or there, if they're the type; God knows the salary's not enough without a little strategic enhancement.

All very *Odo Mongi*. But mixed blood yields strange results. On the *Orok Kiteng* side, there will always be a yearning for something more. Who and what will not suffice – there is a need to know *why*.

It's hard to hang around when you have a mission. Slack time evaporates. Boot polishing is kept to a minimum. Paperwork takes on a new dimension. Read closely enough, patterns start to emerge in the reports. A routine patrol becomes a hunt, of sorts: for things out of place; familiar faces; cars being driven strangely or people walking with no apparent destination. The million different things which say that something's not right or something's about to happen, or someone's got something to hide.

That is how a detective is born.

And often, how they die.

3

Outside *Mji wa Huruma* police post, Kiunga reaches into his pocket and produces a packet of cigarettes. He unwraps it, takes a cigarette out and puts it between his lips, then fumbles for his lighter. His nose twitches as he glances at the petrol-soaked Mollel.

—Perhaps I'll wait, he says, putting the cigarette away again. —You get cleaned up. I'll fill out the paperwork. Then that's it.

There's a tone of regret in his voice which hints at more than just disappointment over the cigarette.

Mollel knows what 'that's it' means. The two of them have worked together for over five years now. Along the way, he's become fond of Kiunga. Come to rely upon his presence, his common sense.

The best relationships, Mollel reflects, are those which fill in your own blanks. With Chiku, his wife, Mollel had only discovered the blanks once she'd gone. The fact that she'd been snatched away from him so suddenly only made the loss more stark. Her compassion had been a deep well which Mollel had fallen upon like a parched man, and over the years, had come to take for granted – so much so, that he'd never learned how to access the same source within himself.

*

Kiunga's most valuable asset was energy. Mollel had energy, too, when the case demanded it; but it was a nervous, dissipated kind of energy that easily switched to long periods of apathy. Yet Kiunga always had it, like a fully charged battery. It proved useful for all those routine jobs which took up the majority of their time: the domestic rows, the abandonments, the petty thefts, the drunken brawls, the bag-snatchers and the dope-dealers. After a while, they could wear you down. But Kiunga treated them all with the same even temperament and diligence, as though every case were his first.

It is that resilient energy which is now taking him elsewhere.

Mollel tries to suppress any tone of resentment as he replies: —Time to move on.

—It's a good opportunity for me, says Kiunga. —Bogani's going places.

That appeared to be the consensus in Nairobi. Joseph Bogani, Superintendent of *Mji wa Huruma*, had been making a name for himself in the city lately. Young and good-looking, he played well in the media, busting the stereotype of the fat, middle-aged senior policeman. His talk of 'zero tolerance' had struck a chord in a society where for too long people felt that a blind eye had been turned to the inconveniences of petty corruption and extortion – such as the *matatu* gangs whose protection rackets pushed up fares and turned every journey into an exercise in fear. Bogani had even persuaded Central to give over two of their top detectives to help break the racket. And now he wanted to keep one of them.

—I'm sure he could find a job for you, too, says Kiunga. —I could have a word.

—Oh, I'm too old, replies Mollel. —I couldn't work for a boss younger than me. Let me stick to what I know best.

—You know what they call him? asks Kiunga. —*Duma*. The cheetah. A legacy of his days at the Academy. He was the country champion, you know. Four hundred metres. Could have gone to the Olympics, they reckon, if he hadn't put his career first. Some say he prefers running circles around the old rhinos at Vigilance House.

—Old rhinos, eh? What does that make me?

—You, boss? You're an elephant. Strong.

—You mean stubborn.

They both laugh. —You're very alike, says Kiunga. —You know what they say about him? *He's too good to be true.* In other words, successful but not obviously corrupt. No smoke without fire. Except in his case, there really is no smoke. But people still think there must be a fire somewhere.

—Let's not talk about fire, please. At least, not until I've changed my clothes.

Kiunga laughs again. —Shows how cynical we've become. But you know, I think he's different. That's what I like about him, Mollel. He reminds me a lot of you.

Mollel tries to keep his voice neutral. —It's a good move for you, Kiunga.

Kiunga goes inside to file the report, while Mollel strolls around the back to find a place to wash. There are two new cars here, gleaming black-and-white paintwork, spotless apart from some traces of mud on the wheels and bumpers. They are quite different from the shabby, dented old Land Rover pickups most police posts are reliant upon. Bogani's high media profile has led to him securing investment from headquarters at Vigilance House – or perhaps the rumours of probity are true, and Bogani's actually spending money on the service which, elsewhere, would have disappeared into someone's pocket.

Mollel finds a tap connected to a hosepipe, turns it, and squats on his haunches between the two saloon cars, using the trickle of cold water to wash the petrol from his hands and face. He takes off his shirt, and holds the pipe over his head. The water runs down his back. He really is like an elephant, he thinks.

—Don't worry too much about the mud, says a voice. —If the cars are too clean, people will think we never use them.

Mollel straightens up. His shirt is balled up in his hand. It looks like he's holding a rag. Bare-chested, in his gumboots and wet trousers, he's not surprised to be taken for the car-washer.

He is surprised, though, that Superintendent Bogani is talking to him. Tall and lean, in his crisp uniform he looks almost as shiny and new as the cars.

—I suppose I ought to get some mud on my boots, too, for the same reason, says Bogani. —I just came out here to look for someone. Perhaps you've seen him. A Sergeant called Mollel?

Mollel raises his eyebrows sheepishly, and Bogani's eyes shift slightly towards Mollel's long, looped earlobes. Mollel sees realisation dawn on his superior's face, and steels himself for a rebuke. Mollel has had enough commanding officers over the years to know that *their* mistake usually turns into *your* problem. He puts down his shirt and snaps into a sharp salute.

Bogani's lips part into a smile. —You don't have to salute me, Sergeant. At least, not now. I'm sorry I didn't recognise you, but we've not officially met. I hear you did good work with the *matatu* gang.

—Sergeant Kiunga made the arrests, says Mollel.

—Kiunga. Yes, a good man. He's joining us here, did you know?

He does not wait to hear Mollel's reply. —I'm hoping you'll help us out with something else before you return to Central. We've had a specific request for your services. At least, I assume it was you they had in mind. They asked for the Maasai policeman and we don't have anyone else around here who fits that description. Now, if you have a change of clothes to hand, perhaps we'll take a ride in one of these nice new cars?

*

Mollel, though a non-driver, has ridden as a passenger long enough to appreciate different driving styles. Kiunga's temperament behind the wheel is decidedly *matatu*: blasting the horn, the engine roaring, nose of the vehicle cutting its way through traffic. Cars, bikes, pedestrians: they'd better get out of the way. Mollel does not relish those journeys.

With Bogani driving, those obstacles seem to just melt away. He is calm and assured behind the wheel, and somehow conveys this authority to the vehicle itself. Of course, the police livery helps. So does the suspension, which glides over the potholed road with barely a judder. The noise and chaos of the city play out beyond the tinted windows like an action movie on a muted television screen. This is the privilege of power, thinks Mollel: to observe. No wonder the politicians don't see the need to change anything.

Bogani is a politician, despite his aura of neutrality. But he's a different sort: the very fact that he's at the wheel, rather than lounging in the back seat, makes that abundantly clear. Instead, Kiunga sits in the back. Mollel can almost feel his discomfort at being the passenger for a change.

As if reading Mollel's mind, Bogani says: —I like to be seen. I like people to know that I'm here.

And then, after a pause: —Do you know why they call this place *Mji wa Huruma*? City of Mercy.

Looking out at the remorseless grey concrete blocks, the teeming people forced into and among the traffic, the storekeepers in their pig-iron kiosks and street hawkers trying to eke out an existence, Mollel shrugs. He had always assumed it was another example of that acute Nairobi sense of irony that imparts a little humour – if not humanity – to such scenes.

—There was a convent here, long ago. The Home of Mercy convent. They had a farm, gardens. It was a lovely spot. Or so they say.

A man driving a donkey-cart glances at the passing police car and lowers his stick – and his eyes – deferentially.

—The thing was, the sisters never had the heart to turn anyone away. Even as the British were evicting the smallholders and chopping down the trees for coffee, the people just kept coming. They planted cassava in the flower beds. Shelters and shops sprung up all around the chapel. And word got out, there was mercy to be found here. Food doled out from the convent kitchen. A clinic. A school which taught the white people's language and didn't even charge.

—In Swahili, *Mji* can mean *home*, or *city*. Gradually, this place turned from one thing, into the other. The quality of mercy changed, too. The convent couldn't afford to look after the community around it. The sisters got old, or tired, or died. But the city stayed.

—And the home? asks Mollel.

—It still exists, replies Bogani. —There's even a nun or two, buried around here somewhere.

He pulls the car off to the unpaved side of the road. Ahead, a crowd has gathered.

—If I'm not mistaken, this is our destination. Looks like I'm going to get my boots muddy after all.

The faces say it all: something unusual is happening. There's almost a carnival atmosphere. Nothing brings quite so much pleasure to the masses as someone else in trouble. Women chatter and speculate, eyes dart around, ears strain for the next sensation, necks crane for a better view. Children duck and weave through legs.

—Make way, says Kiunga, separating those ahead of him with wide sweeps of his arms, as if he is parting corn. —*Polisi.* Coming through.

Mollel follows in his wake.

A scream, and looking up, the crowd sees a number of small white discs blooming at a window high up on one of the grim grey housing blocks. The discs fall, wobbling, seemingly suspended, before there is a crash as they shatter on the ground below. The crash is greeted with cheers and clapping. A large woman in a dressing gown rushes forward and picks up one of the shards. —My plates! she shrieks. Her distress is greeted with laughter. All part of the show. She turns to berate the crowd. —You wouldn't laugh if it was you! Who's going to pay for these, eh? That little witch. When I get her . . .

A policewoman, only slightly less large than the lady in the dressing gown, steps forward and grabs her arm. Just in time, she pulls the woman back. A round aluminium *sufuria* lands with a clatter just inches from where she had been standing.

—I'll throw it all! cries a shrill voice from above. —I'll set fire to the place! I'll burn the whole building down, if you don't get the Maasai here!

People start turning, pointing. Mollel feels all eyes upon him. Despite his ordinary clothes, his earlobes mark him out unmistakably as Maasai.

Apparently he has a role in this drama – he just wishes he knew what it was.

—Thank goodness you're here, Sir, says the policewoman to Bogani. —We've got a thief in there. Grabbed a bag from one of the stalls and ran into the apartment building. Pushed her way into the communal kitchen and locked herself in. She's been making no end of trouble for the last hour. As I told you on the phone, she keeps saying she wants to speak to the Maasai policeman.

Bogani turns to Mollel.

—That has to be you. Any idea who she is?

Mollel shakes his head. —She sounds like a child.

—She is, Sir, says the policewoman. We've been trying to trace her parents, but we've not found anyone here who knows her.

A sound, a little like rain, and then small, hard dots hail down on their heads. Mollel raises his hand. Others around him are doing the same. The children fall gleefully to the ground, like chickens scrabbling for meal. Kiunga bends to pick up something between his fingers. He shows the small, brown bead to Mollel.

—Cowpeas.

The crowd, having already clocked Mollel as a player rather than another spectator in this free performance, turns expectantly towards him.

He steps forward, coughs.

He calls out. —Hello?

His voice seems laughably weak. He tries again. —Hello? This is Sergeant Mollel. You're . . . are you asking for me?

A hundred faces turn away from him – disappointed, he feels, in his failure to rise to the occasion.

—Come up, the child's voice calls back.

Instinctively, Mollel looks over at Bogani, who nods.

—You *are* going to arrest that little witch, aren't you? demands the dressing gown woman.

—What are you going to charge her with?

Before Mollel has a chance to respond, Kiunga quips: —Disturbing the peas.

The crowd has got the punchline it wanted. To the sound of raucous laughter, Mollel plunges forward and enters the building.

Immediately he's struck by the familiar smell of numerous families living in close proximity. A smell simultaneously cosy and repulsive: cooking, charcoal smoke, laundry soap, sweat, drains, bleach. The narrow stairwell, with steps of gritty unfinished concrete, is unlit. He puts his hand out to the wall. A strip of glossy sheen in the darkness shows where countless others have done the same.

It's a relief to escape all those eyes upon him. He's confident Kiunga will be doing his thing: playing to the crowd, keeping a lid on things. The mood out there was good-humoured, for the moment. But now the action has moved indoors, there is a danger they'll start to look around for some other distraction. Get restless. It doesn't take much to turn a crowd into a mob. Bogani says he wants to be seen; let him see what that feels like when he's facing down dozens of restive locals.

But somehow, Mollel knows that between them, Bogani and Kiunga will manage the situation. They'll get this lot moving, and make them think they're doing so of their own volition. It's the kind of cajoling Kiunga does so well.

The landing is a press of bodies. Backs: wide ones, scrawny ones, flowery-patterned ones and grey, threadbare ones. All female. Mollel coughs again, then, as no one turns, he barks: —Police! Let me through!

Their eyes recognise his status, if only grudgingly his authority. *This is our affair*, they seem to be saying, *steer clear of it*.

Nonetheless, with a bit of pressure on some fairly solid flesh, he pushes his way through. The kitchen door is heavy, as a communal door needs to be. Mollel has seen enough of these apartment blocks to know that the pattern of kitchen and bathroom will be repeated on each floor, with the tenants of each landing possessing keys to both. That way, if your *ugali* is pilfered or your toilet fouled, the last of the suspects is limited to your nearest neighbours.

—The key? he demands.

Four or five hands jangle keys at him.

—Don't you think we've tried that? replies one voice, louder and more scornful than the others. —She's bolted it from the inside.

—Are you the mother?

—God, no. She's no one's child. No one here. She doesn't belong here at all!

The woman reinforces her point by banging on the door. The dull thud of her fist tells Mollel everything he needs to know about his chances of kicking it in – not that he was planning to.

—Hello? he calls, tentatively. —This is Mollel. The policeman. The Maasai. You were asking for me.

Silence, then a metallic rasp. A bolt being drawn back. The door gives, barely perceptibly. The ladies on the landing rise as though to strike. Mollel stills them with a glare. He turns to see a large, dark eye looking up at him through an inch-wide gap.

Then the gap widens a few inches more, and the person steps back: an invitation, not a surrender. Mollel slips inside, and the door slams shut behind him. The bolt is slammed back into place.

—I don't think you'll need that, says Mollel.

The girl looks down at the meat cleaver in her hand, its solid blade stained with rust and blood. She laughs.

—It wasn't for you. It was for *them*. I thought they might try to force their way in.

—And you'd use it?

She shrugs. She places the cleaver on the counter beside her. Although he hadn't felt threatened, Mollel is policeman enough always to appreciate the sight of a lowered blade.

With the weapon no longer his focus, and his eyes growing accustomed to the light of the kitchen compared to the dingy landing, Mollel appraises the girl. And with a shock, realises he recognises her.

—Yes, she says, seeing the look of recognition. —You saved me from the *matatu* gang.

—It wasn't you they were after.

—You saved me, just the same.

Mollel feels awkward. He's never appreciated hero worship – especially when it's unwarranted. The girl had been in the way. So he'd put her to one side. Truth be told, he'd forgotten about her the instant he'd turned away from the ledge, leaving her to get down, somehow, by herself: a big jump for such a small girl.

He looks around him. The little kitchen does not show as

much disarray as the sounds from the street had led him to believe. Two pans rest on the ledge of the window. These, Mollel assumes, were the source of the banging. A plastic bag, one or two forlorn peas still clinging on in the corners, sits beside them.

—I'll pay for the peas, the girl says. —I'm not a thief.

—I didn't say you were. So this, then . . . it's your way of saying thank you?

She shakes her head. Casts down her eyes. Suddenly, plump, shining tears form under her dark lashes and fall swiftly down her cheeks.

Mollel would rather be banged up in an interview room with the toughest convict than face this.

Her shoulders begin to shake.

How can this tiny creature, convulsed with silent grief, be the source of the shrieking hurricane which had, just minutes before, brought an entire city block to a standstill?

Mollel knows the answer, for he is a father. Extremes of passion are one of the few privileges of that mysterious condition known as childhood. And his fatherly instinct gives him understanding, if not guidance. It had been the work of an instant to pluck this girl from the bus, when she had been in mortal danger, and place her out of harm's way. Yet now, when she would probably appreciate it even more, Mollel cannot bring himself to extend a consoling hand.

Displays of emotion were not permitted when he was a child. Tantrums had been unknown to Mollel. Tears had come, occasionally – usually in relation to pain – but had to be hidden. Half a lifetime later, he'd watched his own son go through the same learning process. It had been with a strange mixture of regret and relief that he'd seen Adam, even before he could speak, conclude that Mollel was not a father to turn to for comfort. Thankfully, that was a role the boy's grandmother had been eager to fill.

The girl in front of him appears to have come to the same realisation about him. Without changing her stance, her chin rises. A sleeve is quickly brushed across her cheeks. The transformation is settled with a sniff and defiance returns.

—I had no other way to contact you, she says. —I don't have a phone. They watch me all the time. At school. At home. My only time alone is on the *matatu*. That's why I won't let my mother drive me to school. Not that she'd want to, anyway.

A look of sadness. Then:

—When I saw you on the bus, I thought you'd be able to help me.

He begins to understand now. All week he'd been riding that *matatu*, and he'd hardly noticed her. Yet she'd been fixating on him, to the point where even speaking to him was loaded with so much hope and fear of disappointment that she hadn't dared to do it. Then, when she saw that he had completed his mission, she had realised she would not see him again.

If his pride is flattered by her faith in him, as a stranger, it is also dented by the realisation that his disguise had been so easily seen through. Thankfully, most people are not as observant as a child.

—All day at school I kept kicking myself. I'd lost my chance. Then on the way back, I realised it was now or never. I didn't know where I was, she explains. —I just yelled for the *matatu* to stop and jumped out. I had to get the attention of the police somehow. I ran into this building and started a riot. I knew you'd come when I asked for you.

A thump on the door. —Get a move on in there! People want to cook.

—Go cook your head!

She's a changeable one, this girl, but Mollel admires her spirit. They share a grin. Then her smile drops. She's been waiting so long to say it, she hardly knows where to begin.

—It's my sister. She's missing.

Now that he is on more familiar territory, Mollel's instincts harden, his awkwardness evaporates. He does his job. He conducts the girl through a patient, well-worn catechism: *What's your name? What's your sister's name? How old is she? When did you last see her? Parents? School? Friends? Boyfriend?*

This is what he learns. He is speaking to Maryam Lepui. Maryam is twelve years old. Her sister, Fatuma, is sixteen. She'd recently been sent away to boarding school.

—Boarding school? interjects Mollel sceptically. Surely all this fuss couldn't be down to something as simple as a girl pining for her sister?

Maryam shakes her head. —That's where she's missing *from*. She promised she would write to me every week. I got letters for the first six weeks. She was meant to come home for mid-term break, but she never did. And then no more letters, either.

—Have you asked your parents?

—My mother, *he's* not my father, they say don't worry. Everything's *sawa sawa*.

Mollel's brow wrinkles.

Something tells him that everything is not *sawa sawa* – far from it. He trusts this little girl's instincts. After all, she had had the sense not to walk straight into *Mji wa Huruma* police post with this story, which would probably have got her nowhere. She had, just by looking at him, known that he would listen to her – and she had been right.

—Which school is it?

—It's called Brightstart Academy. In Dandora.

—Have you tried calling?

She shakes her head. —No phone.

—You know it could be nothing, don't you? She might just have got bored of writing letters.

Again, Maryam shakes her head. —She wouldn't.

—Did she ever write about anything that was troubling her? Any issues?

—They weren't that sort of letter, says Maryam. —They were more like . . . poems.

Mollel guides Maryam out of the building, past the mutters and curses of the assembled women. Outside, Kiunga and Bogani are chatting – or at least, Bogani is talking, and Kiunga appears to be nodding at appropriate moments. Mollel notices that his colleague's hand keeps twitching towards his jacket pocket. It must be agony for him, being with the boss. Usually, Kiunga would have consumed at least two or three cigarettes in this time.

—Ah, says Bogani, seeing them approach. —So this is the young lady who thinks the best way to call the police is to make a scene. What do you think, Sergeant? Do we take her in?

—I think a word with her parents will be enough, Sir. I'd like to take her home now, if you don't mind me borrowing Kiunga and your car.

—Very good. You can drop me on the way.

The first thing Kiunga does, after dropping off Bogani, is pull out his cigarettes. Mollel, on the back seat beside Maryam, coughs. Kiunga takes the hint, sighs, and places the packet on the dashboard.

—Where to? he asks the girl.

—Runda.

—Really? Kiunga turns around in his seat. —You mean, you want me to drive through Runda?

—No, says the girl, calmly. —I live *in* Runda. Frangipani Avenue.

—Well, says Kiunga, —I didn't realise we had a VIP on board.

The boundary between *Mji wa Huruma* and Runda is as stark as the line between a freshly ploughed field and virgin turf. Which is, of course, exactly how it began. A place of scrubland, woodland and a few small-scale farms was given over to the coffee bush. Those who had previously lived there – and those who came for jobs – congregated beside it, around the convent, and thus the City of Mercy was born.

The beans proved to be far from magic, though. By the 1980s, as Nairobi grew and spread, the plantation owners realised there was more money in real estate. There was a growing market for what were dubbed *Ambassadorials* – sprawling villas on half-acre plots, with en suite bathrooms, guest annexes and servants' quarters. They were snapped up by politicians, business people, and the diplomats working at the newly created UN African headquarters nearby.

And so the City of Mercy found a new purpose – as a dormitory to the housegirls and garden boys, the nannies and drivers, the cooks and night guards required for this blossoming Nairobi Beverley Hills. The workers were welcome – as long as they knew their place. So a high wall was built, and a barrier placed across the access road running between *Mji wa Huruma* and Runda, attended by guards with smart uniforms and ugly batons.

One of those guards now gives Kiunga and his passengers a surly salute as he releases the chain to swing the barrier gate up and allow the police car to pass.

The sound changes immediately as the road beneath them shifts from dirt to tarmac. On either side, protected by kerbstones, there run that most unusual of Nairobi sights: pavements. Spaced evenly alongside them are streetlights, which, equally unusually for Nairobi, still have bulbs and will presumably all be working come nightfall.

Maryam directs them, left here, right here, until they come to a street sign – another endangered species in this city – announcing Frangipani Avenue.

—This one.

They pull up at a large metal gate and Kiunga, almost

apologetically, parps the horn. A guard, who must have been waiting directly behind, opens the gate a crack and glares out. He frowns when he realises he's facing down the bonnet of a police car, and walks lugubriously towards the driver's window. Kiunga whirs it down.

—Police, Kiunga says, somewhat redundantly.

—What do you want?

—We want to come in.

—There's no one home.

Kiunga presses another button and the window beside Mollel rolls down. The guard looks inside, scowls at Mollel, then sees Maryam.

—Wait here.

He retreats behind the gate, but does not open it. After a short wait, a plump woman in an apron and headscarf emerges. She goes immediately to Maryam's side of the car and opens the door.

—Come on, she says to Maryam. But the girl does not move.

—Wait a minute, says Mollel. —We want to come in, too. We need to talk to her parents.

—They're not in.

—Where are they?

—Out.

Kiunga sighs loudly from the front seat.

—You have a phone? asks Mollel. The maid nods and produces one from her apron pocket. Mollel rattles off his number, which she keys in.

—Tell *Mama* to call me when she gets back, he instructs her. Then to Maryam: —Will you be OK?

She nods.

He nods back, sealing a small unspoken contract between them. Then the girl hops out of the car, and the maid ushers her swiftly inside the gate.

4

—You think Bogani needs his car back? Mollel asks Kiunga.

—Eventually, sure. Why, where do you want to go?

Dandora is about ten miles and half a world away from Runda. If *Mji wa Huruma* is a micro-slum on the periphery of Nairobi's smartest estate, Dandora is a township in its own right within the capital. Not quite a slum, not quite a suburb. Slumburbia.

The most noticeable change, even from the air-conditioned saloon car, is the climate. Runda rests in Nairobi's high, leafy west; Dandora is on the edge of the city's eastern plains. The sun seems to beat harder here and a season appears to have passed in the duration of an hour's drive.

This is the hottest part of the day. Forget the blazing noon – around four o'clock is when the city seems to stop absorbing any more heat, sighs, and simply gives up. Instead, it throws the heat back out, from every tin rooftop and concrete wall, the asphalt and the pavements.

But there are no pavements here, unless you count compacted trash as pavement. There are streetlights – or rather, there are poles for them, standing intermittently and skewed, the occasional fitting hanging useless from their peak. The lights serve a different purpose now, as posts for improvised advertising, proclaimed loudly on hand-lettered placards attached with wire. Many of the advertisements are for *Mganga*: healers, as the polite term for them; Witch Doctors as they're more generally known.

Dr. Ibrahim from Kitui, says one. *Dr. Mustafa from Zanzibar. Dr. Akili from Tanzania*. Where they're from seems to be very important, as though their origins might bestow a certain degree of magic. Below the name, many offer a list of ailments they profess to cure:

JOB TROUBLE
MONEY TROUBLE
MARRIAGE TROUBLE
MAN POWER
INFERTILITY
ILLNESS
SADNESS
BAD LUCK
LOST ITEMS
LOST LOVE
DRUGS
SMOKING

—Get out of the way, you *mwanaharamu*! Kiunga curses at a handcart-puller who is not shifting fast enough in front of him.

Mollel, now in the front passenger seat, glances at the packet of cigarettes on the dashboard. Kiunga has left them untouched, presumably for fear of stinking up his new boss's new car.

—Have you ever thought about going to one of those? asks Mollel, thumbing at one of the signs on a nearby post.

—An *mganga*? What for?

—They say they can help you stop smoking.

Kiunga laughs. —I don't want to stop. Smoking is my greatest pleasure in life. Move it, *mfuko ya lami!*

—Some pleasure, scoffs Mollel.

—Oh, you're a non-smoker. You could never understand.

Didn't you ever scratch a mosquito bite? Sometimes it's worth having the itch, just for the sake of the scratch.

—We must be nearly there, says Mollel. You'll be able to smoke to your heart's content then.

—I'm going to, promises Kiunga. —I'm going to smoke one, then I'm going to light the next one with the stub, and smoke that. And after that, a third.

There are no street signs in Dandora, but the locals, enterprising as ever, make up for it. Every shop, kiosk, place of business, clinic and bar has put signs up somewhere – not only on the streetlamps, but notices painted on walls, or on their own metal boards, which bristle at every junction. It's not long before Mollel spots a sign, with a helpful arrow, for Brightstart Academy.

Kiunga swings the car down a narrow side street. A tiny child pulls an even tinier one into a doorway and the car lurches into a pothole; a dog hurriedly gets out of the way. The final building, capping off the street into a dead end, presents a high concrete wall with narrow, barred windows and a metal door on which is painted:

BRIGHTSTART ACADEMY
OUR MOTTO: OBEDIENCE IS LEADERSHIP

As there's nowhere else to go, Kiunga parks the car right up against the wall. They get out, and are immediately assaulted by the noise and heat of Dandora, though that's not the first thing they notice.

—Jesus! says Kiunga, putting his hand to his mouth. Mollel, too, winces at the smell. It's the acrid stench of burning rubbish, undercut with the equally unpleasant odour of putrefaction.

—The wind must be coming off the dump today, gasps Kiunga. —How can people live here?

Dandora boasts the distinction of being Nairobi's garbage

pile. Home to what is – incredibly – the only formal landfill serving this city of millions, the land has been filled a dozen times over and the garbage, piled high, spills into the streets all around. At least in this narrow alley they can't actually see it. But the towering heap certainly makes its presence known. Smell is too mild a word. Odour, reek – they all imply that the nose is the only organ offended. This presence stings the eyes and burns the throat. You'll be coughing it up days later and taste it again when you do. It will stick to your clothes and your hair. This air is malevolent.

Mollel pounds on the door and the centre of the second O of MOTTO opens, an eye appearing behind it. Mollel holds up his ID. —*Polisi.*

There is a clank of bolts being drawn back and the door opens. Behind it is an old man wearing grey overalls, a grubby checked scarf wound tightly around his neck, despite the heat. He holds the door open to admit Mollel and Kiunga.

They step into a dark courtyard. The sun illuminates no more than a corner of it. Windows – barred, like those on the exterior – line the walls, which rise to three storeys. For a school, it's awfully quiet. No buzz of the classroom; no dirgeful chants of rote-learning; no shrieks or playful whoops. The school day does not end at a boarding school, Mollel knows, until the sun is down, so the calm sits ill with him.

Instinctively, Kiunga has drawn a cigarette from his packet and placed it in his mouth. The old man catches his eye, shakes his head and wags a finger.

Kiunga gives a heartfelt sigh and returns the cigarette to its packet.

—We're here to see the head, says Mollel.

The old man points to a sign which says ADMINISTRATION.

—Nice talking to you, says Kiunga, with a wink.

They follow the sign through a doorway and go down a

half-flight of stairs. They must be below ground level now, and a gloomy light pervades. At least the smell is not so bad here. Or they're getting used to it.

The school gives the impression of having grown, rather than having been built. Angles are askew, walls bulge and the ceiling drips with damp. A sudden window appears to look out onto nothing other than a cinder-block wall; a patch of mildew-spotted wallpaper suggests that this corridor was once part of a room. Indeed, one whole side of the corridor is not a wall at all, but a partition of sorts, made, it seems, from old doors – one of which is open.

Sitting behind a laptop computer at a desk in the windowless room is a young-looking woman in a black *buibui* wrapped tightly around her scalp, framing a pleasantly round face.

—We're looking for the principal, says Mollel.

—You've found her.

She half-rises and indicates two plastic chairs in front of the desk. —Please, sit. To what do we owe the honour of a visit from the police?

—How did you know we're police? asks Mollel.

She smiles, and waves her hand at the mobile phone on the desk. —Peter might not be the most vocal person you'll meet, but he's got the fastest texting thumbs in Kenya. Welcome. Please excuse my humble office. We prefer to spend our money on the students here.

Mollel looks around the room. She is right: there are no fripperies. The only nods to decoration are a set of framed certificates: degrees and diplomas in Psychology.

—How many pupils do you have?

—One hundred and twenty-six, she replies. Mollel and Kiunga sit.

—Not one hundred and twenty-five?

—No. Why?

—We're here about Fatuma Lepui. Is she a pupil here?

Mollel has been watching the head's face closely. Her smile does not flicker.

—She was, Detective . . . ?

—Mollel. This is Sergeant Kiunga.

—I'm Sharifa Gatanga. They call me Mama Sharifa. *Mollel.* Why do I know that name?

Mollel does not answer. He wants to be the one asking the questions.

—Tell me about Fatuma.

—She was a pupil here for a few weeks. Not long. Her parents took her out of school about a month ago.

—Did they give any reason?

Still the smile—this time, accompanied by a barely perceptible shrug. —It happens.

—Did they say which school she was moving on to?

—They didn't say anything, at least not to me. They came at night, so the night-duty teacher dealt with them. It's not unusual. Parents often have second thoughts about boarding school when their children have been away for a while. If they want to take them out, we can't stop them. The fees were all paid up, so . . .

She lets her smile complete the thought.

That smile. Perhaps it is because her *buibui* frames her face so completely, leaving no hair or ears or any adornment visible, that the smile demands so much attention. Mollel can't help questioning how sincere it is. Just as he is wondering whether the smile ever changes at all, it suddenly widens, giving a glimpse of even white teeth, and her eyes crinkle attractively. The difference between the fake, guarded smile and the genuine one is like the sun coming out.

—Mollel. I *do* know you! You're *the* Mollel.

He cringes reflexively.

—The one from the American Embassy blast. The one who

kept going back in to save all those people. I remember you from the TV. I must have been about eighteen at the time. You were quite a hero.

Mollel feels his cheeks get hot. —Fourteen years ago, she continues. —Well, well. The famous Mollel.

Whatever hope he'd had of keeping the upper hand in this interview has gone. And before he can speak, she turns the questioning upon him again.

—Why do you want to know about Fatuma?

—Routine enquiries, says Kiunga, coming to his aid.

—Have you spoken to her parents?

—We haven't got hold of Mr and Mrs Lepui yet.

The smile fades for an instant. —Mr and Mrs Lepui? Oh, I see. You mean Mr and Mrs Ngecha. He's the stepfather, you know. I believe her own father died many years ago.

Ngecha. Now it's Mollel's turn to search his memory. As though reading his mind, Mama Sharifa prompts: —Hussein Ngecha. City councillor for this district.

Of course. Now the house in Runda makes perfect sense. City councillors seldom fail to capitalise on their position, and Hussein Ngecha is well known for having what are euphemistically called 'business links' throughout the community.

—I've heard him on the radio, muses Kiunga. —He's always vowing to clean up Dandora. Get the rubbish under control.

Without breaking her smile, Mama Sharifa says: —And yet, nothing ever changes.

—Strange, isn't it, says Mollel, who has regained his composure, —that he should choose to send his stepdaughter to school here?

This time, there is a barely perceptible flicker of irritation in her eyes and the sunshine disappears.

—You mean, why would a rich man send his stepdaughter to a school in the slums, when he could presumably afford something so much better?

—That's not what I meant, says Mollel, backtracking. —From what I understand, he's a vocal opponent of the dump, says it's a health hazard. And yet here you are, next door. But you're right that a man of his means could have chosen anywhere. So why here?

Mama Sharifa sighs.

—This is not just any school, you know, Detective.

—Go on.

Her face is serious now, the smile just a memory.

—We offer some very specialist services here. We don't advertise the fact. But this is a school for what you might call *troubled* girls.

She looks Mollel in the eye, and he holds her gaze, even though it makes him uncomfortable. He feels as though she is looking into his soul. She doesn't need the certificates on the wall to prove she was once a psychologist: the look says it all. For Mollel, who has had experience with the profession – and none of it good – it is an unsettling moment. A reminder of the time, following the explosion, when he found himself at his most raw and exposed, and the police psychologists in whose care he was placed took advantage of that fact.

—I'm sure I don't need to tell you, Detective, she says, —that some conditions carry a certain stigma in our society. It's unfortunate, but there it is. Well, we provide a very discreet service. It's something that many of our parents, especially those in the public eye, appreciate.

Sure, thinks Mollel. Out of sight, out of mind. And what better place to dump a troublesome stepchild?

—Don't get me wrong, says Mama Sharifa, picking up on the tiniest frown of disapproval which had flickered across Mollel's brow. —It's not about hiding people away. It's about giving them the space and security they need to recover. We're delighted when one of our pupils progresses well enough to return home.

—Just a minute, interjects Kiunga. —First you said that she was taken out because her parents missed her. Now you're saying it's because she got better?

Mollel feels a glow of pastoral pride in his protégé. When they'd first worked together, Kiunga would not have picked up on a slip like that. But Mama Sharifa is sharp-witted, too.

—No, Officer. I didn't say either of those things. I said those are both reasons why parents withdraw their children. Like I said, I wasn't here at the time. If you want to know more, I suggest you ask them. Now, am I allowed to ask what this is all about?

Kiunga remains tight-lipped – he's batting this one to Mollel. They don't have a missing person report. Just the word of a twelve-year-old girl.

—Routine enquiries, says Mollel, and quickly counters: —You say this place is for troubled girls. What, precisely, were Fatuma's troubles?

—Do you have reason to be worried about Fatuma, Detective?

Mollel does not answer. Concern rises in Mama Sharifa's face. She takes a deep breath, as though weighing a decision before she replies:

—Fatuma was not easy in her own mind.

—How so?

—She'd been leaving her home at night mostly. Impossible here, of course. Our security is very tight.

—She couldn't have been slipping out to see a boy?

—It wasn't as straightforward as that. There were stories.

—Stories?

—Neighbours reported disturbances. Nothing serious, at first. Strange noises in the dark. Suspicions of a prowler. The stepfather looked out of the window one night, and saw her in the garden. Stark naked.

—How did she explain this? asks Kiunga.

Mama Sharifa shakes her head. —She couldn't. She claimed

to have no memory of the incident at all. But the mud on her body told another story. Over the next few nights, the disturbances got more extreme. Stones being thrown onto roofs and through windows. Mysterious screams. The whole neighbourhood was being terrorised. And then, someone discovered a cat. Its head was wrenched clean off. Only the Ngechas knew about Fatuma's absences. They wanted her to get treatment before she got worse, or was caught.

—Could be quite an embarrassment for a city councillor, says Mollel.

—That's not even the half of it. Have you heard of night runners?

Night runners. The name can bring a shudder to even the least superstitious Kenyan. They're the bogeymen that parents use to chill their children into compliance; the Bloody Mary that teens invoke for thrills. But unlike those characters, night runners are real.

—I was stationed in Western province for a few years, says Kiunga. —That's where the story originates. The Luo, Luhya and Kisii people have always spoken of people being possessed by spirits. From time to time, we'd get a call to investigate vandalism, or a naked person seen at night. It usually turned out to be a prank, or a dispute between neighbours. The occasional pervert. But they were lucky if we were the ones who caught them. If a mob laid hands on them, they'd be lynched.

—What are you saying? Mollel asks Mama Sharifa. —That Fatuma is a night runner?

—It's not really about what we believe, Detective. It's about what *she* believes. At times of severe psychological stress, deep-seated beliefs, such as a belief in night runners, can convert into physical behaviour. We call it 'conversion disorder'. You might say that the subject is checking out on the pressures and stresses of their everyday life, and converting into a different persona. One that is mischievous and unconstrained.

—And naked?

—Free from the trappings of society.

—Did Fatuma have anything to be stressed about?

Mama Sharifa smiles. —You were never a teenage girl, Detective. It's not an easy world for them.

—There are a lot of expensive therapists and psychologists in this city. Why did Ngecha choose you?

—As I said, we have experience in this field. We work with a very well-respected doctor. He takes the view that you have to work *with* the pathology, not against it.

—Meaning?

—Perhaps you should meet him. He can explain this so much better in person.

—I will, says Mollel.

—I'll give you his details. Is there anything else?

She looks at them as though she considers the interview over. Mollel, however, is far from finished with this school. —Was she close to anyone in particular? he asks. —One of the other girls?

—There is Dorcas. Her bunk-mate. I think they were close.

—Can I talk to her, please? Perhaps while I'm doing so, my colleague can speak to the teacher who was on night duty when Fatuma was removed from the school. Is she here?

The smile returns, thin this time. Mama Sharifa shakes her head. —I'm afraid Mr Abdelahi isn't with us any more.

—*Mister* Abdelahi? blurts Kiunga. —You mean to say the night-duty teacher is a man? When did he leave?

—Around the same time. Perhaps a day or two later.

—And you didn't think to mention this to us?

—I assure you, Mama Sharifa says, hardness in her voice now, —the two facts are completely unrelated.

—Where did he go?

—Back to Somalia, I believe. He's Somali by birth. He'd been talking about some interpreting opportunities there for aid agencies. They pay good money for that sort of work. Better than we could afford.

—Do you have a forwarding address for him? Any contact details?

—Perhaps in the files, she replies, glancing at her computer.

Mollel nods at Kiunga, who gets out his notebook. —I'd like to see Dorcas.

Mama Sharifa picks up her phone and selects a number. She sees it connect and then hangs up. The slight figure of the old man appears instantly at the door. He'd obviously been waiting just outside.

—Please take Detective Mollel to see Dorcas.

Peter nods, and indicates for Mollel to follow him. As he goes out into the corridor, he hears Kiunga saying sternly: —Now, tell me more about this Abdelahi.

Silent Peter leads Mollel back out into the courtyard, across it, and through another door, which he opens with a key. This time, instead of descending, they go up. The staircase has the same cavernous quality as the one leading to the head's office; the stairs are made of unfinished concrete and the treads are uneven, nearly causing Mollel to stumble.

A gentle repetitive sound, like blood murmuring in the ears, grows steadily louder as they ascend. Turning on to a landing, Mollel sees a room with the small, barred windows which had been visible from the street. Peter opens the door. A couple of dozen teenage girls, in blue-and-white uniforms, sit at desks within, softly incanting their times tables. They stop as he enters, and the teacher, a portly woman wearing the same style of black *buibui* as Mama Sharifa – only more voluminous – eyes him expectantly.

—I'm looking for Dorcas, he says.

There is a synchronised scraping of chairs as the girls pivot to stare at one small figure at the back of the room. Mollel is left in little doubt that this is Dorcas.

—Well, go on, girl, barks the teacher. Dorcas rises hesitantly, and shuffles to the door. She's small: Mollel judges the girls in this room to be mostly around sixteen and many of them look like women already, despite their uniform and close-cropped hair. But Dorcas is hardly bigger than twelve-year-old Maryam. What a difference between them, though. Dorcas shares none of the younger girl's boldness. She keeps her eyes cast down submissively and her shoulders hunched. Her hands are bunched inside the ends of the sleeves of her threadbare navy-blue sweater, as though she wants to disappear inside it.

Mollel closes the classroom door. It's an inversion of this morning's scene, when he'd been shut inside a room with a fiery girl, and a corridor of curious females outside. This time, it's the girls inside the room who are trying to see through the mottled glass of the interior window. Their faces ripple behind the pebbled panes. What's more, there's a shadow at the corner of the stairs which Mollel is prepared to swear belongs to Peter.

—There's no need to be frightened, Dorcas, he says. —I am a police officer. You can trust me.

Even as he says it, he realises how ridiculous most Kenyans would find that statement. It was so much easier with Maryam: she was the one who had chosen to trust in him.

—You're Fatuma's friend, aren't you? Did she ever speak about her little sister? Maryam?

For the first time, Dorcas' eyes rise to meet his.

—Maryam is a friend of mine, continues Mollel. —She told me about Fatuma. She told me about her poems. Did she ever share her poems with you, Dorcas?

Dorcas nods.

—You were her bunk-mate, weren't you? Could you show me your dorm?

Again, the girl nods. And then, to Mollel's astonishment, she frees one hand from her sleeve and takes his, then leads him up the corridor to another flight of stairs. She goes ahead, her hand trailing behind, softly holding Mollel's as she shows him the way.

This place, thinks Mollel, *is odd*.

The staircase doubles back, and leads out onto the top storey of the building. The whole floor is open at this level. Above them, timber A-frames support a tin sheet roof. The brightness of the timber and the metal suggest this whole level is not more than a few months old; a supposition borne out by the fact that the roof is not even properly sealed against the top of the cinder-block walls on which it perches, and twisted scrag-ends of iron jut out of reinforced concrete pillars which stop just a few feet above the floor, like an amputee's stumps.

This is a common building technique in Nairobi: put on a temporary roof, and stick in another level if and when the bank balance allows. Mollel wonders how many more storeys will follow in the years to come. He tries not to think about the structural integrity of this house-of-cards style of building. He's seen what happens when they come down.

At the far end of the room is a row of basins, some toilet cubicles with no doors, and a plastic curtain which Mollel supposes conceals a communal shower. Along one of the long walls are benches and hooks with shoes underneath and towels, shirts, jumpers and knickers on top. At the other long wall, a set of trunks made out of thin sheet-metal and all painted the same glossy, chipped and scratched blue. Between the two walls there stretch two parallel rows of wooden bunk beds with thin grey sheets and thin grey blankets pushed back here and there to reveal thin blue mattresses. The smell is of soap, sweat and socks, and because the ill-fitting roof renders the space only semi-enclosed, the stench of Dandora makes an unwelcome cameo appearance.

—Which is your bunk?

Dorcas shows him a bed like all the others. She points at the upper bunk.

Mollel indicates the lower one. —And this was Fatuma's?

Dorcas shakes her head.

—The top one, she murmurs. It's the first time he's heard her voice. It is soft and distant, as though she is talking to herself.

—After she left, you swapped?

Dorcas nods. Perhaps the air is fresher up there, Mollel guesses – or perhaps she wanted to be close to her lost friend.

He looks up at the rafters and the pig-iron roof. Not an inspiring sight to look at every night.

There's nothing to be gleaned from this bed, and he moves over to the wall of trunks – metal boxes, of the kind sold on the roadside by the *fundis* who make them on site. All dented and showing signs of rust to varying degrees, but more or less identical. The only way to tell them apart is by the names painted onto them in black brush script, or occasionally stencilled. They all have hasps, but no locks. Mollel guesses that's not allowed.

—Is Fatuma's here?

Dorcas shakes her head. —It was taken.

—When she left?

Again, she shakes her head. —It was here after she left. When I came up from class the next day, it was gone.

This was not what he was expecting. If Fatuma's parents had collected her, why would they leave her trunk behind?

—What did she keep in it?

—Same as everyone else. Some clothes.

—Can I see yours?

Dorcas hesitates, then points at one of the boxes. As she raises her hand, her fingers slip out of the bunched-up sleeve. Her wrist is tiny and birdlike.

Mollel takes her hand: she does not snatch it away, but she holds it firm against his pull. Her eyes meet his, and then fall, ashamed, as he pushes up the sleeve to her elbow. Her forearm is covered in shiny scars, dark against her brown skin. They run sideways; some of them are still scabs.

—Who did this to you?

Not looking up, she whispers: —No one.

—Someone did this.

He takes her left hand and looks at her left arm. It is even worse.

—Are there more? Elsewhere?

She shakes her head, rapidly, definitely. He believes her, but he's unsettled.

—You do it to yourself, don't you?

This time, no response at all. He releases her hand. She quickly balls both her fists up into her sleeves.

He remembers how Mama Sharifa described the pupils here – *troubled* – and does not want to push Dorcas any further. She looks fragile enough to be broken by a word.

Instead, he turns to her trunk. He slides it out and places it on the floor. He glances up at her as he opens it. Her head is turned away.

She's right; inside there's nothing unexpected. Some more items of school uniform, a nightdress, toiletries, some casual clothes. And a notebook.

He picks it up. It's an unremarkable notebook, the kind you'd buy at any local store. It is battered and dog-eared. Mollel flicks through the lined pages. It's full of scrawled letters in childish writing.

—A diary? he asks.

He tries to make out some of the text. The writing is hard to decipher, full of crossings-out and whole sections densely overwritten. He doesn't even know many of the words.

—Is this Sheng?

Sheng is the ever-changing urban patois of Nairobi – a mixture of Swahili, English and tribal languages. Despite hearing it around him all the time, Mollel has never managed to hang on to more than the occasional word. Sheng is slippery – deliberately so. It's not a language for policemen.

Looking closer, Mollel notices that many of the lines have a structure, ending abruptly instead of spanning the whole page. And there are blocks, too. Stanzas.

He recalls Maryam's words about the letters from her sister. *Poetry*.

—This is Fatuma's, isn't it?

Dorcas does not respond.

—I need to take this.

—No!

The girl makes a grab for the book, but Mollel whisks it out of reach.

—Please, she begs.

—I'll give it back. Did she give it to you?

Dorcas shakes her head. —She kept it under her mattress. I could see it from my bunk.

Mollel has an image of Fatuma writing in her book long into the night, stashing it carefully away before rolling over for sleep. He can't believe she would willingly have left it behind. Just like the unclaimed trunk, this does not fit with an orderly departure.

Mollel leaves the school with the notebook, the conviction that something is amiss, and three new names.

The first is Hussein Ngecha, stepfather of Fatuma.

The next is Abdelahi Abdelahi, the missing teacher.

The final name, written on a piece of paper which Mollel has folded into his pocket, is that of the doctor the school head said was treating these troubled girls. Mollel has more than a few questions for this Dr Kanja.

There's also a sense of being observed: looking back at the gate, Mollel sees the eye-hole in the letter O blink.

A sudden cry of anguish from Kiunga makes him turn. Their shiny new police car is covered with swirls and smears, scrawls and splashes and child-sized handprints. A cigarette, unlit, falls from Kiunga's hand onto the muddy ground.

5

Mollel believes in night runners like he believes in Maasinta. He believes Maasinta existed, but not that he was a giant, or that he lived for two hundred years, or possessed magical powers. Night runners exist. They exist because people believe they exist.

He first heard about them when he moved to the city. Night runners are not a Maasai myth. They are creatures of villages, town or cities. They emerge in places where you don't know your neighbours, or you do, but you distrust them. In a Maasai settlement, suspicious noises at night are met with a warrior's spear; in the city, going out to confront the disturbance is the last thing anyone wants to do. There, a noise at night is more likely to result in the bedclothes being pulled up, and imagination filling in the blanks.

Every so often, especially in those community police posts stuck onto the fringes of low-income, tightly packed neighbourhoods, one is brought in. Usually, they are battered and bloodied. It takes a mob to restrain a night runner, and there is little care or compassion in the capture.

Sometimes they are subdued, 'those blows to the head won't have helped'. They won't answer questions. There is a smell of drink or *bhangi*. Other times, they seem almost to be playing a role. They spit and jabber and roll their eyes. They lunge at their improvised restraints and when words emerge from the torrent of sound, they are vile, violent curses that rain down on the heads of all around, the hapless police in particular.

Occasionally, though, the night runner will retain some kind of composure. That's the most unsettling of all. Something in the cool detachment with which they observe the chaos around them suggests a kind of amused superiority; as though they belong to a higher level of existence and it is everyone else, not they, who is confused. Children. The ones to be pitied.

All three types, though – the stupefied, the skittish, and the serene – have much in common. Firstly, trying to get any answers out of them is futile. It's like conversing with someone in a different language. They can't, or won't, explain why they were abroad at night, prowling round other people's compounds, looking in their windows, rattling their door handles.

The second thing they all have in common is that they're naked.

No one knows why nakedness is a defining factor for night runners. It's unusual to sleep naked inside the homes of the areas the night runners frequent. These are places where people seldom live alone; there are often whole families, or multiple families, within the single-room structures. When nature calls, it means a trip to a communal latrine and possibly picking one's way across sleeping offspring, siblings and cousins. This is not the place to be naked. Besides, up-country the nights are cold, and in the lowlands mosquitoes are always close by and eager to home in on exposed flesh. No, nakedness is reserved for babies, conjugals and ablutions. Their nakedness is the most visible sign that there is something wrong, and otherworldly, about night runners. They're not just sleepwalking.

Hence it is the first sign that they're coming out of their spell – or whatever it is – when they wrap their police blanket around them in their cells.

Answers are not forthcoming. Sometimes, not often, they may confess to remembering at least some of *what* they did.

Never will they admit *why*. Ask them, and the shutters go up, the eyes pivot away, and the lips press tightly shut. For, just as it is *known* that night runners prowl around naked, it is also *known* that they cannot, or will not, explain what they do.

And there is some sense in this. While the mystery remains, it provides a form of defence. After all, you can't be guilty when you're out of your mind.

Out of your mind. That's what the *wazungus* call it. Like an unattended car, a train with no driver. You've stepped away for a moment, and there's no telling what damage may be caused in your absence.

But even that suggests some responsibility. When Kenyans speak about it informally, they don't use such a passive tone. You don't slip out of your mind the way you let a cloak slip from your shoulders. Someone takes it from you.

No one goes out of their mind. *Someone else* gets into it.

The blame is usually placed squarely on witchcraft. Mollel's seen plenty of it over the years. Jumpers from bridges. The ones who lie down in front of the Kibera train. The ones who step out just as an eighteen-wheeler truck is roaring down the Mombasa Road. They're the worst; they usually manage to take the driver with them.

These are your everyday depressives. Possessed, certainly, but not by any supernatural means. They might be possessed by the love that forgot them, or the debt that won't. Or maybe it's just the inescapable insight that whatever they do, whether they live or die, the world will go on without them, exactly the same, which is to say, badly.

It's a curse that all detectives have to live with. All, except the worst ones and the best ones. The best ones learn to leave their badge at the station, they go home and have a beer and put on the TV. No doubt those guys sleep well at night, too. Mollel envies them. They'll make it to retirement without having a heart attack or blowing their brains out with their service issue automatic. The worst ones are pretty much the same, except they never gave a shit to start off with.

The mediocre middle-rankers, though, they often find it far too easy to let someone get inside their head. Usually it's a victim.

There isn't a cop in Kenya who hasn't seen their fair share of dead bodies, even long before they've signed up. And chances are, the first few corpses will be treated simply as cases to be looked into, names to be logged, items to be removed. Especially if there's a crowd, wailing and weeping, with someone pulling the corpse to their breast. They've got people looking out for them, and you've got a job to do.

But then, before long, there's a case that will get through the defences. It's as though the body is asking for help. There's a bond. And the more lonely or despised they were in life, and the less mourned they are in death, the more likely they are to get inside a detective's head. Get a drink or two into them, and even seasoned officers approaching retirement will tell you about their *one*. The victim who never leaves them. For Mollel, it's the killer who really worms his way inside his skull. The victim becomes more like a book that he is reading in order to find out about the killer. How were they killed? Slowly and cruelly? Quickly and efficiently? Maybe it was angrily – a crime of passion is what every detective starts off looking for, because these account for the vast majority of murders. Fury makes for a sloppy alibi, and remorse is the best witness. Look for the guy with the red-rimmed eyes and the bleeding knuckles. Such cases are easily closed.

But with those one in a hundred cases where it's not so clear-cut, Mollel has come to learn that it's not just a case of allowing the killer to get into his head. He has to open the door, and invite them in. Let them take full occupation, if need be.

And that opens up some pretty dark places. Parts of him he didn't even know he had when he started out. It makes him look at the innocent, innocuous little details and wonder – is this it? Is this the thing? For instance, the victim has a crushed windpipe. Where did he put his thumbs? Are the marks still there? And if they are, Mollel puts himself in the killer's place, imagining his own thumbs there, just where the marks are. And he imagines, what is *he* feeling right now? Is it hatred? Anger? Jealousy? Or is he getting off on it?

And then he looks at the corpse, so pristine, nothing else done to it. Just those thumb marks on the windpipe. This was done well. This was done properly. This was something the killer had been thinking about for a long time.

And Mollel thinks, yes, he was getting off on it.

And then he thinks, maybe *I'm* getting off on it.

And there *he* is. Boom. Inside your head.

6

After a brief stop at a roadside pressure wash to blast away the dirt – Kiunga insists – they head back to Runda, and the Ngecha residence. Darkness has fallen on the city, but the streets are still teeming with life. This is not the time for night runners. Not yet.

Pulling up, they don't have to wait for the gate to open. This time, it swings back as soon as they crunch across the dropped kerb. The guard must have received orders that the police were to be admitted.

A curtain twitches within the house, and shortly afterwards the front door opens. A tall man, heavy-set but sleek, and snappily dressed in pinstripe trousers, buttoned waistcoat and a white cotton shirt, walks towards them purposefully.

—Officers.

He extends a hand, which in turn, they shake. —What's all this about? Our housegirl called my wife in hysterics. My step-daughter won't tell me a word.

—Shall we step inside?

—Is this going to take long?

—I hope not, says Mollel, casting a look at the guard, who is standing at the compound gate, pretending not to listen. —But I think we can talk more comfortably inside. May we?

The house is dark and cool, but there is something unhomely about it. The large, vibrant squares of art on the wall of the double-height hallway, the complicated modern chandelier, and the row of low red leather benches give the feel of a hotel lobby rather than a private house.

Their footsteps echo as they pass through into a lounge. Again, it is populated with designer furniture and unremarkable space-filling art. Ngecha offers the policemen a mahogany-armed leather sofa, into which they both, simultaneously, sink. Mollel and Kiunga quickly haul themselves back to a more upright position, perched at the very front of the cushions. Ngecha, meanwhile, chooses to remain standing, hands on hips, and they have to look up at him. The positioning is no accident: he's a politician.

Before he speaks, there is a *clack-clack-clack* and a figure appears at the upper landing. She gazes down at them like a stork upon a rooftop. Her elbows are tucked in at her waist, her forearms raised, wrists cocked, fingers splayed. She has long, blue fingernails. Her hair is meticulously braided against her scalp on one side, on the other it explodes wildly.

—Is this them? she squawks. Without waiting for a reply, she flicks her fingernails at the unkempt hemisphere of her skull and continues: —I'm in the salon and I get a call from Wanjiku, sobbing, to say the police have brought my daughter home. I have to run through the whole mall like this, the whole world *gawping* at me, because I think she might be dead, or hurt, or something. Can you *imagine*?

She clacks towards the staircase and totters furiously down it.

—As you can see, gentlemen, says Ngecha, —my wife is unhappy. And when my wife is unhappy, I am unhappy.

She is wearing skin-tight yellow jeans, a low-cut pink vest top and platform heels the same flashing sapphire as her nails. Mollel, knowing the way his partner's mind works, senses Kiunga's struggle to keep his eyes in his head.

—So what's this all about? she trills, taking her place alongside her husband, mimicking his hands-on-hips pose. In her heels, she's as tall as him; her half-mane gives her the slight advantage.

—We were called out to a minor disturbance this afternoon, says Mollel, —Turns out the minor was your daughter Maryam.

—That one's more trouble than she's worth.

There's something about the way Ngecha's hand twitches towards his belt as he mutters this. As though it would be the work of a moment to unbuckle it, slide it out from its loops, and wrap it once, twice around his palm.

—It was nothing, says Mollel. —We're more concerned about her sister.

A glance passes between the married couple.

—Where is Fatuma now? Mollel follows on, casually.

—At school, says the mother. —With relatives, says the stepfather, simultaneously.

—Which is it? At school, or with relatives?

—Both, says Ngecha. —It's quite simple. We've sent her upcountry to stay with relatives, and join a new school. We didn't like where she was. Did we, Noura?

—No, we didn't, says Noura.

—She's better off where she is.

—Do you have a phone number for these relatives? An address?

—Sure, replies Ngecha. He strides over to a bureau and scribbles in a notebook. He rips out the page and hands it to Mollel. —But it's pretty remote, so don't be surprised if you don't get an answer. They only have network coverage when they go in to town for shopping. It could be just once a week.

Mollel looks at the piece of paper. —This is your relative?

—My wife's relative, says Ngecha. —Her aunt.

—I'm impressed. You didn't need to look up her number or address. I'm not sure many men would know their wife's relatives' contact details by heart.

Ngecha smiles humourlessly. —We're a close-knit clan.

—Detective, says Noura. —I don't know what kind of stories Maryam has been telling you, but she's always making things up. She's a lying little . . .

Ngecha puts his wide hand on her bony wrist.

—She has an active imagination, he says. —All children do. And she misses her big sister. She's been here all her life. It's natural for her to wonder why Fatuma's not with us at the moment. So, no doubt she's made up a story to explain it all away. Something a bit more exciting than the boring old truth, that her sister's gone away to school. I'm sorry you've been dragged in to this, officers.

—Can we see Fatuma's room? asks Mollel.

Anger flashes across Noura's face.

—No, you cannot. We've put up with enough of this silliness!

Again, Ngecha's hand steadies her. This time it slips around to the small of her back, where Mollel and Kiunga cannot see what kind of pressure is applied.

—It's no trouble, he intones. —The officers have a job to do. We have nothing to hide. Please, come this way.

They follow him through a kitchen – Mollel remembers the apron-clad cook who ushered Maryam inside earlier, and doubts that Noura's elaborate fingernails ever risk being chipped on these marble surfaces – and past a well-stocked pantry. There is another door, but standing open against the wall in front of it is a white-painted barred gate, with a heavy padlock hanging open.

Mollel swings the gate slightly. Its purpose is to seal off this inner door.

In answer to his unspoken question, Ngecha says: —It's a security gate, Detective. Surely you've seen one before. All the ambassadorials have them.

—Perhaps we wouldn't need them if the police did their job, adds Noura, sniffily. —Going after the gangs, instead of bothering decent people.

—We have the same on the landing upstairs to seal off the upstairs bedrooms, says Ngecha.

—We lock them every night.

Mollel glances at the barred windows. He remembers Mama Sharifa's description of how Fatuma had been found wandering abroad at night.

—So there's no way out?

—There's no way *in*, Ngecha corrects him. —Maryam has a key, so do we. In case of fire.

Ngecha leads the way into the room. As he does so, his fingers reach up to the ledge above the door, and he takes down a silver key.

—You see, Detective? We're not prison warders.

The room is comfortably furnished with a single bed, a chair and a desk under the window. Despite the built-in wardrobes lining one wall, there are clothes draped on every item of furniture. Fatuma seems to share her mother's love of fashion, if not her taste. These items – carefully ripped jeans, a slashed grey-and-black layered T-shirt, a studded leather jacket – look expensive, even to Mollel's untrained eye. A row of shoes – high-top trainers and heavy black boots, ranging from ankle to knee-length – are stashed under the desk. Mollel walks across the room and looks through another door which leads to a bathroom where colourful bottles and lotions crowd the surface around the sink. Make-up and nail polish in an array of sombre plums, greens and pure blacks.

Despite the clutter, nothing is untidy. The housekeeper, presumably, is to thank for that. It's all a very different world to the bare, open dormitory on the third floor of Brightstart Academy. But Mollel is not sure which feels lonelier.

Returning to the room, Mollel looks at the bookshelf above the desk. He recognises some of the names on the books: his wife, Chiku, had loved poetry too. Khadambi Asalache, Micere Mugo, Ngũgĩ, of course. And Plath, Dickinson, Byron, and a host of other *mzungu* names he does not know.

On the desk are a pair of speakers like little black-and-chrome obelisks. They're linked by a wire, which trails forlornly into the only clear space on the desk. Mollel picks up the small cylindrical jack which comes off the end of the wire.

—It's for a music player, says Kiunga.

—I know that, replies Mollel.

His son Adam has one which his grandmother bought for him. Apparently these things can contain a million tracks, or something of that order. How they work, Mollel has no idea.

—That's the reason she's down here, in case you're wondering, says Ngecha. —This is the guest room, really. This way she can play her music without bothering those of us who have to work for a living.

—At night? asks Kiunga.

—You don't know how peaceful it's been lately, sighs Noura.

—I see the speakers, but not the player, says Mollel.

—She must have taken it with her, replies the mother. —She has her headphones on whenever she gets the chance.

—This dreadful *rap*, adds Ngecha, nodding at the posters on the wall. They display a variety of figures, many holding microphones, others striking ludicrous poses, all scowling, the men in slouchy, low-slung jeans and oversized sports jerseys, the girls in tight pants and bikini tops. Plenty of exposed brown flesh for swirling blue-black tattoos to disfigure.

—Do you know any of these guys? Mollel asks Kiunga, who is the closest thing present to an authority on youth culture.

—Some of them. This one, Kiunga replies, pointing to a poster emblazoned with the words *Nyambisha Karao*. The same face glares out of many of the pictures on the walls. —He's pretty popular right now. But not really my cup of *chai*.

—Have you seen enough, Detectives? Noura asks wearily. —Convinced, now, that we don't have our girl locked up here against her will?

—We have, thank you, says Mollel. Then, with mingled disquiet and caution: —I hope you won't be hard on Maryam. As you say, she's just missing her sister.

Ngecha laughs. —Oh, don't you worry about Maryam, Detective Mollel. We'll take care of her.

7

—Let me get this straight, says Captain Bogani, steepling his fingers as he sits behind his desk.

—You want to take my newest detective, before he's even spent his first day in the post, and send him up to Nyahururu to look for a girl who's not even, technically, missing?

—It's some way beyond Nyahururu, Sir, Mollel concedes. —It will take Kiunga most of the night to get there. But in a good car . . .

—Oh I see. You want him to take one of my new cars, too?

—Sir, interjects Kiunga. —I've worked with Detective Sergeant Mollel for years. I trust his instincts. If he's wrong, well, I'll make up the hours. I'll even pay for the petrol. But if he's right, there could be a young woman in a good deal of trouble.

—Relax, Sergeant. I'm not like Superintendent Otieno, only concerned with a quiet life and procedure. I'm just a few years out of your rank myself, you know.

And a few years younger too, Mollel thinks.

Bogani sighs.

—We've got a photograph of her, right?

—From the school file.

—So we email it to the local police post, they swing by in the morning, see the girl, let us know.

He opens his hands, palms up. The gesture implies that this is his offer of a compromise.

—It needs to be Kiunga, insists Mollel. —We left the parents half an hour ago. If they're covering something up, they've already got a head start. I need a detective on the case, not a pair of local beat cops.

—And what will you be doing while Kiunga takes his little safari?

—Looking for the teacher, Abdelahi. And checking out one or two other leads.

Bogani gives a sharp nod. —OK. Do it. But by this time tomorrow, I want answers, understand? Either Fatuma Lepui alive and well, or some proof, *real* proof, that she's not.

Mollel and Kiunga spring to their feet.

This is possibly the best time of day to see Dandora. The trenchlike streets are too dark for the detritus underfoot to be visible, and the sides of the canyons are illuminated by the windows above and the bright squares of storefronts at street level. Wares are stacked high, and people gather and chat in the comforting glow. Mollel had been up before dawn, riding a different *matatu* route, but that seems a lifetime ago. On days such as this, Mollel often forgets to eat: his only appetite is for his mission. Even on quiet days, he regards food as little more than fuel. He'll grab a starchy fried *mandazi* or a bowl of sticky *matoke* from one of the street vendors if he needs to. But this day has a long way to go yet.

Hopping off the *matatu*, Mollel follows the directions the school gave Kiunga for Abdelahi's address – a street in an area known as Phase 6, just a few blocks away from Brightstart Academy.

The building is exotically called MALE HOSTEL. A set of rates is painted on the wall by the door: *bed 50/-; room 200/-; self contained 300/-.*

Immediately inside the door, there is a small open window, through which the sound of a TV can be heard. It's just after

7pm, so the nationwide ritual of the evening news is being played out. It's a national article of faith. All the stations in Kenya broadcast news at the same time, and wherever you are – in a bar, or a home, or in a police station – the news is turned on, turned up, and then religiously ignored.

Peering through the hatch, Mollel sees a lounge, of sorts. A couple of grubby armchairs. The TV is perched high on the wall, inside a metal cage. Mollel catches a glimpse of his own boss, Otieno, on screen, being grilled by a parliamentary committee. He's seen the routine often enough to know that it will consist of point-scoring and grandstanding by the MPs, and attempts to make Otieno look as foolish as possible. His boss's wide, dark head hangs deflated on his shoulders as he wearily defends his record. The on-screen caption reads CRIME RISE: CHIEF GRILLED.

This, thinks Mollel, is where Bogani's ambition will lead him someday. He's welcome to it.

Mollel raps his knuckles on the counter. A wiry, grey-stubbled man in a vest rises from his armchair.

—Bed or room? he asks.

—Neither. I'm looking for Abdelahi.

The man snorts.

—Which one? We get a lot of Abdelahis.

—His name is Abdelahi Abdelahi.

The man tuts. —I got a Mohamed Mohamed, and an Ibrahim Ibrahim. We get a lot of *sujuu* in here.

Mollel tries not to show his irritation at the racial epithet – a corruption of the Swahili word *sijui*, meaning *I don't know*, in mockery of the Somali's supposed poor mastery of the language.

It reminds him of his first experiences of Nairobi. Back then, a newcomer to the city, he barely spoke a word of Swahili, and no one, apart from his own kind, understood his Maa.

What's more, he's always felt a certain affinity with the

Somalis. Many are pastoralists, too, and the sizeable diaspora here in Nairobi share the Maasai's sense of loss of a homeland they loved.

—He's no *sujuu*, says Mollel. —He's a teacher.

The man makes a noise in his throat which suggests he has as much respect for teachers as Somalis.

—I know the one. Self-contained.

He's referring to the room, rather than its occupant – self-contained means it has a bathroom attached – but from what little Mollel has learned so far, the title could equally apply to Mr Abdelahi.

—Did he have friends here? Any visitors? Did he go out at night?

These enquiries are punctuated by pouts, shrugs and sighs on the part of the hostel-keeper. Eventually he throws up his hands. —If I paid attention to all the comings and goings here, I'd never get anything done.

Mollel wonders what *anything done* means. Judging by the greasy window panes and dust collecting in the less-trodden areas, he doubts it's cleaning.

—Look, continues the man, I ask no questions, I see nothing, I hear nothing. That's the way people like it. What do you think they're coming here for, the *ambience*?

—Is anyone staying in the room at the moment?

The hostel-keeper's eyes narrow. —No. But you're not getting in. Not unless you're a city council inspector, or you've got a letter from a judge. Like I say, my customers appreciate their privacy. And that means no police officers.

Mollel thinks ruefully of what some of his colleagues would do in the face of such a statement. Otieno would have the man's scrawny throat in his hands by now. *Do you still want that letter from a judge?* Kiunga, more subtle, would be looking round for code violations – or threatening to conjure up a few.

Mollel enjoys taking a different approach. He opens his wallet and removes three one hundred-shilling notes, slapping them down on the counter.

—I'll take it, he says.

—Take what?

—The room. Now I'm a paying customer. You're not going to turn away business, are you?

He can see the man weighing his options. He clearly values his establishment's reputation as a place of discretion, and yet his eyes keep returning to those three grubby notes on the counter. Finally he snatches them up, reaches behind him for a key attached to an outsized wooden fob, and slides it over to Mollel.

—Check-out's at eight, he growls.

—Oh, I'll be gone before then, replies Mollel.

According to the school, this hostel had been Abdelahi's home for several weeks, so either Abdelahi was phenomenally unmemorable, or the man downstairs was lying about not being able to recall him. Mollel had hoped that during that time, some impression of his personality might have been left in this room. He is immediately disappointed. There is nothing to be learned about Abdelahi in this anonymous square.

The self-contained part of it is a quarter of the square, partitioned off with gloss-painted plyboard and a curtain. Behind it is a toilet, a sink, and a shower head jutting out of the wall barely higher than waist-height. The only way to shower would be crouching over, or sitting on the toilet – perfect for multitaskers.

The room has a small window which looks out onto a wall, almost, but not quite close enough to reach out and touch. There is a waste basket with a shopping bag liner; a wardrobe, empty; a bedside table with a drawer, also empty; and a bed, a little wider than the average coffin, but no longer.

It's a space more private, but barely more comfortable, than the girls' dormitory.

Mollel's attention turns to the bed. It is made up. There is a single flat pillow, two sheets, and a scratchy brown blanket. The top sheet is folded over the top of the blanket, which in turn is tucked tightly under the mattress.

There's something about the way the bed is made which is too fastidious for these surroundings. It looks like a lot of effort, unless the intention was to save an even greater effort.

Mollel strips away the blanket and tosses it onto the floor. He holds the top sheet by two corners and spreads it out to the light. He is greeted by the bitter smell of stale sweat. He was right. The bed had been neatly made to distract from the unchanged sheets.

Dropping the top sheet, Mollel pulls the bottom sheet away. Again, he holds it up to the light. This time, something glints. He examines it more closely. Flakes of shiny residue. So it's not entirely true that Mr Abdelahi made no mark. Mollel carefully bundles the sheet so that the semen stain is in the centre, then removes the shopping bag liner from the waste bin, and stuffs the sheet inside.

As Mollel is leaving, the hostel-keeper looks up. —Hey! Where are you taking that?

—I thought you never noticed comings and goings, replies Mollel.

Mollel knows that the next thing he has to do is call this Doctor Kanja. He can feel the piece of paper with the phone number in his pocket. For some reason, he's feeling a powerful resistance to calling it. Mollel has interrogated psychopaths in their cells, and politicians in their offices, and none of them have daunted him. But the prospect of seeing this psychologist has him rattled. He has a history with psychologists, and it's not a happy one. He's not sure that the questioning would be as one-sided as he'd like. He decides it's probably too late to call, anyway. He'll do it in the morning.

Since he is in Dandora, he wants to get a feel for the place. He's not very familiar with this part of the city and, with almost anywhere in Nairobi, it's not the sort of place you stroll around aimlessly, especially after dark. But at this time, there are still enough people to make the streets feel fairly safe, so Mollel adopts a purposeful stride and heads off towards the setting sun.

He's barely taken a few steps before he corrects himself. That's not the setting sun – sunset was two hours ago. The sky glows red behind the rooftops, but those are not clouds illuminated from below; that's smoke. He sees it billowing now. For an instant he thinks there must be some kind of catastrophe just beyond the next block, and he listens for the danger signs – the screams, the sirens. But then he realises that the catastrophe is of a far slower sort. The sort that will kill many more people, and attract far less attention. It is the perpetual fire of Dandora's dump. Not even Nairobi's regular deluges could douse this blaze. No one screams at a disaster that happens all the time.

As he approaches, Mollel realises that the smell – which he thought he'd never get used to – has become familiar. He knows this because as the first wisps of smoke hit his nostrils, he becomes nostalgic for when it was merely a reek. He gags slightly and gulps in more air, which has the opposite of the desired effect. Looking up, he sees that the people around him have scarves or cloths covering their mouths and noses. He has the bed sheet, but he's not about to use that. Instead, Mollel makes do with his sleeve, burrowing his mouth into his elbow as he searches for a way out of this smoke.

Ahead. Cutting through the gloom, there are flashing lights. The vibrant colours seem to imply a cheerful haven. As Mollel approaches, he sees the ropes of twinkling lights are draped around a painted sign, with a cartoon of a winking, grinning man strapped into a chair, one hand giving a thumbs-up as sparks fly out of the helmet on his head. THE ELECTRIC CHAIR, the sign reads. BEER N BEATS.

Getting closer, details emerge. The walls beneath the sign are covered with posters, most of which feature a familiar face: Nyambisha Karao. The same rap artist Fatuma Lepui had plastered over the walls of her room. Across one of these is painted, in white letters: HAPA, MOJA KWA MOJA, KILA FURAHI-DAY.

Furahi is Swahili for fun, so *Furahi-day* is a cross-lingual pun. The whole slogan means *Here, Live, Every Friday.*

A shame, thinks Mollel, that this is Tuesday. He'd like to see Mr Karao perform some time. Check what all the fuss is about.

He pushes open the door and tentatively sniffs the air. Nothing more noxious than stale beer, roast meat and the faint whiff of piss. In other words, the air is the same as in any bar, and Mollel immediately takes deep, refreshing lungfuls of it.

The bar is mostly empty – it has the air of a place that won't even start to get going until way after any sensible person's bedtime. A lone drinker sits at the counter nursing a bottle of Tusker in a manner which makes it impossible to tell whether it's his first or his tenth of the day. At the far end of the room is a raised stage, with some large speakers behind it, and what look like DJ turntables. Although the stage is unlit, Mollel can see a figure standing at the front, holding on to a microphone stand as though it's a crutch.

There's no one behind the bar to serve him, so he is spared the charade of buying a drink. Instead, Mollel slips into a booth and sits where he can observe the stage.

It's a young woman up there. She's wearing jeans and a white vest top, with long braids bunched behind her head and trailing between her shoulder blades. She has a large pair of thick-rimmed spectacles on her nose, and just beneath them, on one nostril, the flash of a stud or ring.

In her right hand – the one not gripping the microphone stand – she holds the microphone and a thick wad of paper. She has been raising this paper close to her face, squinting through her glasses, and lowering it, her lips moving and head nodding.

—OK, she mutters. —Let's do this.

She turns back to the turntable deck and does something with the equipment. Immediately a throbbing bass fills the room. The drinker at the bar jerks his head up, ascertains it's nothing to worry about, and returns to his bottle.

Mollel watches as the woman sways back to the microphone stand. Without the music, it had been propping her up. Now, the beat seems to hold her. Her hips rock and her braids bounce in time. She fixes the microphone in the stand, stuffs the wad of paper in her pocket, and removes her glasses.

Suddenly she thrusts her face to the microphone, her lips almost seeming to brush it. Eyes closed, her teeth flash white as she starts to spit loud, clear words at machine-gun pace. Mollel struggles to catch what he can.

—Karibu Dando, hii ndio ile mtaa natambua yako,
Place hautaget maua Mtaa imejaa tako.
Tako iko kwa ubaro ni ika ile imejaa kwa mongo,
Ndio nainywaku, naipumua, nailipa hongo.
Law hakuna, siyo rahisi.
Na madindo wanoma wanaitwa Polisi.

At the word *Polisi* she opens her eyes and seems to look directly at Mollel. The spell which had come over her is instantly broken, her rhythm disrupted. She fumbles for the next word but she's lost the beat now. She pushes the microphone stand away from her in disgust and it falls to the floor with a boom that reverberates around the room.

—Hey! comes an angry shout from the bar. Mollel looks over and sees a fat man with a proprietorial air emerging from a stock room. —I told you before. You break that mic, you pay for it.

The music stops suddenly as the woman attends to the turntables. The steady, booming bass begins again from the start.

—Oh no you don't! the man shouts. —We've got customers here need serving. You can mess around on your own time.

The woman casts a contemptuous glance at him, and then at Mollel. She snatches something from the deck – Mollel thinks it is a music player, like the one missing from Fatuma's room – and pulls a wire out of it. The music instantly stops once more. She puts her glasses back on, takes a cloth from a nearby stool, ties it around her waist, and with an angry, grim smile at her boss, she stomps from the stage.

Within seconds, she is at his table.

—What do you want, Policeman?

He does not need to ask how she knows. Over the years, Mollel has come to learn that about half the people he meets instantly recognise him as a policeman. It might be something in the way he looks around him, in the way he holds himself. Whatever it is, to those people, it marks him out as surely as if he were wearing a uniform.

—Nice rap, he says. —I couldn't follow all of it. My Sheng's not up to much. But I got the bit about the police. *There is no law. Life's not easy. And the biggest crooks are the Polisi.*

She shrugs. —You can't deny it.

—I don't, says Mollel. He takes the photograph of Fatuma from his jacket pocket and slides it across the table. —Do you know her?

The woman takes the photograph, adjusts her glasses, and peers at it.

—No. I mean, maybe. Is she in trouble?

—I hope not. That's what I'm trying to find out.

The woman looks over at the bar.

—Look, can you order something? A beer and some *nyama choma*, at least? Then we can talk.

When she returns, with a cold beer dewy with condensation, and a steaming plate of goat meat wobbling with fat, she slides into the booth next to Mollel.

—The boss doesn't mind me talking to paying customers, she explains. —In fact, he encourages it. Keeps the dirty old bastards coming back.

She gives a shudder. Mollel judges her to be about twenty years old, and he feels guilty at being cast, even unwittingly, as a *dirty old bastard.*

—I'm Mollel.

—You can call me Dora, says the woman. —It's kind of a stage name, but it's what they call me round here.

—A stage name?

—Yeah. I used to perform with a guy called Dan. Dan and Dora. Dandora. Get it? Nah, nobody thought it was very funny then, either.

—What happened to Dan? asks Mollel.

Dora shakes her head. —Dandora happened to Dan. He didn't make it.

—I'm sorry, says Mollel. Sensing her sadness, he does not want to push it any further, but he makes a mental note to look up violent deaths in Dandora when he gets back to the station.

—So, about Fatuma, he says.

—Who? Oh, the girl in the picture. Is that her name? I never knew it.

—But you know her?

—I didn't think so at first. But look.

She takes the photo, and laying it flat on the table, she uses her fingers to crop the face. The schoolgirl's close-cut hair and prim collar disappear. —Imagine her with long, glossy hair, a fringe way down to her eyes. And she's wearing a blouse and leather jacket. Yes, I know her. I've seen her here in the club, quite a few times.

Mollel thinks of the school. Just a few buildings separate it from this place, but they seem entirely different worlds. Schoolgirls and bar girls. Could there be an overlap?

He looks at the face in the picture and tries to imagine the girl Dora describes. Certainly the image fits with the clothes and make-up in her bedroom. But the glossy hair? They'd not found a wig, yet.

Dora takes her fingers away from the photograph and Fatuma's image reverts to childish innocence. Mollel has the disquieting sensation – he can't quite pinpoint where it comes from – that this new, sophisticated Fatuma might be even more vulnerable than the simple schoolgirl.

—Did you ever notice who she was with?

Dora thinks for a moment. Mollel prompts her. —Could it have been a Somali man? Fairly young, slim-built?

She shakes her head. —I'd remember someone like that. We don't get many Somalis in here. They're not exactly big drinkers.

—The notes you were rapping from, says Mollel. —Can I see them?

She grimaces, but then stands so she can get into her jeans pocket. She produces the wad of paper Mollel had seen her consulting on stage.

As Mollel had suspected, the paper is packed with tightly written verse, heavily crossed through in parts. The handwriting, though, is quite different from that in Fatuma's book.

—Can you point out the lines I heard?

She makes a show of reluctance, but Mollel detects a glint of pride in the way Dora straightens her shoulders and pushes her glasses up her nose as she reads from the paper.

—*Karibu Dando*, she speaks, softly. She's inhabiting a very different persona from the one she adopted on stage. Up there, she was fierce. Down here, shy. —That's welcome to Dando: Dandora. Here. The only home we know. A place where rubbish blossoms and no flowers grow. The only freedom I have is inside my head. I eat it, breathe it. I pay bribes. And then there's that bit you understood. About the police.

She casts her eyes down prettily. It's almost as though she's embarrassed now about casting aspersions on the integrity of Nairobi's finest.

—You wrote this yourself?

Her eyes rise and blaze at him. —You think I'd rap someone else's words? This stuff has to come from the heart, or it doesn't mean anything at all.

She snatches the notes back and stuffs them into her pocket. As she does so she glances over at a group that has just walked into the room and is looking around for service. —I got to go now. I hope you find the girl.

—Wait, says Mollel. But Dora is already clearing away his mostly untouched plate of meat.

—Trust me, she hisses. —You don't want to attract the attention of this lot.

She leaves him and goes to the bar to attend to the new arrivals. Picking up his carrier bag with the hostel's sheet inside, Mollel follows her up to the bar and slaps a few notes down on the counter.

—*Asante sana*, he calls out. *Thanks a lot.*

Dora throws him a dismissive wave. Mollel turns, getting his first clear view of the group. There are a couple of girls, dolled up for a night out. Neither of them could be mistaken for Fatuma, even in the semi-darkness. The two men are leering over the girls. One, dressed in a sharp suit, is middle-aged, with a bald head. The other is tall, in baggy jeans and a tight T-shirt over which he wears a deep red velvet jacket with black lapels. A patterned bandana is tied around his head, with the knot above his eyes. As Mollel passes, those eyes swivel up to meet his; the young man whispers something into his companion's ear, and then he grins.

There's something about the amused, assured glance he gives Mollel that instils an unnerving sensation of recognition. But it's not until Mollel is outside the club once more and looking at the same face over and over again, on poster after poster plastered on the walls, that he realises his earlier wish has come true. He has just met Nyambisha Karao.

8

Mollel has always felt like an imposter in any role he has tried to fill – or that was forced upon him. Son, warrior, father, detective. All of them have sat uneasy on his shoulders. But his younger brother, Lendeva, always seemed to know exactly what was required of him. He played the part of the *Odo Mongi* perfectly. And yet, to him, it was all an act. No one else saw it, but Mollel saw the look in his eyes. A look of detached amusement. As though he knew that all the tradition, and the ritual, was silly, and also knew that Mollel knew he knew it. But he would continue doing it anyway, because it gave him something. Kudos. Status. An authority that Mollel never had. People listened to him. Respected him. He had become a man, both physically and in terms of authority, before Mollel did. He was handsome, lean and muscular, whereas Mollel was gawky and awkward. The imbalance played out in their relationship.

They first came to Nairobi in the second year of the long drought. Mollel was nineteen, Lendeva sixteen, and Lendeva was already the one making decisions for both of them. Mollel's authority – the natural authority of an elder brother – held no sway. He had wanted to stay and protect the herd, the village. But Lendeva said: what herd, Mollel? The goats are all dead, and the cattle that remain are only good for leather. There won't even be a village if we wait much longer.

Enkare'nyrobi: the name of the city means *cool springs* in Maa. That seemed auspicious. But it was hard to disguise the fact that what the brothers were about to do, in Maasai terms, amounted to defeat. They were selling out.

You won't find many businesspeople more hard-headed than the Maasai. Yet they have a curious contempt for money. Money only has value in so far as it buys cattle, and that is the measure of wealth: *he is a rich man. He has a hundred head.* But the drought had hit Mollel's community hard. Money was needed to buy fodder for the remaining stock, and meat for the elders, and corn and sugar for the women and children. It was a shameful situation, one step away from beggary: but it was better than death.

So Mollel and Lendeva were going to have to find work.

Maasai learn a wide variety of skills. How to find your way home at night by the patterns of the stars. Which leaves will balm the bite of the golden spider, and which tracks will lead you to the pangolin's den. Which small red berries are refreshing, and which are lethal. All crucial skills, but none of them very useful in the city.

There, brawn counted more than brain. For eager young men, there was always some way of earning a few shillings, even if it meant fighting for it. For close to a year, Mollel and Lendeva pulled carts in the markets, jostled their way to the front of the pack waiting to help unload cargo at the railway sidings, broke rocks with huge hammers for the roadbuilding teams. It was tough work, and poorly paid, but they had few expenses, so managed to send home what they could and still break even. In the process, they got to know the city. How it operated. How to survive. They also mastered Swahili, which was a foreign language to them when they first arrived. The labour strengthened Mollel, turned his physique from gangling into a wiry, lean strength. But he never regained his status with Lendeva.

*

Had he been in charge, Mollel can admit to himself, things might have stayed the same. But Lendeva was restless. Ambitious. He knew that in the city the Maasai had one trait which made them very much in demand. Fairly or unfairly, they were seen by all other Kenyans as fearless.

This, in a way, is what corporate types would no doubt describe as their brand value. These days, most other tribes in Kenya have more or less abandoned their traditional styles of dress. This makes the Maasai distinctive. Even when they do, individually, give up their *shukas* and sandals in favour of trousers and lace-up shoes, they often retain the scars of their upbringing – either in their bearing, or their speech, or in cases such as Mollel's, on the lobes of their ears.

These are the marks of the Maasai.

The marks can be useful. They mean that – depending on their motive – when people see a Maasai, they are either reassured, or deterred. Because Maasai make up the largest informal security operation in the whole country.

Lendeva managed to persuade a contact – a Maasai standing guard outside a grocery store in Kitengela, on the very edge of the city – to put them in touch with his boss, who was not the owner of the store, but another Maasai who subcontracted the work for this client, and a dozen more across the suburb. That night, on the promise of enough money to buy themselves a meal, this man gave them a try-out. They sat on old paint tins in the crippling cold for what seemed like a lifetime, guarding some run-down warehouse, until the first glow of dawn emerged in the sky and another tired, grey-looking pair, who had been in the city for many years, came to relieve them. They expressed surprise to find both of the brothers awake. Apparently they had done a good job.

The level of crime in Nairobi, or the fear of that crime, or the complete lack of trust in the police, meant that there was no shortage of work. Before long they were able to pay for more than their own meals – even after the deduction for rent, which meant the privilege of sleeping all day on flattened cardboard boxes in the corner of the warehouse.

But while Mollel was content to sit and wait and hope that trouble never came, Lendeva had other aspirations. One morning, as they finished their shift, they heard news that a private house on the other side of Kitengela had been robbed during the night. The two Maasai guards – young men, who the brothers were on nodding terms with – had been overpowered and tied up, while the family had cowered at gunpoint and the home was ransacked.

Their boss had told them this as a warning to be extra vigilant. But for Lendeva, this was not enough. He was furious.

—We have to do more, he insisted. —We can't just let them get away with it. If we do, it will only happen again.

—What do you want to do, track down this gang? asked the boss. His tone was mocking, which made a pulse beat visibly in Lendeva's temple. —If you want to catch those guys, you're in the wrong job, he said. —You ought to join the police.

Mollel was arranging his blanket and cardboard mattress for the day when Lendeva told him to come. —You can sleep later, he said. —We've got work to do.

Together, they swung by all the usual places where the night guards hung out during daylight hours. Most of them had been warriors, back in their village days, so the brothers had a pretty good idea of where to find them: under a tree somewhere, lying on the grass.

They found the pair at the third or fourth place they looked. It was where the main road, coming into town, split in two; an island in the stream of traffic. A noisy place, but one where you could be guaranteed to be left undisturbed for a few hours at a time, if you did not mind the fumes and car horns.

—We heard you had some trouble last night, said Lendeva to the two men. In reply, one of them held up his wrists to show the red weals where the ropes had been.

—Funny, said Lendeva. —I don't see any other marks on you. No bruises on your arms or face.

—They had guns, said the other man, rising from the ground. —What's it got to do with you, anyway?

Lendeva removed his *rungu* from his belt. The stout ebony club ended in a thick, heavy bulb, plain on one side, the other carved into a sharp, nipple-like point. It was a skull-splitter. You wouldn't want to be hit with either side of this weapon, but if you were, you'd want it to be the plain side.

—You can't think we were in on it, protested the first guard, also scrambling to his feet now. There was fear in his eyes. —You're wrong. We have no idea who they were. It was dark. They had guns. We did everything we could.

—You don't get it, do you, boys? replied Lendeva. With a sudden movement, the *rungu* crashed into the ribs of one of the guards. As he doubled over, Lendeva brought his knee up and slammed it into the man's groin.

The second man was reaching for his dagger. Mollel didn't need to be told what to do. His right fist struck him on the nose, which flattened with a jet of blood under his knuckles. The man fell back against the tree, and Mollel twisted the knife from his hand, feeling the tendons crack in his palm. The man sank to his knees.

—I never said you were in on it, chuckled Lendeva. The two men were dazed, one doubled in pain, the other trying to stem the flow of blood from his nose. —But *this* is what you boys should have looked like after last night.

Even then, Mollel almost laughed out loud at this seventeen-year-old addressing the two grown men as *boys*. But Lendeva had always had an authority well beyond his years.

—You see, he continued, we Maasai have a reputation to uphold. No reputation, no work. So you'll understand if we have to beat you up a little more. You'll thank me for it, one day.

9

Dandora, at night, is not a place to be by choice. Mollel finds himself looking for a *matatu* or *boda boda* through instinct. There are no signs or official stops. *Matatus*, obviously, tend to ply the main routes, and so he navigates towards what feels like a more important road, but it's empty. *Boda bodas* – motorcycle taxis – are more likely to congregate at corners and junctions, so he continues until he comes to a crossroads, but it is similarly deserted. A ghost town.

A petrol station up ahead looks promising: the sort of place you might find a *boda boda*. But as he draws closer, Mollel realises the place is closed. The lights are on but the solitary, decrepit pump has a chain wrapped around it. A hunched figure sits on a stool in the doorway, a red-checked blanket wrapped tightly around him, pulled up high over his mouth. A *rungu* lies in his lap, and a faint snore rises from his vicinity. Mollel considers, briefly, disturbing the guard to ask for directions out of this place, but sympathy for this alternative self – the person he once was, and might still be today, had things gone differently – stalls him.

A distant beat still drifts towards him from the Électric Chair, catching the currents of the air, but now he picks up something else. His head has risen and his skin has started to prickle before he even processes what it is.

Distantly – but unmistakably – there is the sound of screaming.

He turns his head, scanning for the source of the noise. It twists and tangles with the bass boom from the nightclub, but the two sounds eventually separate enough for him to decide they're coming from different directions. Even accounting for echoes, he ascertains that the screaming originates from somewhere near where the dark night sky is lightened by the glow of the garbage fire.

As he approaches, hurrying now, the screaming takes form. Not one person, that's for sure: no one could keep the noise up as incessantly as this. There are multiple voices, and all of them high in register, piercing. These, surely, are children's screams.

He realises the source almost as soon as he turns another corner and recognises where he is. Brightstart Academy is at the end of this dead-end street. Here, in the tunnel created by the high buildings either side, the screaming ricochets and reverberates.

He breaks into a run.

The immediate and obvious thought is that this is a fire. He reaches the metal gates and pushes and pulls at them, but they do not give. He starts to pound on them with his fists.

The screaming from within is not abating; if anything it grows more hysterical at the sound of his banging. There are a dozen voices or more raised in this shrill chorus.

Mollel recalls the windows of this building with their thick bars, and the barred gates at the end of each corridor and at the single door to the dormitory, and he thinks of the heavy padlocks he saw. With a rising sense of panic, he wonders if he is hearing children being burned alive. But even as he considers this ghastly prospect, he is aware there is something wrong here. Something is not as it should be. Normally, in this sort of neighbourhood, he'd expect such a noise to bring all the residents of other buildings out into the street to investigate – but the street is empty. It's unheard of for a fire to drive people indoors rather than out.

Could it be that they're mistaking the glow of flames and smell of smoke for the smouldering mass of the nearby dump?

Or could it be that Mollel is the one mistaken?

The seed of doubt prompts him to re-evaluate. Stepping back from the gates, he can't see any light flickering at the windows above. No flames licking around the rooftop. The screaming continues, but now he's not so sure the tone is one of panic. It's too sustained for that. Almost theatrical.

Looking at the gates again, he remembers the peephole in the second O of MOTTO. He steps forward, places his fingers against it, and sure enough, with a little pressure the circle slides to one side. The last time he saw this peephole open, there was an eye on the other side. This time it is Mollel who lowers his face to the metal, and looks within.

What he sees surprises him more than any of the images of catastrophe his fearful mind had conjured up. At the far side of the courtyard, sitting at a school desk, is Peter, the guard who had let Mollel and Kiunga inside during the day. Under the light of a single bulb suspended high on the wall, he is shovelling a fork into a plate of beans, while reading a newspaper. The very picture of relaxation, despite the continued screaming.

Mollel reaches down and feels with his fingers in the dirt until they touch a suitably sized stone. He picks it up, then puts his hand to the spyhole and, as best he can, flicks his wrist and flings the stone towards Peter. Given the constraint, he's gratified to hear the stone rattle far away in the yard, and quickly swapping his hand for his eye once more, Mollel sees Peter looking down in puzzlement. He then looks up, scanning the courtyard – and his eyes meet Mollel's one eye at the hole. Peter pushes his plate aside, gets up, and cautiously approaches.

—It's me, Sergeant Mollel. —I heard the screaming. Can you let me in?

Peter, who is now at the other side of the gate, pauses, cocks his head, then raises a finger. He points at one ear, and shakes his head. Then he points at his lips and mouths them open and shut, like a fish.

Mollel gets it. The man is deaf and mute, but he can lip-read. This explains why he didn't speak to him or Kiunga when they visited in the morning. Now Mollel steps back from the peephole, and tries to stand where what little light there is will fall upon his face. It seems to do the trick, and he hears the bolts being withdrawn and the gate opens wide enough for him to step inside.

It's all he can do to stop himself leaping forward and grabbing the man by the collar, but he knows this will be futile. Instead Mollel gestures wildly, pointing up at the upper floors from where, even now, screams from a multitude of voices come tumbling.

Peter puts up his hands. *Slow down*. Again, he points at his lips. *I can lip-read.*

—The screaming, says Mollel, trying to make his mouth articulate the words clearly. Forcing himself, against instinct, to slow down. —I heard it a block away. We've got to get up there. We've got to help them.

A slow smile spreads across Peter's face. He nods, and gives a silent chuckle, as though to say *that? That's nothing.* His hand reaches into his pocket and he pulls out a big bunch of keys. Then he beckons Mollel to follow him.

Through the first door they go, and the effect is like stepping into a sawmill or a workshop with machinery screeching at full blast. But this is the sound of the girls.

As they mount the stairs, Mollel follows Peter, frustrated at the man's ponderous pace. But he is calmed, somewhat, by the deaf man's blasé attitude. He might not be able to hear these screams – so remains immune to their bone-chilling effect – but he's aware that they're happening. And if he's not concerned, then Mollel's initial impulse, that there was danger at hand, must be wrong.

Down the corridor, unlocking a gate, and on to the final staircase leading to the dormitory. Now Mollel can hear that there is as much sobbing as screaming, though naturally those cries don't carry as far as the full-throated shrieks.

One thing is for certain: there is no fire here. No smoke fills this narrow passage; there is no heat in the concrete walls Mollel places his hand against as they climb the stairs; no crackling and flicker of flame. Peter reaches the door of the dormitory and unlocks it. He stands aside for Mollel to enter.

When the Maasai round up their herds at night, they usher them into the *boma*, a circular compound whose walls – as much as ten feet high – are made from branches of acacia and whistling thorn. These are plants which have evolved over millennia to resist the leathery hide of the elephant and the sandpaper tongue of the giraffe. They do so with cruel, needle-sharp spikes. The branches are cut down with *pangas* and collected with padded leather mitts to be stacked high and intertwined – a barbed corral, not to keep the animals in so much as to keep the predators out.

Not that it discourages them. Leopards, in particular, are adept tree-climbers, so they're always tempted to try their luck. Any gap of a few inches which a careless or tired boy might not have noticed when constructing the *boma* is enough for the cat to slip through. A leopard only wants one – preferably a young one it can suffocate swiftly and silently, and pull out the way it came in. They're sly. More often than not, the first the villagers know about it is when the boy does a head count in the morning.

After it happens, though, everyone gets twitchy. The boy who left the gap, still sore from the beating he received for his negligence, will whip the animals in early so he can inspect the thickets and make any reinforcements necessary before nightfall. The warriors will stay closer, and their edginess will infect the dogs, who will already be excited by the scent of cat and blood. The livestock detect all this and the tension crackles in the air like lightning. They become skittish and wild-eyed, tossing their heads and snorting.

It doesn't take much to tip them over into full-blown panic. A gust of wind makes the branches creak, or a dog yelps outside the compound. Goats scream like humans when they're terrified. A couple of hundred of them, alongside the bellowing and charging of cattle, is enough to sound like the end of the world.

And whatever damage a real leopard does, this ghost leopard is worse. In their desperation to get away from their non-existent attacker, the animals will trample each other and impale themselves upon the spikes. Any Maasai foolish enough to try to enter and calm this boiling tumult risks the same fate. Better to wait for the first signs of exhaustion, and pray that a whole village's livelihood is not wiped out.

So Mollel does not step immediately into the dormitory. From the doorway, he sees flitting white gowns flying in all directions as the girls move around. The room reminds him of a bottle of soda, shaken up, the bubbles agitated and bouncing off each other. Now, with the door eased open, that energy has a chance to dissipate.

The smell emanating from the room is at once familiar and strange to Mollel. He is a graduate of police college, where recruits are put up in dorms much like this one. He has to use a locker room nearly every day. He's even familiar with the smell of prison. For him, the scent of living bodies in close confinement holds no surprises, but here, alongside the thick fug of sweat, there is something else. Something powerful; electric. Mollel is well aware that girls smell different to men. But could hormones produce such an atmosphere?

The force of the screams is waning now, and the noise begins to separate like a sweater unravelling from a solid block to individual strands of wailing dismay. Mollel can almost hear each girl detaching from the group and regaining her sense of self – and with it, shame.

A small, black-shrouded figure pushes past Mollel's elbow into the room. She reaches out and snaps on a light. It is Mama Sharifa.

—Now *what*, she demands, folding her hands over her chest, —is the meaning of all this *foolishness*?

Mollel wonders where she came from. He'd been drawn by the noise from streets away. She can hardly have tolerated being in the building with this racket going on. He suspects Peter must have used his lightning text skills while Mollel was not looking.

Mollel steps into the dormitory. The screaming has disappeared along with the darkness, the light pushing it out through the cracks in the brickwork. The only noise now is a mixture of suppressed sobs and snivelling. The girls stand, shivering and shell-shocked, blinking bleary-eyed in surprise to find themselves back *in* themselves.

They begin to pull at their nightdresses or raise hands to flatten wild manes of hair. A girl near Mollel has fresh blood on her knees, as though she has leapt from an upper bunk and landed on them. Another has a trickle of blood on her upper lip. All of them – there is not one exception among the thirty or more present – have red eyes and tear-streaked cheeks.

—It was Dorcas again, says one of the girls quietly. —She started it.

He looks around for Dorcas. She's one of the smallest girls, and most likely to be hurt in a stampede. He can't see her until he realises that the crumpled blanket on her bunk – which he had initially taken to be vacant – is rising and falling slightly.

He walks over and places his hand on the cold metal tubing of the bunk. The bundle reflexively shrinks.

—Dorcas, he says gently. —It's me, Mollel. Are you OK?

The blanket shifts in a movement which could be interpreted as a nod.

—She woke us all up, says a girl. —She was screaming, pointing. She terrified us.

—Says she saw a ghost, chips in another.

—Not a ghost, adds a third. —A *night runner*.

They are in Mama Sharifa's office. The principal, Mollel, and Dorcas. Dorcas, despite being wrapped in a dressing gown and her blanket, is still shivering. Her tiny bare feet dangle down from the chair.

—This is not the first time, Mama Sharifa is saying. —She's had these night terrors before. The trouble is, you have all these girls in a small space and they react off each other. It turns into hysteria.

Mollel does not want to hear Mama Sharifa's analysis. He wants to hear from Dorcas.

—Is that right, Dorcas? You had a bad dream?

She shakes her head. —It was not a dream.

She's so quiet he can hardly hear her. He leans forward.

—She was here. Right next to the bed. As close as you are.

—Who was, Dorcas?

—Fatuma.

—Projection, sighs Mama Sharifa. Mollel casts her an irritated glance and says: —Can I speak with Dorcas alone?

Mama Sharifa pouts and gets up brusquely from behind her desk. —I'll wait outside, she says.

—Now, Dorcas, says Mollel, when she is gone. —Tell me what you saw.

—It was Fatuma, she breathes. —She'd come back.

—The lights were off. Are you sure it was her?

She nods vigorously. —There was light from outside.

—And yet none of the other girls saw her.

—As soon as I started to scream, she disappeared. Then the

others started, too. There was so much noise . . .

—She's your friend. Why did you scream?

—It was her, and it wasn't her. She was different.

He stays silent. He does not want to prompt her. After a moment, she adds:

—She was a night runner.

Again, he does not speak. She wants to talk; he gives her the space to do so.

—Her face was different. Her skin was grey. Her eyes didn't know me.

—And yet she came to your bunk.

—She came to *her* bunk, she corrects him. —She wanted to return. That's what night runners need to do, to return. I stopped her. And now she's gone.

10

—You know what they call us? Lendeva asked Mollel one day. —Night runners.

He was proud of the fact. It confirmed, for him, their burgeoning reputation. That reputation was the foundation stone upon which they would build their new business. Or, more accurately, his new business – for although Lendeva insisted the proceeds were evenly split, there was little doubt about who was effectively in charge.

The rains had come and the drought had passed, but the brothers remained in the city and did not return to the plains. They were earning too much money.

It was all Lendeva's idea, naturally. They had become a sort of independent sub-contractor, hired to test out the responses of private security guards all across the city.

They came at night. And like night runners, they specialised in surprise.

It started off as a favour to their current employer, but Lendeva soon worked out they could get more money by approaching clients directly. And it suited his personality; instead of waiting around all night, hoping nothing would happen, this new venture brought in many times the fee for just a few hours' work.

Their approach was not without its dangers, of course. For a start, they could hardly announce their arrival in advance, so they became, in effect, the thieves they'd previously been guarding against. They had to adopt their mindset. Get into their heads.

They planned out their operations in advance, starting with surveillance. What time did the shift change? When did the guards go to the toilet, or make *chai*? And those who slept on the job – which turned out to be most of them – where and when did they think they could get away with it, and for how long?

Together, Mollel and Lendeva would identify the weak points in the perimeter. If there was an electric fence, was it the sort that could be stormed with a blanket thrown over it, or the sort that could be disabled with a few clipped wires? If there was a wall, was it topped with shards of glass? And was there likely to be a dog on the other side?

They were scrupulously fair. If the fault was with the property owner – the place was vulnerable because the owners hadn't invested in an alarm, or spotlights, or had tried to save money by having only one guard patrol too large an area – they were sparing on the guard when they broke in. Usually, he was so terrified by the sight of the intruders – and relieved when he realised they weren't robbers, and he'd live – that the shock in itself was enough to keep him on his toes.

When it was the guards' fault, though, it was a different story. What made the budding business successful—their *unique selling point*, corporate types would call it – was the combination of enforcement and deterrence.

An individual guard represents an investment to a business. It's not just his wages. It's his recruitment, the basic checks – criminal record, word of mouth – and even the most basic training costs money. The traditional way of dealing with a guard who'd been neglectful of his duties was just to dismiss him. But the brothers went one better. A guard who'd been caught napping, and bore the bruises to prove it – yet kept his job – was a guard who would be doubly vigilant in future. And his face would be a living, walking advertisement to others who might be tempted to slack off.

Lendeva, in particular, was always up for whatever means necessary. Mollel was the voice of caution, both in terms of the risks they took in breaching the properties, and when it came to meting out the punishment. More times than he cared to think about, Mollel had had to hold Lendeva back.

Of course they benefited, in those days, from the fact that guns were fairly rare and it was not legal for guards to be armed. So the prospect of breaking in to a place to find themselves staring down the barrel of an AK-47 seemed comparatively remote. Perhaps because they were buoyed with confidence after their early success, they never considered the possibility that one day they might turn up when a real break-in was already in progress.

Mollel and Lendeva took pride in planning entries that produced the maximum confusion and surprise. Even with the caveat that they could not inflict any physical damage – on the property at least – there was plenty of scope to be creative.

Their target that night was a used car lot on the Langata Road. It belonged to an auction house and a selection of the best models was kept out front. Big Japanese off-roaders, chrome fenders and flashy lights; saloons with blacked-out windows and spoked alloy wheels. There were cards in the windscreens with slogans such as FULLY LOADED and NEW MODEL, and prices that seemed astronomical to the young Maasai, but which they later learned were vastly below the market value.

—It gets the customers through the door, explained their contact, a young woman who worked in the office. —They're not even for sale, those cars. If you look, you'll see they have no plates. They're import jobs awaiting customs clearance. Already bought and paid for by the clients. No, the idea is to entice the buyer in, then give them the hard sell on some of the older models out back.

*

She'd been assigned to look after the brothers by the owner of the car lot, as their insider. She wasn't keen. She was grudging in her answers when they asked her their questions: how many guards? Where do they like to sit? Do they listen to a radio or read a book?

—It just seems sneaky to me, she said. —Like you're trying to catch them out.

Lendeva was concerned that she'd tip off the guards. —She's indiscreet. She told us about the owner's pricing scam, didn't she?

Mollel wasn't so sure. What Lendeva saw as indiscretion, he saw as a natural inclination towards fairness. She seemed to be interested in what was *right*, not because it was convenient, or because that was the way things had always been. Right was a good enough reason in itself.

Her name was Wanjiku. Chiku for short. She was nineteen, and worked at the car lot as a runner and fetcher and general helper. The owner said she was the only one with the time to babysit the two Maasais who had started hanging around. The cover story was that they were interested in buying a pickup as they were starting a transportation business. No one seemed to care enough to challenge such a ludicrous story. And anyway, the further a client went towards the back of the car lot, the more old, beaten-up trucks there were; exactly the sort of thing that was often seen trundling down a dirt track with a dozen young men hanging on to it.

An initially prickly relationship began to soften over the few days needed for the brothers to scope the site. Their lilting, Maa-tinged Swahili made Chiku laugh, and she corrected their occasional mistakes. She also taught them new words, in an even more exotic language: English. It was a must, she said, if they wanted to succeed in business. That was enough to have Lendeva, at least, convinced.

*

She'd always been fascinated, she said, by the Maasai. She was a Kikuyu, and just a generation or two ago they'd led very similar lives. At nineteen, she'd have been a mother by now, with a shaved head and a leather apron, and a baby on her breast – and probably an older child playing in the dust at her feet. Instead of which, she was the daughter of a teacher, working hard to save for her dream, of one day attending secretarial college. She wore a smart dark suit with a knee-length skirt and white blouse, which she must have laundered and pressed every evening, because she was always fresh and immaculate. She woke at five and walked an hour to work, changing from her dirty trainers into shiny high-heeled shoes which, being more for show, rubbed her all day, so that she'd slip them off when she was with Mollel and Lendeva at the back of the lot, sitting on an old tractor tyre.

—The Kikuyu and the Maasai often intermarried, she said. —Just think. I could have been a Maasai bride instead of an office dogsbody. I wonder which is better?

The very fact that she'd asked the question supplied an answer of sorts. Mollel was taken aback, and thrilled. It had never occurred to him that anyone would prefer this city life. He had always seen city folk as slaves. Ants in this vast colony, busily marching in their tracks, oblivious to the scale and scope and beauty of the world outside. He hadn't realised there was a choice. That they had options.

—We're wasting time on this job, said Lendeva, after a few days. —It's not that complicated. Besides, if we hang around much longer, people will talk.

—They're already talking, laughed Chiku. —It's not a problem. I told them one of you is my boyfriend.

—Which one? Lendeva and Mollel spluttered together.

—Oh, I don't know, she said, slipping on her shoes and rising to return to the office. —Which one of you would you want it to be?

They watched her hips sway out of sight.

—That's it, said Lendeva. —We strike tonight.

It had been a busy day at the car lot, with a car-carrier of duty-free vehicles arriving from Mombasa. They were not strictly new, but they were Kenya-new, and the sales staff had drooled over the metallic paint and leather interiors. An old saloon or two and a hardbodied truck had also come in, so the layout of the lot had changed significantly as vehicles were shifted around to accommodate all the new arrivals. Any decent security company would have trained their guards to anticipate trouble at a time like this. They should have been familiarising themselves with where the new shadows fell, stepping up their patrols, being extra vigilant. They weren't.

Over the road, lying under an acacia bush, Lendeva and Mollel had already planned their attack.

They had identified a place where the chain-link fence ran close to a drainage ditch. In this season, the water in the ditch was low and the earth of its banks was dry and crumbly. They had taken the opportunity, when visiting Chiku, to kick and prod the support which kept the fence in place at that point. This would be their point of entry.

Their exit would be even easier, thanks to the lax security around the new shipment. One of the vehicles at the front of the lot, a 4x4 with a roof rack and ladder, had been parked only a few inches from the fence. It would be the work of an instant to scale it, leap over the razor wire and drop down the other side. They would be in and out within minutes, having caught the security men off-guard and with no damage to the client's property. Then they could move on to the next job.

Mollel was taken by surprise at the pang of pain he felt at that thought.

Darkness came. The traffic ebbed, and the city settled into the slow watch of the night. Choosing their time carefully, the brothers made their first move. They got in without a snag – almost. As Mollel wriggled up and under the chain-link, he felt a jagged edge of wire tear his calf. No matter, he thought. But Lendeva, following, had a better view.

—We have to bind that, he whispered.

—Afterwards.

—No, first. It's deep.

There were two guards on duty. One was supposed to be on patrol while the other manned the sentry hut at the gate. But the Maasai knew, from their surveillance, that both men were squeezed into that small hut, listening to the radio and dozing. They crouched in the shadow of a box truck, Lendeva peering closely at Mollel's leg as he tore a strip from his *shuka* and wound it around the tear.

That was when they heard it: a squeak of metal on metal. The box truck they were leaning up against shifted slightly on its suspension. There was movement inside. Feet shuffling. Voices, low. And then the door of the truck body, ever so slowly, creaking open.

Mollel drew the knife he always kept in its leather sheath at his waist. Lendeva already had his in his hand, from cutting the bandage. They shrank up against the truck wheel as the body rocked. They counted eight pairs of feet descending; heard whispered instructions, and six men passed on one side. Dim orange light from the street played on the barrel of a low-slung gun. The men were headed for the office. There, on the wall behind the counter, was a metal cabinet which contained all the keys. It was locked, but that would present little difficulty. The other two intruders were presumably headed for the guard hut.

Night hunting requires stealth and communication; luckily the Maasai have a system that combines both. Lendeva's hand gripped Mollel's left wrist and his thumb tapped twice, then his little finger tapped once on the inside, where the pulse ran. That meant that he would go to the left, and the office. Mollel would head right, and hope to find the guards with their throats not yet slit. He used the shuffle-run he had learned as a child, with a straight back but knees bent. It looked ridiculous but it was swift, kept the head upright, and prevented his profile from breaking above the undergrowth – or in this case, rising above the bodies of the cars. He allowed himself the most fleeting glance through a window from time to time, before darting across the spaces between the vehicles.

Mollel could see the rectangle of light coming from the doorway of the hut – a naive error on the guards' part, as it allowed people to see in, whilst obscuring what lay outside. The two thugs were standing with their backs to the entrance, a gun pointed at the guards within. Their faces were ashen and their eyes rolled with fear, but they were still alive.

A gun, in Nairobi, is usually a rental. You pay a few bob for an hour or two – bullets and training cost extra. The renter usually forgoes the training – anyone can handle a gun, right? This guy certainly couldn't. The stock was folded down and he held it pistol-fashion, one-handed, elbow away from his waist. Definitely an amateur. But that was little consolation. An amateur in charge of a high-powered automatic rifle held inches away from someone's head was probably even more dangerous than a pro.

Mollel had one advantage, though. The thug's stance left a gap between his right arm and his body. Reluctantly, Mollel set his knife down on the ground; he needed both hands free for what he was about to do. He wanted this to be silent, and for that, he was taking a gamble that relied on two things: that the second thug didn't have a gun; and that the captive guards would not have been rendered stupid by fear – or were just plain stupid to start with.

Silently, he rounded the corner, covered the three paces to

the guard hut, and rose to his full height. Then Mollel moved to let the light from the hut fall upon his face. This was the moment when all could have been lost. He wanted the guards inside to spot him, and one of them did. He was the one everyone called Uncle. To young Mollel, he seemed ancient, but he was probably only in his forties. Their eyes met and, as best as he could, Mollel tried to smile.

Then he slipped his left hand over the mouth of the thug with the gun. At the same time, he pushed his knee into the small of the man's back, put his right elbow around his neck and squeezed. The man struggled for a while until Mollel felt him go limp. The gun fell with a useless clatter to the ground.

As Mollel had hoped, Uncle knew what to do. While Mollel was incapacitating the first, he had leapt forward and punched the other thug in the stomach, making him double up. The second guard, less quick off the mark, seemed to have nonetheless grasped the situation by now, and had stood to assist his colleague. He reached for the whistle that hung on a cord around his neck.

—No, Mollel hissed.

The gunman was lying on the floor, unconscious, while the second was now being sat upon by the two guards, one of Uncle's hands clasped across his mouth. He looked close to suffocation.

—Careful, Mollel warned. —You don't want to kill him. Bind them both.

Uncle opened his mouth as though to protest: why should they care what happened to the intruders? If the situation had been reversed, little mercy would have been spared on them. Besides, even injured robbers were still dangerous.

But Mollel silenced him with a furious glare before he even spoke.

Trusting the guards and their wards to silence, Mollel trotted off with the gun. He had no idea how to use it, but he figured he could hold it convincingly enough to disguise that fact.

It was only now that he had a chance to think about Lendeva. The other group were almost certainly armed, too, and there were more of them. What did his brother have in mind?

He didn't have to wait long to find out. He saw the intruders first – his eyes drawn by the beam of their torch at the doorway of the office. They'd obviously gained access to the cabinet inside and he heard the jangle of keys. He had seen those bunches – each as big as a fist, with sets of keys for many cars on each oversized ring. Paper labels with a registration number scrawled on it were attached to each set with string. If the lot could be called organised at all, then it was organised according to when the cars came in, rather than their position. Mollel assumed the intruders were sifting through, looking for the keys for the best cars at the front. This, at least, would buy him some time.

So where was Lendeva?

Mollel needed to get as close as possible to the main gate. This, after all, was the only way for vehicles to get out. There was more light in this part of the lot, due to its closeness to the street. Moving between the cars would have been too risky, so Mollel decided to go underneath.

The gun he was carrying had no strap, so he shoved it down the back of his *shuka*, lodging the folded stock under the part that passed over his shoulder blades and trying not to think about the muzzle, which was now lodged close to the base of his skull. Had he known of such a thing as a safety catch, he would have checked it was on. It did occur to him that it would be a stupid way to die – blowing his own head off – but he didn't have much choice.

The first car was easy enough – a jeep-style vehicle with sixteen-inch wheels. He swung himself underneath and rolled on to his belly, cursing the fact that the undersides of cars were so lumpy. He didn't know the names of things like the exhaust or the differential. All he was concerned about was not banging his head, or worse, the gun muzzle, and making a noise that would bring attention.

The disadvantage of the jeep was that it was short. Hardly had he got under it than he needed to shuffle forward under the next car. He was moving snake-style – using the sideways motion of his hips to drive himself forward – except that snakes are graceful, and he was anything but. What Mollel was, though, was silent.

The most terrifying part was the gap between each car. The space in the lot was limited, so the cars had been parked nose to tail, but there was still a couple of feet space between each one. There was no way Mollel could stick his head out and check that the coast was clear, so he just kept crawling, and trusted to the darkness.

Occasionally, he would raise his face out of the oily dust and breathe for a moment. It was at one of these points that he saw Lendeva.

His brother was high on the chain-link fence. He was climbing up, negotiating the coils of razor wire which frothed along the top. Mollel could only make out his silhouette against the gleams of light on the cruel barbs, but he knew what his brother was doing. It was the way they would get in and out of the thorny *boma* when they were boys. He had threaded his leather belt through the spirals and was now pulling it, inch by inch, to create a space where the razor wire would be more stretched out. His *shuka*, beltless, hung off one shoulder. As Mollel watched, Lendeva slipped his free hand across and removed the garment altogether. He would be naked now – a perilous state in which to straddle razor wire. Lendeva bunched up his *shuka*, placed it over the stretched strand, and then he was up, over – and gone.

Mollel hadn't even had time to make a noise to get his attention. That was probably for the best, as just then he heard the blip-blip of a car being remotely unlocked, and bright orange lights flashed on the car ahead of him. He scrambled and slid his way forward and underneath its chassis. He heard the car door open, and the undercarriage creaked and rocked above him. Meanwhile, his head was reeling with what he had seen.

How could Lendeva have done this? Not only had his brother abandoned him, but he'd actually sent Mollel into danger while knowing he intended to flee.

Mollel's heart was pounding and he could barely control the violent shudders that were running up and down his body. This was not the adrenaline of action kicking in; this was a visceral response to betrayal. Mollel tried to get a grip; to shut down the shuddering. His body was reluctant to respond, but it didn't matter, anyway: at just that moment, the world moved around him and there was a roar as the car's engine leapt into life. Hot, oily smoke enveloped him, and he screwed up his eyes and buried his face in his shoulder.

Mollel prayed that the car would move straight forward – otherwise he'd be crushed. The alternative was hardly more appealing. Mollel had no idea whether any of the gang would be around to see him lying exposed and helpless – as he would surely be – once the car rolled forward, so he began to shuffle backwards. It was trickier than going forward, with the added disadvantage of not being able to see where he was going. His left calf brushed against the exhaust pipe of the car, and he cried out in pain. At least, he thought, the sound of the engine would have disguised his yelp.

He didn't get much further before the wheels started turning, and his shelter began to slide away. There was a further blast of heat along his spine, and a merciful moment of fresh – or, at least *fresher* – air, which he gulped greedily.

The respite was short-lived. He glanced at the bumper of the jeep behind, which was now creeping towards him. He thanked God that these guys had not put on their headlights, or they would surely have seen the heap on the ground rise slightly, then throw itself back down again. Instead, they just rolled over it, and once more Mollel covered his mouth and coughed at the exhaust fumes.

Mollel suddenly figured out what they were doing. Rather than spend time jockeying the best vehicles into place for removal, they had selected a column and were simply going to drive those cars straight out of the gate. Mollel made a mental note to check – if he ever got out of this – whether one of the salesmen had been responsible for repositioning some of the more valuable vehicles in the run-up to that night. This had something of the inside job about it.

He was resigned to lying low, hoping that no one would pay too much attention to their rear view, and praying that there was no low-slung sports car edging towards him, when he sensed the car above him picking up speed. The engine roared; the gate, he assumed, must be open now. He felt utterly defeated.

Then there was a sudden jolt and Mollel felt as though the car had been dropped on him and that he would be crushed. The gun on his back rammed into his body. There was a crump of metal, and a tinkle of broken glass. Then the engine died.

From his prone position, Mollel rolled to the side, pulled himself out from under the car and rose warily to his feet. He pulled the gun from the back of his *shuka* and attempted to look as though he knew what he was doing.

What had been a column of evenly spaced vehicles was now one continuous line. The car he had been under had gone straight into the back of the car in front. Inside, an airbag had exploded. It was slowly deflating now, revealing a slightly bloodied, very dazed-looking young man. His eyes lolled towards Mollel, and Mollel tried to suppress his own surprise and look threatening. He didn't need to bother acting: the gun did most of the work for him. The young man raised his hands meekly.

Deciding he was unlikely to cause trouble, Mollel moved

along the line of cars towards the gate. Voices began to break the spell. The front two cars were locked together, their fenders entwined, and as the second car jerked forward and back, its front wheels began to spin and an acrid smell of burning rubber filled the air. These cars were going nowhere.

One of the thieves had obviously decided the same, and he leapt out of his vehicle. Mollel raised his weapon and attempted to shout, but the fumes had rendered his voice little more than a croak. The man ran towards the gate, but didn't get far. A horrifying figure, lean and bare, stepped forward. The driver stopped in his tracks, and gave a short scream. With one swift punch, the freakish figure laid the driver to the ground.

The figure, illuminated in the headlights, threw back his head and roared with laughter. The remaining thieves – and Mollel – were transfixed. He was naked, his body streaked with mud and blood. He seemed possessed with a euphoric, supernatural energy. His mere presence seemed to carry more power than the gun in Mollel's hand.

—What are you waiting for? he asked Mollel with a grin. —Round them up, brother.

11

—I'm sorry, Boss. Nothing to report.

Mollel finds it touching that even now they're both sergeants, Kiunga still calls him Boss. But his heart sinks at what his colleague has to say.

—When I got to the aunt's house there was no one home. I waited outside in the car all night, but there was no one there this morning, either. The place looks like it's been empty for a while. I'm going to go into the village now and ask around the locals. Someone might know something.

—Let me know what you find out.

—*Sawa sawa*, Boss.

After he's hung up, Mollel stands looking at the phone for a few moments. The feeling of dread, which has been creeping up on him since yesterday, is growing stronger. It's out of proportion, now, to the news that Kiunga has just given him. It's no surprise that Ngecha's alibi for Fatuma's whereabouts has failed to check out – especially if the Fatuma Dorcas claims to have seen last night was not just a figment of her imagination.

No, there is something else bothering him.

He sighs, takes a deep breath – and punches a number into the phone.

—*Habari*. Is that Doctor Kanja? This is Sergeant Mollel of Central CID. Could I come and see you, please?

Mollel does not like psychologists, psychiatrists. Anyone

with the prefix *psych* – though he has met more than a few perfectly charming psychopaths in his career, both behind bars and behind expensive desks.

This dislike dates back to 1998. The year when Bin Laden's men drove a truck bomb into the US Embassy, killing over 200 people, including Mollel's wife.

He had searched for Chiku tirelessly, pulling people out of the rubble, and leaving them at the roadside when he discovered they weren't her. After several hours, they took him away. Covered in blood – only some of which was his own – which ran in black, caked lines down his ash-covered skin, and with his ragged, torn clothes, they thought he had been in the blast himself.

Days later, waiting to see the police psychiatrist, the taste of pulverised concrete still accompanied every hacking cough. His damaged eyes hurt every time he closed them; and he didn't want to close them, because of what he saw when he did.

There was no talking that first visit. The psychiatrist – a sympathetic but harassed-looking man with a fountain pen and a thick prescription pad – had taken one look at him and scrawled a script.

The drugs had helped. They helped Mollel stand up, at least. They helped him dress. They helped him hold his baby, coax the teat of a bottle between the boy's lips, shush him when he cried for more familiar arms.

Mollel had had no idea how many pills he'd been taking when he agreed – or they told him he'd agreed – to go in front of the cameras. The police were getting a lot of criticism in the wake of the attack. Here was a good-news story. An off-duty policeman charging into the disaster, saving dozens of lives. A genuine Kenyan hero. Never mind that he didn't consider himself a hero. After all, if he'd found Chiku, he would never have returned to save anyone else.

All he had to do, they said, was stand there, and shake the

hand of the Commissioner, and blink as the cameras flashed. But that wasn't all he had to do. They had wanted him to talk, too. A foreign reporter, a white man from an American newspaper, had been asking for him – said that his photo had made the front pages. He was *iconic.*

Coaxing the words forth had required more pills; pills the police doctors were quick to supply. Small yellow ones, big red-and-black ones. Even that thick, white, toothpaste-tasting drink they had served him in a little paper cup just before each interview.

He was a hit. Somehow, the scale of the tragedy – more than two hundred killed, more than four thousand wounded – defied comprehension. Horror, dismay and fear came easily. But real empathy required something more intimate to latch on to. A human face. A story. An attack of this magnitude required a certain amount of coverage, and here was a new angle, a way to recast it through the experience of one individual. It was a gateway to what all the journalists wanted, which was empathy, and they lapped it up.

It was a throwaway remark in the third or fourth of these sessions that started all the trouble. Mollel couldn't even remember what he'd said at the time, but there were plenty of people who saw the interview on TV that evening and told him about it later.

The interviewer this time was a young woman, a Kenyan not yet jaded by her profession. She had seemed genuinely moved by what Mollel was telling her, and she reminded him, a little, of Chiku. Perhaps for this reason, or perhaps it was because of the drugs, he had let his guard down.

She had asked him why he had joined the police. He hadn't really thought about it until then. Chiku had never said as much, but he suspected that, having agreed to marry him, she had wanted him to become something more respectable than a night guard and security consultant.

But it went back further than that. Back to before he had met Chiku. Back in the Maasai village, he'd been a warrior, a member of the proudest caste. Warriors were the most respected of all: even more so than the elders who set the law, for they were the ones who enforced it.

Perhaps that was why, a few days after his arrival in the city, and as the initial shock at the noise and the cars and the buses and the bustle had begun to diminish, and he was able, at last, to pick out individuals in the crowd rather than just a blur, he began to notice the policemen.

These were the warriors of the city. Their uniforms marked them out, much as the red *shuka* tied over one shoulder, and fine, long dreadlocks set the warrior apart. At the policeman's waist, in a hoop on his belt, sat a baton, just like the Maasai *rungu*. Some of them even had a gun, holstered but ready, as the Maasai carried a knife in its leather sheath.

When he first put on his cadet uniform, Mollel had fumbled with the buttons, but he relished casting himself a smart, snapping salute in the mirror.

It didn't take him long to lose some of his illusions. His fellow cadets smoked, drank and slacked off. They mocked him for his diligence. Didn't he know he could just slip the examiner something under the table to ensure graduation? They openly discussed the best way to exploit their new-found status in society. Traffic Division, it was universally agreed, was the place to be. They swapped stories of tricks and tactics for extortion and profit: a broken tail-light here; an accusation of speeding there. The best ruses involved nothing more sophisticated than holding up every passing *matatu* and demanding full paperwork until a driver's licence was handed over with a note or two folded inside.

None of this appealed to Mollel, and his fellow cadets quickly came to resent the way he fell silent when they spoke of such things. How, they seemed to say, could you trust someone unless they were as untrustworthy as you?

Perhaps this was what informed Mollel's answer to the TV interviewer. Why had he become a police officer?

—Not for the money, he told her, tired of the questioning and the stock answers. But maybe because it had sounded gruff, and his judgement was muddied by exhaustion, and grief, and pills, he had added: —if it was about making money, I'd have joined Traffic Division.

—What do you mean by that? asked the interviewer.

Mollel was taken aback. He had thought everyone would understand what he meant. That he wouldn't have to elaborate. That the statement would speak for itself.

—Well, uh, you know . . . There's always opportunity for *baksheesh* there.

—*Baksheesh*? Are you saying that there is corruption in the Nairobi police?

Again, Mollel was dumbfounded. He was being asked to confirm what was evident. What could he say, but *yes*?

He had broken an unspoken rule. He had uttered something aloud which everyone knew to be true.

The next day, more questions. A journalist on his doorstep asked him precisely *what* went on in Traffic Division – and Mollel, his natural caution suppressed by chemicals, told him. He also told him about a certain procurement scam which was common knowledge in the department, and which implicated half of the senior management.

Within hours, Mollel had been detained. Bundled into a car and taken to the Police dispensary – a prison in every regard, except the wings were called wards.

It was for his own good, they said.

Had he just been any regular cop, they'd have conjured some trumped-up charge against him, and he'd have been gone – bitter, perhaps, and broke, certainly. But at least his integrity, and his mind, would have remained intact.

But they couldn't sack him. He was a hero.

The journalists were told – he later learned – that his trauma had made him act erratically. And so his doses went up dramatically. He began to lose hours, days at a time.

The police therapist asked him once: —Why did you feel the need to invent such a tale? Why the need to lash out at your employer with lies? Could there be some unexplained anger to blame?

And Mollel, too drugged up to demur, had been forced to talk about his childhood, his heritage, his past, his long-gone father, while the psychiatrist nodded, and made notes in which words – glimpsed upside-down on the pad – like *fabulist* and *fantasist* seemed to recur frequently.

So no, Mollel does not like psychiatrists. But he consoles himself with the thought that, this time, he should have the upper hand. He will be the one asking the questions.

At least, he hopes so.

Mollel's morning ritual involves a cup of black instant coffee – anything else makes him too queasy – and a little yellow pill. It feels like something of a victory to have reduced his intake to one pill a day over the course of thirteen years. He'd tried going completely without at various times, with results he either couldn't remember, or wanted to forget.

Pill and coffee consumed, he showers, shaves his cheeks and scalp, and washes away the grit in the sink. Then it's time to check on Adam.

His son is already awake. The faint thump-thump of music from his room makes Mollel hesitate before he knocks and enters. Opening the door, he is greeted by a familiar face, one he had seen in real life just a few hours previously. Adam must have had these posters on the wall for some time, but Mollel had paid them no particular heed before.

Adam is in front of the mirror, tying his school tie. —Sorry, Dad. I'll turn it down.

—No, it's all right, mutters Mollel, distractedly. —I didn't know you liked Nyambisha Karao.

Adam looks over at him with surprise. He obviously hadn't expected his father to know who it was. The boy squirms with embarrassment.

—Oh, not really. I mean, he's *OK*. I don't really listen to the words.

—But you understand them? You know Sheng?

Adam drops his eyes. He's not used to his father taking an interest like this, and Mollel gets the feeling that the boy has become accustomed to a certain level of benign neglect.

—Wait here, says Mollel.

He returns with the small, densely inscribed notebook he found in Fatuma's bedroom.

—This belongs to another fan of Nyambisha Karao, Mollel says, handing the book to Adam. The boy opens it, flicks through and then stops at a random page. His smooth brow creases as he examines the handwriting.

—These are rap lyrics, he says.

—Yes. Can you understand them?

Adam shakes his head, but slowly. Then he pauses.

—It will take a bit of work, he says —I don't know some of the words, but I can ask around. I think I can do it, yes.

He raises his eyes and Mollel is struck by how much of a young man the boy has become. And strangely, how much he also looks like his mother.

—Is it for a case, Dad?

Mollel nods. —Cool, says Adam.

Following the directions Doctor Kanja had given him over the phone, Mollel finds himself in a part of Dandora he's not been to before. It is called Phase Five.

Dandora, hard as it is to believe nowadays, was once planned out as a model community. The swampy, low-lying area between the city and the plains had previously only been of note as the site of a battle between the British and the *Mau Mau* prior to independence. But as the city grew around it, in that post-*Uhuru* period of optimism and growth, nothing seemed simpler than to drain the swamp, draw brisk, straight lines of avenues across a map, and populate it with the happy, productive workers Nairobi needed.

Unfortunately, Nairobi had other plans. Dandora was already serving a purpose. No problem, said the planners: the dump would be landfilled and closed by the 1980s. But the dump had never closed. It had reached its capacity, as the planners had predicted, around three decades ago, but then it had just kept on growing.

And it had devoured Dandora. The Phases were set out in the 1970s, with each phase consisting of several street blocks separated by a wider avenue, each with their own facilities and services, shops and community. Phase One was the section furthest from the dump. The idea was that by the time they built Phase Nine the dump would be gone, and a wide, open green space beside the Nairobi River would be available for parkland.

As it was, the city got as far as Phase Six, but even as the first houses were being opened, the ever-growing pile of trash was encroaching upon its borders.

Like some huge, slow volcano, the rubbish heap swallowed everything in its path. Houses that had been homes just weeks before were buried. The occasional chimney or ribcage of a stripped roof were all that remained to show where a dwelling had once been.

Dr Kanja's clinic – his treatment room, he called it – is in the first house of the last street in Phase Five. The last house is already part of the dump.

—I apologise in advance for the location, he had told Mollel on the phone. —I run a community service.

Hadn't Mama Sharifa said something similar?

Turning the corner onto this street, Mollel gets his first full-frame view of the dump which he has previously only had fleeting glimpses of between buildings. Now he gasps at its size. It rises high, several times higher than the structures around it. But that's not all that makes Mollel gasp.

In this morning light, it is beautiful.

The wind is behind him, which means he can breathe, and so is the sun. The sky is a delicate blue, and the smoke rises from the heap like mist from a mountain, rolling and twisting into a wispy white strand. The mountain itself shimmers and sparkles. Flashes of gold and white play across its slopes. Occasionally one of these shapes – a plastic bag or a piece of paper – is caught by an updraught and floats high, spiralling, like a bird.

And there are birds, real ones. These are less graceful than their imitators. They walk on tall legs, wings hunched, long necks pivoting spear-like beaks in search of pickings. Cranes. Above them, swooping occasionally, are fork-tailed kites, which fight and bicker over the choicest takings.

But these are not the only inhabitants of the slopes and foothills of Dandora's mountain. They seem hardly human at first; the inhabitants of this place look like they have been created out of the very matter they traverse. They shamble and pick their way across the landscape, bent over with swollen grey packs on their backs, looking somehow like ticks or lice. Indeed, the whole structure is nothing as solid as a mountain, but more like a fallen giant, dead and decomposing, but in turn a source of sustenance and life.

The sign on the door says simply DOCTOR KANJA. It is slightly open, as though to catch the fresh air while it lasts. Set into the concrete step, there is a raised metal lip: a necessity in this street, where the spillage from the tip has resulted in a soft, organic sludge underfoot, even now in the tail-end of the rainy season. Mollel makes use of it and unclogs a clod from beneath each heel, banging his soles for good measure before stepping inside.

—I'm here to see the doctor, says Mollel, to a woman who is sitting beside the door. She looks up at him with bloodshot, desperate eyes, which roll around the room, as though to say: —We all are.

Then she produces a grubby-looking handkerchief, which she balls up in her hand and stuffs into her mouth.

Mollel looks around at the others present. On a bench against the far wall are more women, and one sorry-looking man. No one speaks: they seem bound together by an unwritten pact of misery.

One of the women rocks solemnly back and forth, a low moan escaping from her lips. Her face is drawn, her skin papery over high cheekbones. She reminds Mollel of the AIDS sufferers he used to see all the time about ten years ago, but who have become much less visible in recent years, since antiretroviral drugs became commonplace. The man beside her is clearly not her companion, though one knee twitches as if beating out a silent accompaniment in sympathy with her rocking. He is about thirty, Mollel judges, and gaunt, though not obviously unwell. His hands grip the front edge of the bench and his knuckles are pale, straining slightly too hard, as though he is hanging on for his life.

The third woman in the room sits back on the bench. Mollel would not have been able to tell whether she was pregnant or merely large, were it not for the protective hand that runs up and down her round belly.

They're a diverse group, but anguish takes many forms.

Mollel should know.

He looks up at an inner door and says to the lady with the handkerchief: —Is the doctor in there?

She nods, and quickly turns away, a sob absorbed in the cloth.

At that moment, the door opens, and a tall, smartly dressed middle-aged man, wearing a tie and shirt sleeves, appears. He radiates an air of professional assurance. Next to him is an even stranger character than the inhabitants of the waiting room. A short man – he must be under five feet – wrapped in a dark red sheet. And it is a sheet: a cotton bedsheet, as far as Mollel can tell. Certainly not the sturdy, woven *shuka* of the Maasai. It is tied in a distinctly un-Maasai fashion with knots over both shoulders, as opposed to slung over one. A black singlet is visible beneath. The man's hair is a matted mop of salt-and-pepper, and a wispy grey goatee sprouts from his chin. The lower half of him reveals a pair of bare, skinny legs, sports socks and old tennis shoes. Mollel, who has hardly worn the *shuka* for years, can't help feeling slightly offended. This strange little man seems almost deliberately to be parodying the proud costume of the Maasai.

—Doctor Kanja? asks Mollel, extending his hand to the first man. —I'm Detective Mollel.

The taller man holds Mollel's hand and meets his eye.

—Oh dear me, no, he says, in a confident voice. —No, Detective. I'm very pleased to meet you, I'm sure. But you're quite mistaken. *This* is Doctor Kanja.

He delicately removes his hand and motions towards his strange little companion.

The real Dr Kanja cackles and bony shoulders rise and fall as he rubs his hands together.

—How about that, eh? he says, casting around the room for his audience to acknowledge the humour of the situation. Much to Mollel's surprise, they all seem to have livened up in the presence of the wizened figure. They smile and chuckle appreciatively and even the woman with the handkerchief begins to giggle self-consciously.

—Fancy mistaking *you* for *me*, continues Kanja, slapping the taller man on the back. Mollel distinctly recognises his voice, now, as the person he had spoken to on the phone. —Calls himself a detective, eh? No wonder he needs my help! Eh? Eh?

Mollel, not used to being laughed at, realises he has a humourless smile spread across his lips, and a frown on his face.

—Perhaps we could speak in your office? he suggests.

—Of course, of course. Kanja shakes the tall man's hand. —See you next week, Rehoboth. In the meantime, try to resist. Remember: you are strong! And everyone else, I won't be long. At least, I hope I won't be.

—Goodbye Doctor, says Rehoboth, with a nod at Mollel. Mollel follows Kanja into the inner room.

—Well now, says Kanja, taking a seat, and indicating one for Mollel. —You're a Maasai.

Mollel eases himself down onto one of the two small, concave wooden stools that are the only items of furniture in the room. In fact, *room* is too grandiose a term for what is little more than a large cupboard.

Kanja is sitting on the stool opposite him, splay-legged, and Mollel can see – to his huge relief – a pair of shorts under the old man's robe.

—Yes, says Mollel. —I'm a Maasai.

—People often mistake me for Maasai, says Kanja breezily.

A Maasai wouldn't, thinks Mollel.

—In fact, I'm Kamba, the old man continues. —We have much in common, but we come from very different traditions.

—I know, says Mollel. He is thinking that no Maasai would ever allow himself to look like this. And then he thinks: no *psychiatrist* would allow himself to look like this. What is he dealing with here?

Kanja leans forward and pats Mollel's knee.

—I'm glad you've come to me. This is not the first time I have been consulted by the police. There was a case, about three years ago. An eight-year-old boy had been playing with friends not far from here. When the mother came looking for him, he was gone. None of the friends had noticed him leave. We had the whole community out, you know. Even the trash-sorters came down from the tip. Their gang-masters had told them: look for the child. The police were mystified. But one of them, he knew me of old. He said to me, Doctor Kanja, *you* can find him for us. I know you can.

The old man had closed his eyes during the telling of this tale. Now he suddenly snaps them open.

—And I did. I found him for them. He was inside an old refrigerator, up on the heap. He had been playing hide and seek.

He gives a sad smile. —If only they had come to me sooner. Well, now. We have a girl gone missing, right? Let us hope we're not too late this time. Do you have any of her personal possessions?

Mollel stands. The little man looks smaller than ever from here. He does not even look up as Mollel towers above him.

—I think I'm mistaken, Mollel says. —I thought you were . . .

His voice cracks slightly. —I understood you were a therapist of some sort.

—Indeed I am, replies Kanja, looking up with a grin. —Now, the possessions. These are very important. We need something with a direct link to her. The energy fades after a while, you see. If we can harness that energy while it lasts, it should lead us to her.

Mollel can't help himself. He gives a short snort; part disappointment, part derision.

Kanja's face clouds. —You don't have to believe it, Detective. But you have to *want* it to work.

—You're an *mganga*, Mollel says. Suddenly a lot of things—the out-of-the-way location, his strange dress, the disparate nature of the people in the waiting room – start to make sense. The only thing that doesn't is the involvement of the school.

Mganga – a witch doctor, a sorcerer, a tribal healer. Or a charlatan, a con man, a fraud. There's any number of names for these people. The Maasai call them *Laibon*, and they occupy a privileged role in the community, feared and respected more than warriors or even chiefs. But Mollel, who left that world behind long ago, has nothing but contempt for these tricksters. They even made psychiatrists look respectable.

—Yes, I'm an *mganga*. And it could be that my magic – which you obviously scorn – is the only thing that will find this girl. Are you going to let your prejudice blind you to the truth, Detective? Let me tell you, I've had more sceptical people than you ask for my help. I've had priests, pastors. Imams . . .

—Headteachers? asks Mollel.

—Mama Sharifa, certainly. Ask her. I've had more success with the girls of that school than they ever did with pill-pushers.

Mollel finds himself in the somewhat unexpected position of defending the psychiatric profession.

—With what qualifications? What training? I've seen a girl in that school whose arms are scarred from what is obviously self-harm. What possible help can your spells be to a troubled soul like that?

Kanja smiles up at him.

—Were the scars old or new?

—Does it matter?

—It matters, continues Kanja, —because since I've been treating her, she has not hurt herself again. It matters, because she was doing that all the time while she was under the care of the so-called medical professionals, and yet, once she started seeing me, she stopped. Now, Detective, you may not have any faith in *how* it works – I am quite prepared to grant you that – but you can't dispute that it *does*.

Mollel lets out a sigh, but Kanja is fired up now, and as though to prove his point, he has risen to his feet. He points a bony finger at Mollel's chest.

—Tell me something. The regular doctors have no solution

other than to pump these kids full of drugs. Do you know how these drugs work?

Mollel does not reply, but his pursed lips concede that he does not.

—Right. *Nor do they.* Most of these drugs, these pills, are by-products of all sorts of other research. And yet, because they have fancy, scientific-sounding names, and they come foil-wrapped or in blister packs or nice brown bottles, they must be good, right? Now if that's not a faith-based decision, what is?

Mollel sighs.

—Did it ever occur to you to ask, continues Kanja, —why a man like Ngecha chose to send his daughter to a school in a place like this?

—Stepdaughter, corrects Mollel. But he also gives the very faintest of nods. Because of course it had occurred to him. Indeed, he had asked Ngecha that very question. He just isn't sure he believes the answer.

—They come here after they've tried everything else. Either those treatments haven't worked at all, or they've made things worse. Do you have any idea how heartbreaking it is for a parent to watch their child being possessed by spirits, then drugged into oblivion? Do you blame them for trying something different?

Mollel keeps his face expressionless. He still does not believe it. A rich man like Ngecha would have no problem in summoning someone like Kanja to his home, if he needed to. There is something about his choice of location for Fatuma – out of sight, out of mind, discarded – which makes him uneasy.

—Besides, continues Kanja, taking Mollel's silence for acquiescence, —my form of treatment has been around for a lot longer.

—So the school, and the parents, were both supportive of this course of action?

—Naturally.

—And what, says Mollel, —was the course of action,

precisely? How were you treating Fatuma? And what for?

Kanja shakes his head. —You should know better, Sergeant. I'm not at liberty to discuss my patients in that kind of detail.

For the first time, Mollel is tempted to pick the little man up by his shawl and bash his head against the ceiling.

—So you reject modern psychiatric practice, but you respect doctor–patient confidentiality?

Mollel can barely disguise his contempt. As he becomes more irate, Kanja becomes more passive. He smiles.

—I work on the basis that anything said within these four walls is perfectly private, between me and the patient. It wouldn't do to discuss all the things I hear. Those people waiting outside. They would not be here if they thought their personal problems were going to be aired to the neighbourhood. I am therapist, I am priest, I am healer. I am trusted like no other. You cannot ask me to betray that trust. I am sorry, Sergeant, but I can't help anyone that way. Not even you.

Mollel is about to make another threat, but he is stopped in his tracks by the implied proposition.

—What do you mean, *not even me*?

—You cannot disguise it from me, Sergeant. I have seen it all. And I see it in your eyes. You are troubled, too. Why don't you sit back down? Approach this with an open mind. I may be able to help you.

Mollel does not sit down. He grabs Kanja above the elbow. His fingers almost close around the arm, the old man is so thin.

—You'll come with me, says Mollel, in a cold, quiet voice. —You can explain your scruples to Captain Bogani, down at the station. Maybe a night in the cells will change your mind about your precious principles. Meanwhile, I've got a missing girl to find.

Hauling the small man beside him, Mollel wrenches open the door. He had been expecting to march Dr Kanja past the patients in the waiting room, but they aren't there. Instead, there is a group of men. Three of them – though the way they fill the space, there appear to be more. They are large enough to dwarf Mollel as much as he dwarfs Kanja.

The slightest of the three steps forward. Mollel has to raise his chin to meet his eyes.

He recognises the figure as the man he'd seen at the Electric Chair the night before. The man who'd been with two women, and Nyambisha Karao.

—I believe you've been looking for something, he says. —Well, we've found it.

12

The soft but solid ground under their feet soon changes to something more slippery and organic, as they begin to mount the rubbish pile. The new arrivals at Kanja's clinic are leading the way. Mollel deliberately drops back a pace or two so that he can whisper to the little man scurrying alongside him.

—Who is that?

Kanja lets out a laugh.

—Him? Nicodemus. He runs everything around here, didn't you know? If you've been sniffing around here for a day or more, you can be sure he knows about it.

The words sniffing around seem to coincide with a change in the breeze, and Mollel gives a bitter cough as his mouth and nose are filled with a putrid smell.

Once more, Kanja laughs.

—Stick around long enough, and you'll get used to it. Ten years or so should do it.

They pass a scavenger, a boy of about Adam's age, shirtless and shoeless, ragged trousers his only clothing. He grins at them shyly. He is bent over almost double, carrying on his back a tall, wide package, elaborately tied together with grey and green polythene bags. Inside, there are dozens, if not hundreds, of milky-white plastic bottles. The boy spies another one ahead, and lunges for it. He retrieves it from the soft matter beneath, takes it by the neck, sniffs it, and then drains some of the white, gloopy contents into his mouth.

Mollel suppresses a retch.

—This is quite an ecosystem, says Kanja, offhandedly, as though the sight has not perturbed him in the slightest. —Everyone has his speciality. That young man is collecting plastic milk bottles. Another might be after their caps. There'll be someone looking for green glass, someone for white. Aluminium cans are particularly valued. A day's worth of pickings could bring in fifty, or a hundred shillings.

Fifty or a hundred shillings? Mollel wonders how anyone could survive on that. It's barely enough to purchase one of the half-litres of milk whose empty bottles the boy is scavenging.

Nicodemus and his two henchmen have pulled further ahead. Mollel, who has a Maasai's strength and stamina, is surprised to feel his legs tiring, but then, he is not used to walking on such treacherous ground. Occasionally, he would have had to follow his goats, as a young herder, across banks of mountain scree. But there, at least, he was not afraid of piercing his foot on a shard of glass, or a discarded needle, or stepping into the unsavoury contents of a nappy.

The air, too, is taking its toll. All around him is a low smoke that clings to the mountain, as though the smell has been made visible. It seems to seep and bubble up from within the densely packed material beneath his feet. No doubt there are fires burning, deep within. Occasionally a plume of black or grey punctuates the sky ahead.

He coughs once more, and this time the sputum he produces is bitter in his mouth.

—So all these pickers, says Mollel, —presumably they pay this Nicodemus for the privilege of working here?

Kanja chuckles.

—Sure they do. Or rather, they pay the next one up, who pays his dues. It all trickles up to Nicodemus eventually. He's the king of the hill. Top of the heap. But that's not the half of it. No, the real money comes from . . .

He suddenly pauses. Nicodemus and his men have stopped and are looking back at them. They've joined a group of pickers who are standing solemnly atop a crest of the heap. One of them, a boy, is waving a stick to keep away the kites, which have detected something appetising, and are circling in a frenzy of interest, waiting for an opportune moment to swoop, despite the human presence below.

A thin line of smoke rises from the midst of the group, and a different smell pervades the air. For a moment Mollel's nostrils greet it, as a more pleasant respite from the putrefaction all around. But then, he realises what the smell is, and he has to restrain himself from retching once more.

It is the smell of burned flesh.

Mollel knows what he's going to see even before he sees it. Still, he is incapable, for a few moments, of noticing anything other than the black, steaming skull which gapes eyelessly up at the sky.

He turns his back to regain his composure. From here, he can see Nairobi spreading before him. To the south, the long, flat roofs of the warehouses and factories of the industrial area; the bulbous tower of the airport, and near it, a gleaming passenger plane, climbing in an impossibly slow arc, bound for some other place. Beyond the airport, the yellow plains give way, ultimately, to the knuckle-shaped ridges of hills. To the north, the city's tall skyscrapers pack in on one another. On the exalted heights of Upper Hill, Nairobi's most prestigious district – though from here, little more than a wrinkle in the panorama – cranes bristle around all the new buildings that are springing up like mushrooms after rain. Somewhere further away than the line of green that demarcates the Northern suburbs, Mollel pictures Maryam, the little girl who was missing her sister enough to start a riot, and the two parents who do not seem to care about her at all. His heart, already leaden, sinks further.

With a sigh, he turns to examine the body.

—Here, he says to the boy with the stick. —Give me that.

He uses the stick to prod around the ribcage, which rises in a mound from the pile of ashes. There's not much can be told from this blackened scene; treacly, glistening organs, not yet entirely destroyed, lie beneath the charred bones. There are fragments of burned textile, but not much can be inferred from those either. The hips are twisted to one side; the legs splayed in a parody of a running position.

What is here barely qualifies as a body; a skeleton, certainly. Mollel recollects the red sky he had seen the previous evening. This would have been one of the many fires burning atop the mountain that night.

All around the skeleton, the litter is equally blackened and charred. Petrol, he supposes, must have been splashed around. There's no way a corpse would have burned so completely without the use of some sort of accelerant.

—Who found the body? Mollel asks.

No one answers, until Nicodemus says: —It's OK. Tell him.

—Me, Sir, lisps a small, hunched man, opening his mouth to reveal a solitary brown tooth. His face is wrinkled and his scalp eaten away with ringworm. He is dressed in rags, but on his feet, incongruously, is a pair of tan leather shoes. The spoils of the dump, no doubt.

—What's your name?

He looks taken aback, as though it's been a long time since anyone cared enough to ask.

—They call me Kitu.

Kitu. It means *Thing*.

—Well, Kitu. Tell me how you found it.

—I sleep here. Wherever I can. I have a cover.

He waves, and Mollel sees a filthy tarpaulin some metres

away. If Kitu had been sleeping below that, anyone could have virtually stepped over him without noticing.

—Go on.

—I heard someone come in the night. I kept my head down. I don't want trouble. Trouble, up here, usually ends up like that.

He points at the smoking pyre.

—Did you see the person at all?

—No. But I knew they were carrying something heavy.

—How?

Kitu makes a grunting noise. For a moment Mollel is confused; he thinks the man is having some sort of attack. Then he realises he's imitating a person groaning under a heavy load.

—Then splashing. I smelled the petrol. I began to think, maybe I'd better get out of here. I didn't want to end up being burned myself. But before I could go, there was a flash, and the heat came over me. I had to move, then.

—And still, you saw no one?

—I saw them running down the hill. They fell a couple of times. It's not easy to run here in the dark.

Mollel can believe it.

—Was the body a man? A woman?

Kitu shakes his head.

—I don't see so good. I didn't even see *this* thing was a person 'til the sun came up. I feel a bit bad about it, really.

—Why? asks Mollel, dreading the answer.

—It gets cold up here at night, admits Kitu. —I like a good fire, me, so I warmed myself up for a while. That's all. Wouldn't have done it, if I'd known. But then, why waste a good warm fire?

—We get bodies here all the time, says Nicodemus, his words clearly signalling an end to Mollel's interview with Kitu. Kitu himself, and many of the others, shrink back, providing Nicodemus with the space he requires to speak.

—So what makes this one special? asks Mollel. —Why bring me here?

—My people have been keeping track of you ever since you first arrived in Dandora, replies Nicodemus. —You think I just happened to turn up at the Electric Chair when you were there last night? I wanted to see you for myself. I don't like having policemen on my patch. I know what you're looking for, and I reckon this is it. So, now you've found it, you can clear off.

—We'll have to get a team up here, muses Mollel. —I want the pathologist to do this properly.

Nicodemus shakes his head.

—You're not listening to me. I want you gone, and I want no police here. This is not your jurisdiction, policeman. It's mine. I'll get someone to bag up this roast meat for you to take away. If not, you can leave it here, and within ten minutes it will be under six truckloads of trash. I've got a business to run.

For the first time, Mollel becomes aware of a number of garbage trucks at the base of the slope, battered and belching black fumes.

—Can't they dump elsewhere?

—You see, this, says Nicodemus, —this is what I'm talking about. You people simply don't understand what I'm doing here. You don't want to think about what happens to your rubbish when you get rid of it, so you don't. You have no idea, for example, that the trash has to be dumped in rotation. You really want avalanches of this stuff pouring into the homes and shops of Dandora? You want floods of it in the river? No? Well, then, you need it to be dumped in stages. This area, for example, has had time to settle. The garbage here has begun to decompose. It's been picked through, sifted and sorted. Anything of value has been removed. It's three metres lower than it was a month ago. This is the only place where those trucks can dump safely.

—So whoever dropped the body here, says Mollel, they knew it would soon be covered up?

—Exactly, says Nicodemus. —I hope you appreciate the favour I'm doing you, policeman. Twenty more minutes and this heap of bones would never have seen the light of day. And you'd have been prowling round Dandora, poking your nose in where it's not wanted, for God knows how long. So here's your body. Take it, and leave.

The trash-pickers have constructed a kind of sled out of sheets of cardboard, and they load the skeleton, and as much of the smoking ash around it, as they can, scooping it up with flat, oar-like shovels. Then Kitu comes forward with his cover – a tarpaulin, patched in places, but not altogether undignified. He and the other pickers maintain a quiet solemnity as they cover the body, and then drag the sled carefully down the side of the trash heap.

As soon as they depart, the lorries roar into action, and begin to crawl up to the place where the body had lain.

13

—I'm on my way back, says Kiunga. Defeat hangs heavy in his tone.

Mollel has conducted enough murder investigations to know that this is not the time to give up: that the pursuit of the guilty in the name of the perished will bring its own, determined impetus. But at this moment, he does not feel it.

Kiunga has a six-hour drive ahead of him back to Nairobi. The challenge for Mollel will be to advance the case in that time, and not to dwell on what might have been. He has no way of knowing whether Fatuma was alive or dead twenty-four hours ago, when Maryam first asked him to take on the case. The only sighting of her was in the febrile imagination of a damaged girl. The apparition which so startled Dorcas the previous night must have appeared at around the same time that the body was being burned on the rubbish heap. Mollel recalls stories of ghosts sighted at the very moment their soul left their body. If Fatuma was indeed killed last night, that means he failed. He was responsible for failing to find her in time.

—Did he find anything up-country? asks Bogani, after Mollel ends the call.

Mollel shakes his head. —Nothing to find. She never left Dandora.

*

Mollel, Bogani and Dr Achieng, the police pathologist, are standing around the bones. These have been transported – makeshift sled, ashes and all – to Chiromo Mortuary in a private ambulance.

—So what's your plan? asks Bogani, and Mollel is aware of a certain deference in the captain's tone. Deference, no doubt, to his feelings: every police officer, even the most robotic of careerists, can sympathise with the feeling of having failed to save someone. But there is also a deference to his experience. For all his seniority, Bogani does not have Mollel's years of detective experience.

Achieng, the ancient police pathologist, has been sifting through the ashes.

—When can we get an ID on this body? Mollel asks Achieng.

The old man looks up and down the bones. He has a swab in one gloved hand, which he has been running along the femur.

—Whoever did this did a pretty comprehensive job, he replies. —But not comprehensive enough. Get me some DNA to compare it to, and I'll have an ID within twenty-four hours.

—There's a hairbrush at her home. Will that do?

—Possibly, if there are hairs on it. See if you can get a toothbrush too.

—You're going to see the parents? asks Bogani.

—Yes, replies Mollel. —But I don't want to tell them about the body. I don't think word will have got out yet. Nicodemus might be uncooperative, but he runs a tight operation at the dump. If he's told his men to be tight-lipped, I'm sure they have been. And we only have one other witness.

—The *mganga*.

—Yes, says Mollel. —Doctor Kanja.

—I'd like to meet him, says Bogani.

—Here, says Achieng, and he holds out a latex-gloved hand. In the middle of his palm lies a credit-card-sized mess of twisted, blackened circuitry. A gleam of gold-coloured metal lies at its heart.

—What is it? asks Mollel.

—Care to guess, Captain? asks Achieng.

Bogani does not take the item, but lowers his face to Achieng's hand to study it.

—It looks like an electronic device, he says.

—Indeed it is, replies Achieng. —The rest of the components have melted away. I don't think it's a phone, do you?

Bogani turns to Mollel.

—Do we know whether she had anything like a music player or a camera?

—Yes, says Mollel. —Yes, she did. A music player.

And then, knowing he risks sounding foolish, he adds: —Could we make it work again? Play the music somehow?

The sceptical look from his colleagues makes him regret the question.

—I'm no computer scientist, says Achieng, —but whatever was stored on this, is gone. What we *might* be able to do is confirm the particular device. That would provide some sort of identification, at least.

The holding cell at *Mji wa Huruma* police post is not a place of entertainment. Just as on any other day, there are half a dozen men languishing there, slouched up against the side of the cage with their forearms wrapped around the bars, or sitting on the floor, head in their hands. Many of them are drunks, nursing the after-effects of too much home-brewed *changa'a*, or glue-sniffers who had been found passed out in the gutter. Usually there will be a petty thief or two, probably glad to be in a cell rather than suffering the summary justice of a mob.

But today, rather than suffering in silence, the prisoners are paying amused attention to a small, wizened figure, who is holding court on the other side of the bars in the adjacent waiting room. He's down on his haunches, and has removed his red bedsheet, which he holds by one corner with one hand. He's now in his singlet and shorts. He is moving the sheet in a circular motion, swishing it around on the floor, and making a low, chanting noise, which though quiet, strangely fills the cell, causing the bustle of the general office beyond to fall similarly silent.

A couple of the traffic officers have drifted over to observe the scene. Even the cynical custody sergeant, usually far too dignified to show any interest in the antics of those under his control, has raised an amused eyebrow from behind his desk.

Doctor Kanja stops chanting, and casts his wild eyes around all those watching.

—When I lift my robe, he says, —it will be gone.

The only sound in the room comes from a slumped drug addict wheezing in the corner.

Kanja stands, and whips the red robe into the air. Underneath it, a tin cup spins, rattles and falls over.

A howl of derision fills the cell. Those hanging on the bars slap and shake them. The policemen laugh, too, until they decide that enough is enough, and then they draw their batons and start to bash them against the bars, not paying too much heed about whether they bash a few fingers in the process.

When order has been restored, Kanja remains standing in front of the cage. He picks up the cup, inverts it as though looking for something, then places it back on the ground. Quietly, he ties the cloth around his body once more. Then he smooths its creases, as though nothing is amiss, and walks towards the custody desk.

—Is Sergeant Mollel ready to see me? he asks the duty officer. —When I agreed to come, I did not realise it would take this long. I have patients waiting for me.

—Let them wait! growls the policeman. But Mollel, who has

been watching from a doorway on the far side of the room, calls out: —It's OK. Let him come.

The desk sergeant nods Kanja through. His departure is noticed by the drug addict, who rubs his eyes. A slow smile of wonder spreads across his face.

—It's *gone*, he croaks. —It's gone!

The rest of the prisoners start up their racket again, and the duty officer bellows for calm. But the junkie stands, and extends his hands through the bars to Kanja, who is making his way towards Mollel. —Thank you, he sighs.

Kanja presses his hands together in the praying sign, and bows his head.

—What was he thanking you for? Mollel asks.

—For making his addiction disappear.

—Really? I thought you were trying to make the cup disappear.

—I was, replies Kanja. —But the spirits move in mysterious ways.

They sit in Bogani's office, Bogani behind his desk, Mollel and Kanja before him. Mollel has shifted his chair at an angle so it doesn't look quite so much as though he, as well as Kanja, is the subject of the interrogation.

—The girl is dead, says Bogani.

—What makes you think it's her? asks Kanja. —Nicodemus says they get bodies up there all the time.

—We have a positive ID, Bogani replies unblinkingly. Mollel tries not to react to the lie. He's pulled the same trick himself plenty of times.

—This is a murder case, continues Bogani. —There is no question of client confidentiality any more. We need to know why you were treating Fatuma. We need to know what she said to you. Anything and everything could be important. By staying silent, you're only protecting her killer.

Kanja raises an eyebrow.

—So secrets belong only to the living?

Mollel sees a shadow cross Bogani's usually imperturbable face. He gives the slightest hint of a nod. It is the falling leaf which signals an impending storm.

—Why don't you leave us, Mollel? he says.

—Yes, Captain.

It is not done to eavesdrop on one's superiors, even in the police service. But it is acceptable to linger near an office door, in case assistance should be required – and Mollel, ever mindful of his duty, leans against the wall just a few feet away. He also can't help overhearing Bogani's voice, more forceful than usual, reverberating through the door. The individual words are lost, but the tone is unmistakably laced with frustration, and something more. What little Mollel has seen of Bogani gives him few clues to decode the passion rising in his voice.

Of Kanja, Mollel hears nothing. His responses are the seconds counted between the flash and the thunder. But whatever he is saying, it is enough to make Bogani spring to his feet. The screech of his chair skidding back gives Mollel enough warning to allow him to retreat a couple of paces and spin around, as though he were walking nonchalantly towards the door just as it opened, rather than away from it.

Bogani comes out first. Mollel shoots him a questioning glance, but the captain marches past with a barely audible growl.

Behind him strolls Kanja. He beams at Mollel unperturbed.

—It looks like I'm done here, he says. —You know where to find me if you need anything, Sergeant.

Mollel accompanies him to the doorway of the police station, and remains, watching the little, clown-like character walk splay-footedly to the curb, where he looks both ways as though pondering which direction appeals most, before plunging into the crowd. Mollel is afforded an occasional glimpse of his head, bobbing amongst the foot traffic, until he is gone.

A policeman's instinct is a curious thing. Although he's looking one way, Mollel feels compelled to turn his head to look the other way down the street. Someone is looking at him, he is sure, and he searches for their eyes.

And there – behind the tinted windscreen of a black car – a pair of round, oversized shades on a feminine face. Seeing him look, a slender hand reaches up and pulls down the sun visor. Then, hurriedly, the car starts and pulls out, sending a cyclist swerving, and rumbles past. The side windows are even more heavily tinted than the front, so Mollel sees no more of the driver than a cloudy silhouette. He is sure, though, that it is a woman. He makes a mental note of the plate number and watches the car move off in the same direction as Kanja had taken.

Mollel is aware of Bogani at his shoulder.

—I assume you had as much luck with him as I did? Mollel asks.

Bogani shakes his head furiously. Mollel has never seen the captain so disturbed before. Was it just because Kanja had proved immune to his interrogation technique?

—That Kanja, Bogani says. —People like him, they get into your head. That's what they want. Don't let him do it to you, Mollel. He has nothing to do with this case, I'm sure of that. I don't want to see him again. And if you'll take my advice, you won't, either.

14

When Mollel remembers the raid on the car lot, he wants it to end with the image of Lendeva, victorious. The brothers reunited. Mollel regretful for his suspicion that he could ever have been abandoned. That's how a storyteller would leave it.

Unfortunately, memory does not follow a neat path. It rarely arrives at the conclusion one would hope for. For Mollel, it is impossible to remember the moment of triumph without recalling what happened next.

The older guard, the one they all called Uncle, had been left in charge of the first intruders Mollel had subdued. Everyone agreed, Uncle was such a nice guy. In the days before the raid, Mollel used to meet him, occasionally, as he came on shift. He had kids. He worked nights without a break, week in, week out, to make ends meet. Mollel always thought of him as a gentle soul. He had those eyes – those light-brown eyes, like an *mzungu's* eyes, that you seldom see on a Kenyan, and when you do, they seem to catch the light and laugh.

After he and Lendeva had secured the other intruders, Mollel went back to the guard hut. The first thing he saw, as he rounded the corner, was a pair of bare feet. The toes were pointing at the sky. They were not moving.

The dead lie like no living person. Even in the darkness, Mollel could tell this was a corpse. He barely dared advance, even though the gun was still in his hand. He inched his way around the corner. There, in the light streaming from the interior of the guard hut, he could see not one, but two figures lying prone on the ground. Alongside the dead, two living; one standing, one crouching.

The standing one, trying out his new shoes, was Uncle. He'd removed his heavy black boots and was bouncing his heels up and down in a pair of trainers he'd stripped from the corpse. He looked up with his light eyes as Mollel approached. The other guard stood up now too, removing his hand from inside the jacket of the second body. Something went into his pocket.

—Ah, Maasai, said Uncle. —Just after you left, they tried to escape. Attacked us. We had no choice . . .

He turned up a palm. It glistened with blood. A black slit gaped on the throat of one of the bodies. Mollel looked down at Uncle's shoes.

—Well, he won't need them any more, will he?

15

—You know, Dad, you *could* always learn how to do this for yourself.

Around them, on the walls of Adam's bedroom, Nyambisha Karao and the other exponents of the genre glare down at them. But in the glow of the computer screen, an eager smile is playing across the boy's lips. He wants to appear cool, detached and professional – grown-up – but can barely disguise his pleasure at being able to show off his skills. Not to mention the unexpected opportunity to spend time with his father.

—So we just log on to the vehicle registration database using your police ID and your credentials. What's your email address?

—I don't have one. Do I?

—Oh, come on, Dad! You must have one. I bet your work has set one up for you. You've probably got a million unread emails.

Mollel shrugs. —If people need me, they know how to find me.

The boy is openly grinning now. —Let's just try your name at the Kenya police domain.

The keyboard clatters and the screen changes.

—We're in, says Mollel, patting his son's shoulder.

The boy laughs. —It's not exactly *hacking*, Dad. This is the way the world works now.

Even five years ago, searching out a car's owner using the

registration number would have involved a trip down to the department of transportation, and sweet-talking some fusty functionary into climbing a ladder and pulling out a set of curling yellow files. Kenya had arrived late to the digital age, but was now embracing it. Everyone except Mollel.

—Here's the number, Mollel says, passing his son a piece of paper. Adam glances at it and his fingers dance across the keys.

—Black BMW saloon, he says. Nice wheels.

He sounds like Kiunga.

—Registered owner: one Janet Kimathi, Adam continues. —Wow, Dad. You've got yourself a celebrity stalker.

—I thought she was in America.

—She was, replies Adam. —She's back. Word is, she lost her job because of . . .

The boy makes a cup shape with his hand and mimes drinking. When did he get so worldly?

—I wonder why she was watching you, Adam says.

—I didn't say she was watching me, replies Mollel, who had been wondering the same thing. —She could have been waiting for anybody.

—And yet she sped off the moment she saw you looking at her?

—She might have had plenty of other reasons for acting the way she did. She . . .

Mollel breaks off. He is speaking to his fourteen year-old son as though he is a colleague.

—Never mind. Are those her contact details?

He takes back the scrap of paper and writes down the address and phone number. It seemed obvious now. It hadn't occurred to him before, because she hadn't occupied his conscious mind for many years, but yes, now he heard the name again, he did think that the silhouette behind those round, dark glasses could not have belonged to anyone other than Janet Kimathi.

*

It had been big news in Kenya when the local girl had made good. In the late nineties, none of the US TV networks had correspondents in East Africa. They might have had some grizzled hack in Johannesburg or Cairo, and plenty of them had been flown in to wring their hands over Rwanda, when it was all far too late. But otherwise, the rest of the continent was one big blank space where the latest bad news was related via out-of-vision voice-over to file footage, and a reminder to stay tuned for the weather after the break.

Then the American embassies in Nairobi and Dar es Salaam had been struck, and suddenly East Africa mattered. In the scramble to get the household names out of Beirut and Bosnia someone had the bright idea of patching into the Kenyan stations and picking up pictures that could be matched to a script so American viewers would understand that these dead Africans were significant, somehow.

But there was a pesky – if pretty – young reporter who stood in front of the scenes and wouldn't leave the carnage clear for a nice, professional edit, and in exasperation some executive turned up the audio and heard her words, which to his surprise delivered an engaging and comprehensive narrative in a clear but charmingly lilting Kenyan accent. 'Fuck it,' he said (or so the story went), 'we'll put her on air.'

The horror of the mass murder and the novelty of a young, African reporter who could so eloquently set the scene – *contextualise*, they called it – made compelling viewing and a few phone calls later, she was putting together segments at the direct behest of the US networks. *We need a hero*, they told her on day four of the Nairobi bombing, as the story was beginning to drag. *Find us a hero*, and after this, who knows what awaits you. Maybe a job over here, in the States. We could do with more international faces back at base. But *find us a hero first*.

So Janet had found Mollel.

*

Mollel leaves Adam watching online videos of rap music. He has a sense of unease about those swaggering figures in baggy clothes and the girls writhing around them, but there is nothing strictly indecent about it. Besides, he had felt – for a moment – a rare connection with his son, and he didn't want to ruin it. For too long he had been both mother and father to this boy, and never felt that he had succeeded at either. Occasionally, though, he felt a glimmer of hope that he might be a better father to the man than he'd been to the boy.

He looks at the number written on the piece of paper. It represents all those years that have passed. Now he's the one who feels like a teenager. He picks up his phone and dials.

—This is Janet.

Her voice hasn't changed.

—Janet. It's Mollel.

A silence. Then a laugh. —Mollel. *Bado kufa?*

—No. Not dead yet.

—That figures. I wondered if you'd spotted me the other day. Sorry for not stopping to say hello. I thought I'd seen a ghost.

A ghost. Mollel is reminded of Dorcas, and her night runner.

He shakes himself out of what could only be a fruitless line of thinking. Perhaps he's been spending too much time around the likes of Kanja. Stupid superstition.

And yet . . .

—I'm no ghost. You didn't have to run away.

—Oh, Mollel. It wasn't *you* I was running from. Look, it would be great to see you again. Properly, I mean. How about a drink? Are you free this evening?

—Thanks for coming over, Faith. Sorry for the short notice.

—Always a pleasure to baby-sit my grandson, says Faith. —Not that he'll need it much longer.

They share a look which is simultaneously proud, and wistful. Mollel has never been exactly friendly with his mother-in-law, but they have developed a kind of mutual respect whose foundation lies in their shared love for Adam. —They work you too hard, Mollel, she adds. —It *is* work, isn't it?

Not much gets past this old woman. She may be getting thinner and frailer every year, but her shrewdness just gets sharper. Mollel instinctively clutches his tie. He knew the tie was a mistake. He never wears a tie.

—Let me do that for you, says Faith. She reaches up and he lets her readjust the knot.

—There. Very smart.

She pauses. —You know, Mollel, all these years, you've never seen someone else. No one would blame you if you did.

—It's not like that, says Mollel.

—I don't care what it's like, says Faith. —Your life is your business. I just want Adam to be happy. And honestly, Mollel, do you know what would make him happier than anything on Earth?

Mollel is silent.

—To see *you* happy.

Mollel does not know how to answer. They are both desperately relieved when Adam enters the room. —Hi, *Bibi!* Oh, wow, Dad. Looking sharp! Have you got a *date*?

It's not a date, though. It is work, as Mollel keeps telling himself. It must be, because his policeman's instinct is firing off. Something tells him that Janet Kimathi turning up at this time is more than just coincidence. If she was not hanging around at the police station in order to see him, then it must have been Kanja she was tailing. She's always had a nose for a story. In some ways, she was a better detective than he had ever been, because she didn't care about anything other than the story. She didn't let little things get in her way. Little things like proof, or people.

Mollel feels a flush of anger towards her, which turns into a flutter of excitement as he spots her sitting on the far side of the bar. She is perched on a high stool, her slim legs crossed, the toe of one high-heeled shoe turning slowly as she rolls some white wine around in a tall-stemmed glass. She looks up, sees him, and smiles. He realises he's smiling, too.

She stands as he approaches and offers him a fine-boned cheek to kiss. It's a gesture which would normally flummox Mollel, but he accepts it naturally. And then she looks at him a while.

—You've not changed.

—Nor have you.

He's being honest, though he doubts she is. He is fully aware of the toll the years have taken on his features. She, though, is still a very attractive woman. Hardly a wrinkle on her face – though maybe the soft lighting in this hotel bar has something to do with it.

A cough from the barman, who has appeared beside them. Mollel looks with dismay at the backlit bottles which fill the shelves, the rows of shiny refrigerators with even more bottles within, and he hasn't a clue what to order.

—Just a water, please.

The barman looks at Janet. She picks up her glass and empties it. —Another. Still not drinking, eh, Mollel?

A glass of wine appears, as does a tall glass of sparkling water, full of clinking ice, with a straw and a slice of lemon. Mollel takes a sip of his water and tries to act as though he's used to such a concoction.

—I think our table's ready, says Janet. —Shall we?

The table brings fresh hell for Mollel. There is more cutlery than could sensibly be deemed necessary, not to mention more glassware, and a candle, and a little flower in a little vase, and salt and pepper and some kind of oil and another liquid Mollel does not recognise, and an oversize napkin in an arrangement which resembles a child's party hat. Janet plucks the napkin and shakes it free, smoothing it gracefully on her lap. Mollel knows that were he to try the same thing, glasses would go flying. He doesn't risk it.

—So, he says. —Is this just a flying visit? Or are you back for good?

—I'm back. I wouldn't say for good. But for the foreseeable.

—How was America?

She gives a sigh.

—America's America. It's a long way from here.

He smiles.

—Why are you smiling?

—I just remembered something, says Mollel. —Your habit of saying things without saying anything. It's a good trick for a journalist. Keeps the conversation going, without switching the focus away from the subject.

—The art of interviewing, concedes Janet. —Create the space, and let them talk. Everyone needs someone to talk to. Even a policeman.

—Or a journalist.

Or a psychiatrist, thinks Mollel. And the ridiculous figure of Kanja appears in his mind. That, he reminds himself, is why he's here. Not to renew an old acquaintance. Or play word games.

—So you say you weren't at *Mji wa Huruma* police post to see me. I can believe that. But you were obviously following someone. Am I allowed to ask who?

—You're allowed to ask. But no, I'd rather not say at this time.

The waiter arrives with two oversized menus. Mollel glances at his, sighs, and looks around for somewhere to put it down. There isn't anywhere. Instead, he raises it in front of his face as though reading it, and enjoys a moment's respite from this duelling conversation.

These places, with their subdued lighting, and their soft music, and their attentive waiters, and décor so tasteful and neutral, are designed to be as unobtrusive and restful as possible. Everything is intended to set one at ease. The effect upon Mollel is the opposite. This is not his world. He is a man of improvisation and opportunity. A grabbed meal on the street or a snack sitting on his haunches in the wilderness; either of these would make him more comfortable than he feels now.

And then, there is the company. Janet Kimathi is charming, certainly. She knows just how to ramp up the intensity of her smile or widen her eyes in fascination. But while Mollel had been looking forward to feeling that attention again – he can admit it to himself now – it is beginning to irk him, as he remembers just how well she can use these wiles to attain her end.

Last time, she got the exclusive story she needed, then she discarded him. He hasn't been able to figure out what she is aiming at this time.

He lowers the menu. He had been expecting to be greeted by Janet's eyes upon his, wrinkled with ironic humour – but she is looking aside, her eyebrows pinched in a frown.

Mollel follows her gaze. Another aspect of this type of restaurant is the illusion they try to create of being private, when they are anything but. A few tables away, someone has broken the unspoken rule of these places – that glances must be sideways, snide comments whispered – with photographs strictly forbidden.

Sure, the guy was attempting subtlety. A nonchalant viewer might suppose he was just looking at his phone's screen. But it is held down below the table level at an angle not suitable for browsing. And once he realises he's been spotted, the way he swiftly pockets it, and then glances around, says it all.

—Got your picture? demands Janet. Her voice is loud and level, which amounts to shouting in this environment. Everyone in the room falls silent and people turn to crane and look. The man, who is sitting alone, puts on a *who, me?* face which fools no one. The waiter approaches him and leans in for an exchange of words so discreet that the two might be communing telepathically. The man gets up and leaves.

—I'm sorry, Miss Kimathi, says the waiter, now appearing at their table. — I've asked the gentleman to leave. Can I take your order now?

—I don't know. The mood's gone. Are you hungry, Mollel?

Mollel shakes his head, relieved not to have to navigate this menu.

She dismisses the waiter with a wave of her long-nailed hand.

—Look, I've taken a suite here while I'm settling back into Nairobi. How about we order a drink and take it upstairs? I mean, you can stick with the water if you like, but I want some wine.

Upstairs turns out to be a ride in an elevator as plush and impersonal as the restaurant, with the same low lighting and piped music. Mollel wonders whether this wasn't part of Janet's plan all along.

She has picked up two glasses, despite his abstinence, and holds them cross-stemmed in one hand as she inserts the key card and the door clicks open. Mollel follows behind, holding the neck of the wine bottle, recorked, and sloshing coldly.

A light comes on inside the suite. Janet does a quick one, two kick, and her tall heels come off and clatter against the wall. Her hips sway as she pads ahead of Mollel into the kitchen area. She places the two glasses down on the marble counter.

Mollel has no idea what a suite like this must cost, but if Nairobi had a hotel room ratings system comprehensive enough to encompass both Abdelahi Abdelahi's grubby 'self-contained' and this place, they'd be at opposite ends of the scale. Floor-to-ceiling windows at the far end reveal a balcony, and beyond it, the twinkling vista of Nairobi's towers. Somewhere beyond that – and not even too far, certainly no more than twenty minutes by car at this time of night – would lie the glowering, smoking pile of Dandora. But here the air is fresh and clear, filtered by the leaves of the park whose treetops, tall and elegant silhouettes, become evident to Mollel as he steps further into the room.

The view has distracted him so much that he almost walks into a tripod with a tiny camera upon it; a silver-black three-legged spider with a single beady eye. Like limp webs, wires trail from it, ending with bud microphones, one lying on the seat cushion of each of the two leather chairs. A pair of small lamps on spindly poles stand in the corners. It all looks a lot smaller and somehow, to his layman eyes, less professional than the kit Janet had used when she'd interviewed him a decade ago; she'd had a crew then, too. Mollel doesn't know whether this says more about improved technology or Janet's diminished star power.

—This was your plan, then? Mollel asks. —Bring me up here, and shoot another interview? Hope I'd give you the inside track again?

His mind goes back to the scene of Otieno struggling in front of the parliamentary committee. Perhaps it was his blood she had scented, and she had singled out Mollel as her attack dog.

To her credit, she looks genuinely surprised. Then she laughs.

—Oh, Mollel. Is that what you thought? Well, I suppose I can see what it looks like. But honestly, no. No, no, no.

She laughs and pours a glass of wine. She raises it to offer it to him. He shakes his head; she shrugs, takes a sip, and then picks up a napkin. Walking over to the camera, she unfolds the napkin and places it delicately over the small device.

—There. Now we're alone.

She laughs again.

—Don't be so paranoid, Mollel. This is about me, not you. Take a seat, why don't you.

She picks up one of the bud microphones and drops it to the

floor, sinking into the seat and crossing her legs. Mollel picks up the microphone from the facing chair, and places it on the armrest before slowly taking his place.

—I guess things don't always work out the way we imagine. I certainly didn't think ten years ago that I'd end up back in Nairobi, holed up in a hotel room, desperately making showreels for low-budget lifestyle chat shows.

She reaches forward and picks up a remote control. The flatscreen TV blinks into life, and she scrolls through a menu. There, on the screen, Mollel sees the very room he's sitting in. This time, the camera is pointed at the kitchen. On the counter sits a mixing bowl, and some ingredients in bowls. Janet walks into shot, composes her smile, and speaks.

—Welcome back. Today we're going to make a wonderful dish I learned to love when I was in the States. It's called grits. It's a lot like ugali, but a little more American, if that makes sense. Shit.

The smile vanishes, and the on-screen Janet reaches out of shot. Her hand reappears in frame with a glass in it.

The real-life Janet pauses the video.

—Death and disaster come much more naturally to me, she says.

She scrolls and picks another thumbnail on the video. This time Mollel recognises the empty chair as the one he is currently sitting in.

On screen, Janet sits down on the chair and again composes herself.

—Hello. Today, we're talking about a serious topic. Did you know that an estimated one in five Kenyans suffers from depression? It's something that can happen to anyone, rich or poor, male or female, married or single. And sometimes, people can be very good at hiding the symptoms. And this is something about which I can speak with personal experience. About which I can speak? What the f . . .

—I used to be known as one-take Janet, she says, pausing the video once more. —I don't know if it's my age, or . . . do you ever feel it, Mollel? Feel like you're losing your edge?

He shrugs. —I never had an edge.

—Come on, Mollel. You're *all* edge! I never met anyone edgier than you.

He doesn't answer.

—I'm sorry, you know, she says. —Sorry for what I did.

—It was a good story, Janet. I never blamed you.

—You opened up to me, and I betrayed you.

—The camera was right there. I knew what I was doing.

—You were grieving.

—I said things that needed to be said. The fact that I was grieving was irrelevant. Except that it helped me out at the disciplinary.

—I still feel terrible. I guess I put it out of my mind for all those years, but when I saw you the other day, it all came flooding back. You were vulnerable and I used that. If I could do it all over again . . .

—I'm not keen to go over any of that, Janet.

—I know. But if I could, I'd like to get to know Mollel the man, instead of Mollel the policeman.

He has not been looking at her while she makes this speech. His eyes have been on the freeze-framed image of her on the TV screen. But now he looks up, and sees that her eyes are glistening with tears. She gives a half-sob, half-laugh, and wipes her eyes with the back of her hand.

This is the second time in a matter of days that Mollel has been confronted with tears. Again, he has a feeling that something is expected of him.

There is a buzzing in his pocket. He stands, and Janet stands too, but he turns away as he pulls out his phone and sees that the caller is Kiunga.

—I've got to get this, he says.

She tosses her head and leaves the room.

—It's not her, says Kiunga.

Mollel, hauling himself back into detective mode, has to ask: —Who?

—Fatuma, says Kiunga. —The body from the dump. It's not her.

16

—A tie, Mollel? asks Dr Achieng. —We don't usually insist on such formalities at City Mortuary.

—I'm surprised you're in the mood to joke, mutters Kiunga. —I'd be too embarrassed, if I were you.

—You told us it was a teenage girl, adds Mollel.

—No, bristles Achieng. —*You* told me it was a teenage girl. It was perfectly reasonable for me to go along with that assumption. But upon closer inspection, the facts did not bear it out. Would you like to come through to the autopsy room and see for yourself?

Kiunga shudders. Mollel says: —Just tell us, Doctor.

—You saw the corpse. It was comprehensively incinerated. The trash heap provided an effective pyre, allowing for good oxygen flow all around the body. Some sort of accelerant had probably been used – paraffin or petrol. Given that what we had was effectively charcoal, our initial conclusions were naturally going to be subject to revision.

Kiunga catches Mollel's glance with the slightest hint of an eye-roll. Achieng is on the defensive.

—From what I could tell about the amount of material adhering to the skeleton, this was a neither an obese nor a muscular person. Either case would have resulted in a significantly different combustion pattern. The tissue erosion fitted the hypothesis you presented me with, i.e. that this was a young female. The skeleton height of one hundred and sixty-seven centimetres was also congruent. Traces of fabric were insufficient to provide clues about clothing. Besides which, without access to the locus, there could have been no way of ascertaining whether these came from the body or not. You'll have noted, of course, that there were no shoes.

Mollel frowns. He *hadn't* noticed the shoes, or lack of them, and he's furious with himself. In the heat of this makeshift cremation, plastic or rubber soles would have melted but any metal fittings – such as lace eyelets – would have been preserved. He keeps his eyes lowered, not wanting to catch Kiunga's again. He hardly feels he can rebuke Achieng after this oversight.

—When I came to examine the skeleton, however, I was struck by the compact pelvis. While this would not be uncommon for a teenage girl, it might be supposed that the superior aperture would be elliptical in shape. What I was looking at was virtually circular.

—In other words . . . prompts Kiunga.

—In other words, detectives, your teenage girl was a man. A slightly built and possibly young man, certainly. But a man, nonetheless.

Given the reality of the charred corpse which Mollel had helped to carry down the mountain of trash, there is no relief to be found in this revelation. Someone is still dead—presumably murdered. And Fatuma is still missing.

—Where do we go from here? he murmurs to himself.

—I feel like a drink, replies Kiunga.

—I know just the place.

Not that either of them will be drinking. But they've come to a place where people are. It is fast approaching midnight, and the Electric Chair is just beginning to warm up.

There are cars that you'd never see in Dandora in daytime – Range Rovers and Lexuses, Land Cruisers and Jaguars, all of them black, all of them spotless – parked up on the sides of the streets for a block or more. A security detail whose only uniform is their air of belonging guides new arrivals into place. Wary eyes scan the police car as it glides past. No one rushes to usher this one into a spot; Kiunga has to curse and try to reverse it into a gap himself. Out on the street, the music is already loud enough to set their teeth jangling and the beat bouncing in their chests. The neon light of the BEER N BEATS sign flickers and picks out the figures clustered around the doorway. There's a line, but Kiunga steps to the head of it, and the two huge men standing there part, aware of *what*, if not exactly *who*, they're letting in. Mollel notices that one of them looks up and flashes a hand signal to a small camera perched above the door.

They push past a gaggle of young men and women waiting for the cloakroom. The men wear either slouchy, low-slung jeans with baggy American sports T-shirts or singlets, or they wear sharp, slim-cut suits, with wide-necked shirts and gold chains. Both styles, so diverse, are united by chunky, pristine trainers.

The women wear short skirts or shorts cut so high they nip the base of the bottom; spines and navels are on display; breasts are pushed up and forward; nails and lips and eyelids are painted and flashing.

Mollel would imagine this to be Kiunga's nirvana, but looking at the younger cop, he is heartened to see that his colleague looks decidedly uncomfortable. Mollel himself, while feeling out of place, does not find this environment as intimidating as the hotel he was in earlier. Although he attracts some glances – amused, scornful, wary – they quickly look away as the scene changes and shifts around them. The press of bodies is too heavy, the flow of movement too strong, the darkness too dark and the lights too bright, and the music – the music! – is too distracting for any impression to last more than a few seconds before another emerges and demands to take its place.

The air seems to tingle and throb with the beat, and is thick with the smell of sweat and beer and piss and the sweet, cloying scent of *bhangi*, smoked openly here, joints occasionally seen in a flash of light being passed from hand to hand, or in cherry-red tips glowing in corners.

A hand on his shoulder. Mollel sees Kiunga's lips move.

—What?

Kiunga leans in closer. —I said, I feel old!

His teeth glow in the light from a UV lamp and Mollel can't help smiling back. If Kiunga feels old, how should he feel? But somehow, he feels different. Energised. It could be the loud music or the pent-up energy of the bodies all around him. Or it could be that, now there is a possibility that Fatuma is still alive, the hunt is back on. His detective instincts thrill again at the challenge. And it could also be, he has to concede, the fact that an attractive woman invited him back to her hotel room this evening. Had Janet been making a pass at him? He tries to put the question out of his mind, deciding that there are more important questions to address right now – or preferring, perhaps, to leave the answer ambiguous.

They move through, shouldering their way into the main hall. Up on stage is a double act, a pair of small, wiry boys in red, tag-teaming a rap, mics in hand, throwing their elbows out in wild gestures. The crowd seems only partly engaged; this appears to be the warm-up act rather than the main event. The buzz of shouted conversation is still audible, just, above the antics on stage.

Even so, most faces are turned that way, and Mollel and Kiunga make their way towards the pool of light. Right at the front, a few dozen youths are rowdily thrashing along to the act, hopping up and down and flailing into one another. Mollel is reminded of the way young warriors, often drunk on honey wine, will bounce on their heels following an initiation ceremony. He's seen that result in a broken nose, and he's not keen to get one now, so he pulls Kiunga aside and they ensconce themselves along the wall beside a shelf crowded with empties. They are able to appreciate the vantage point this gives them. With the glow of the stage lights reflected upon their faces, most of the club's patrons can be made out. Instinctively, Mollel starts checking them off against the mental database of offenders, louts, layabouts and chancers he's built up over the years.

His attention is suddenly caught by a movement making its way across the dancefloor towards him. It's not so much a presence, as the absence of one – a gap between the dancers getting closer. It reminds Mollel of the way you can spot a small dog running through long grass.

The dancers part and Dora steps deftly forward. Somehow, through the melee, she has managed to carry a tray with two bottles of Tusker and two glasses. She gives Mollel a smile. Kiunga straightens up, but it's Mollel she speaks to – or shouts to.

—Compliments of the boss.

She tilts her head back towards the bar. Through the darkness and smoke, Mollel can nonetheless make out the stocky shoulders and bald head of Nicodemus. The man raises a glass theatrically to toast the policemen.

—That girl we're looking for, starts Mollel, but Dora cuts him off.

—Don't talk to me, she hisses in his ear as she starts collecting empty bottles. —Listen up. She's not the only one, get it? There are others.

Turning away, so as not to look at her, Mollel puts his hand over his mouth and says loudly: —What others?

But Dora is gone. At least now the shelf beside him is clear, so Mollel has somewhere to put his unasked-for beer. Just in time, too. The duo on stage have stopped gooning around and are lapping up the faint applause and a few lacklustre cheers from the crowd, which seems less keen on congratulating them than getting them off the podium and out of the way for the next act. In fact, a palpable sense of anticipation is beginning to fill the hall.

The room swells as hangers-on drift in. Mollel sees Kiunga scanning the hall. His eyes follow Dora as she ducks and darts nimbly among the crowd, taking orders and carrying her tray. She is quite different from the glammed-up, high-heeled clientele. She is wearing black jeans and a black T-shirt. Her chunky glasses, nose ring and dreads also mark her out as more distinctive and somehow more self-confident, even though her flat canvas sneakers render her much shorter than the average concert-goer.

A whoop comes up from the crowd. A tall, skinny guy, track-suit top dripping off his hunched shoulders, a sun hat pulled down like a bucket over his eyes, round sunglasses on his beaky nose, comes out on stage. He waves and whips his hands in appreciation of the applause. Then he takes his position behind a set of record decks and the lighting changes. His lips approach the microphone.

—*Sasa*, Electric Chair. *Niaje*?

—*Poa*! cries the crowd.

—Yeah, that's what I wanna hear. Thanks to those guys, whatta they called, Mickey and Mikey. Great. But we all know who you're here for, right?

The crowd is becoming more frenzied. The DJ steps back from the mic, grabs his crotch with both hands and thrusts his hips. This elicits peals of delight. He reaches out, pulls the mic from the stand, and announces:

—Give it up! For! Mister! Nyambisha! Karao!

The last name is subsumed in the screams which rise up in greeting: the lights flash, the DJ waves his hands in the air, the crowd follows suit and Kiunga, who had been taking a sip of his beer, has the bottle dashed from his hand.

Onto stage, strolling nonchalantly, his hands in his pockets, slouches Nyambisha Karao. His muscular arms are covered in tattoos, as is his chest, much of which is visible beneath his low-cut vest. His body language exudes power and control. The less excited he is, the more animated the crowd becomes. He comes to the centre of the stage, stops by the microphone stand, and almost as an afterthought, says into it:

—Hey.

Jomo Kenyatta declaring Kenya's independence from Britain could hardly have received a more rapturous reception. Karao holds his hands up to calm the noise.

—Now, I'm here to play to you good people tonight, but you know what I just heard? I heard we got some pigs in the place tonight.

There is a ripple of laughter, but it's nervous, and is quickly replaced by booing and jeers. People are looking around. Quite a few of them are looking at Mollel and Kiunga.

—You guys know me. You know I don't play for no *pigs*.

What was excitement now turns to outrage. Kiunga's hand grabs Mollel's wrist. —Time we were going.

A dozen or more pairs of eyes turn upon them. Someone mutters something. People start nudging and nodding in their direction.

—I agree, says Mollel.

Just then, Karao raises his hand to his eyes against the light. It takes him a second, but then he spots them, and points directly at Mollel and Kiunga.

—Good evening, officers. A lot of people paid good money to see a show tonight. How's it feel to disappoint them?

Faces around them snarl. Mollel feels a sharp pain: a kick in the shin.

—We're not looking for any trouble, protests Kiunga.

—How about we give them something to remember us by? yells Karao.

It's the signal the crowd needs. A sudden surge is upon them; Mollel's shirt loses several buttons as hands grab at him. He struggles and pulls away but more hands lunge forward. He has a vision of sinking down onto this sticky, littered dancefloor and meeting more feet than he can resist, drowning amidst an undertow of high heels and high-top trainers, stomping and lashing at him, one judiciously aimed kick crashing down onto his temple and crushing his skull.

It's not going to happen. Not yet. —Follow me, urges a voice – Dora's – as her small hand grabs his and leads him towards the stage. She's adept at weaving through these crowds, and Mollel has a fingertip's grip on Kiunga's sleeve behind him. They snake their way – a glancing blow of knuckles against the back of Mollel's head, the sudden shock of a mouth full of liquid, spit running down his cheek – and then they're virtually at Karao's feet, looking up at the brightly lit stage. The performer catches Mollel's eye with a look that implies he has total power of life or death over the two of them, and it's simply a matter of whether he can be bothered to exercise it. Then he turns away.

The howling of the crowd grows louder – but it's because Karao has signalled to the DJ, who spins a beat. The lights drop, as do the hands lunging at Mollel and Kiunga. They are suddenly free.

Dora has disappeared from view, but her hand still grips Mollel's. He understands why, as he feels a heavy, scratchy curtain brush across his face. Just at that moment, Nyambisha Karao starts rapping, but the sound is slightly muffled by the curtain, and his machine-gun delivery is too fast, and his Sheng too dense, for Mollel to follow.

—Christ, says Kiunga, behind him. —That was close.

—You're not out yet, cautions Dora. She is standing before them in a narrow space beside the stage, lit by a single dim light bulb. Crates of empty beer bottles are stacked high along the wall, and she pushes the two policemen into a space between them. Mollel and Kiunga just have time to flatten themselves against the wall before they hear voices: —Where did they go?

—You supposed to be back here? Dora demands of the people following them.

Apparently they aren't, because there is no reply, and there is a glimpse of light from the stage as the curtain is lifted again. Dora pulls Mollel's sleeve and takes him to a swing door. There is a corridor with toilets, and a group of men and women hanging around, smoking and chatting.

She reaches into the back pocket of her jeans and pulls out a creased, laminated card. It is black. Upon it are the letters VIP.

—There's a private section through that door at the end. This'll get you in.

—Both of us?

She smiles and nods at Kiunga, and Mollel wonders what is amusing her. —Say he's your guest. They'll believe it. Once you're in, keep going, you'll find a fire exit. Just don't hang around.

—Wait. You said there were more. More what? More missing girls?

Again the light, and now there's another group coming in. One of the stacks of beer crates wobbles, and Dora rushes to save it – as she tries to push it upright, she also manages to pull it out into the path of the oncoming figures. Kiunga tugs at Mollel. —Let's go.

They head through the door, faces down, trying not to catch the eye of any of the group clustered around the toilet doors. A woman coming out, her face bleary, bowls into Mollel and apologises, then looks him in the face, and her eyes narrow.

—I know you . . .

—I don't think so.

He moves her aside and they head for the private area.

—Hey. It's those two pigs! Hey, listen, guys, look! It's them . . .

They keep pushing forward, leaving the voices of indignant protest behind them. They reach a door where a bored-looking female attendant leans against a sign saying VIP AREA ONLY. Mollel flashes the card. She chews her gum and eyeballs the two of them. She looks decidedly sceptical, but whatever her reason, she keeps it to herself. She pushes open the door and they enter.

The pounding of Nyambisha Karao's backing beats still reverberates through this place like the heartbeat of an enormous animal. But they are inside a different part of the beast, now. The lighting is just as dim, but the walls are red and there are red upholstered benches set at intervals, upon which people lounge. They are drinking beer from bottles but also wine or cocktails from stemmed glasses. There is something uniform about all these couples, and the occasional trio: the men are all middle-aged and the girls are all young.

How young is impossible to tell. Their figures are full, possibly surgically enhanced. But their faces are highly made up, and the lights are low. Even so, the contrast between the staff and the clientele – for it is obvious that this is the case – is striking.

—Where do you think this fire escape is? mutters Kiunga. He grabs a handle which is set into the wall and a door, disguised as the wall itself, opens up. They see within some sort of dressing room, with blank-faced styrofoam heads ranged before a mirror. Most of the heads are bare, but one of them wears a wig, long and glossy, just like the one Dora had described to Mollel.

Kiunga closes the door again. He strides across the corridor and tries another handle. There is a female shriek and a male voice cries out —*Hey!*

—Not that one, either, says Kiunga, rapidly closing it.

—She said it was at the end. We've got to keep going.

Further down the corridor, through a plush red curtain, the atmosphere seems to change once again. There are more people here, but the girls have gone. In here, they don't need to yell, but turn into each other's necks to whisper discreetly. They are all men.

Kiunga turns to Mollel with a look of disgust, and Mollel understands Dora's chuckle as she suggested Kiunga could be his 'guest'.

They pass two men locked in a passionate kiss, the one against the wall barely visible except for one of his legs wrapped around those of his companion. Mollel looks at Kiunga, who has a frown on his face.

The two men break, and Mollel sees that the one who'd been pinned up against the wall is a youth, while the other is a stocky man in his forties. It's the youth who is very much in control, though, as he pulls the older man's shirt out of his trouser front, and plunges his slim hand down. —Come on, he smiles, and he leads the other man to a curtained-off section. The youth lifts the curtain, revealing darkness beyond, and they both disappear within.

Mollel nods. —That's got to be the way to the fire escape. There's nowhere else left.

Kiunga groans. —You're kidding me.

Mollel can hear a commotion at the door, and turning back, sees the woman who let them in peering through the gap. There are others clustered behind her, and again he hears the word *pigs*.

—We have no choice.

—All right, Mollel. Look, I worked vice for two years, so I've seen this sort of place before. Admittedly, during a raid, so the lights were on, and people had mostly stopped doing . . . whatever they were doing. But if you'll take a tip from me, don't stop to look around. Just find the door, head for it, and keep walking.

Were it not for the mob on their tail, Mollel would have been quite happy to savour Kiunga's discomfort. It is unusual in his partner, normally so self-assured. He remembers the way the younger cop had handled the scene at the apartment block when Maryam had holed herself up, the way he had taken control. Obviously, everyone had their comfort zone, and Kiunga was well outside of his.

There is a sudden laugh, and the curtain ripples. Three men step out from behind it. One is a shirtless, slightly built Indian. Another looks like one of the regular clubgoers in his baggy sportswear. Between the pair of them, an arm around each of their waists, is a man in a sharp suit, his shirt hanging untucked and open at the top three buttons. He is the one laughing, but his laugh freezes as he glances up and sees Mollel.

It is the patient from Kanja's clinic, the one who had been leaving when Mollel entered. He looks horrified, immediately lets go of the other two, then puts his head down and barges past them, back into the club. Mollel recalls Kanja's last words to the patient, whom he had addressed as Rehoboth: *Resist. Be strong.*

The Indian man shrugs and ignores Mollel, looking Kiunga up and down. —Hi, he says. —You coming in?

Kiunga looks like he's about to punch the guy, so Mollel takes his arm. —He's with me, he says, and together they walk through the curtain.

17

The city has a way of throwing things into sharp contrast. What was merely a difference in personalities back in the village became a rift between the two brothers in Nairobi. The first time it struck home was after the raid on the car lot.

For Mollel, the victory was worth nothing when he saw what the guards had done. Two men were dead, unnecessarily. Lendeva's attitude was that this was just what happened. They were the ones who'd put themselves in harm's way – what was the use in mourning a pair of crooks?

But Mollel knew the fine line between desperation and survival. He could have been one of those guys, too, if things had gone differently. Also, it highlighted a very different interpretation the brothers had of justice. This was something more than just words. It went to the very nature of their beings. For Lendeva, justice was simple. In *Odo Mongi* terms, it should be swift, proportionate, and equivalent. *An eye for an eye.* Compassion is weakness.

Maybe Mollel had too much of the *Orok Kiteng* in him. He believed that people could change, could be changed.

—Those intruders would have killed us, or the guards, had the situation been reversed, Lendeva told him. —Uncle did the right thing. And besides, that's two less robbers we have to worry about in future.

But then Lendeva paused, and said a very curious thing.

—Don't tell Chiku I said that. All right, Mollel?

That was the first indication Mollel had that Lendeva liked Chiku. Up until that point, he'd always thought his brother felt indifferent towards her. He certainly acted that way. He'd often get up and stand aloof when she came along, and seemed to be annoyed when she was around. And she was around, a lot. The brothers always tended to end up near the car lot, even though their work there was done. Lendeva used to say, *it's on the way to a lot of places*. And so they would drop by and see her, or they would lounge about under the trees outside, and wait for her to bring some *chai*, and she'd sit and chat a while. She was pretty bored with her job at that time, and sometimes whole afternoons would go by, her and Mollel chatting, and Lendeva there too, but seldom speaking.

But now he saw that Lendeva was anything but indifferent. Mollel had seen him flirting with girls before, both back in the village and here in the city. They gravitated towards his good looks and easy charm, and he had never been hesitant about drawing them into his orbit. But he'd flung them away again, too, once he'd got what he wanted.

This cool approach to Chiku spoke of higher stakes. Mollel could see that Lendeva wanted her to pursue him, to feel like she was getting a catch. He was serious about her. But was she serious about him?

The question brought a strange elation, followed by a creeping sickness to Mollel's stomach. Elation, because he realised for the first time that he was falling in love with Chiku. Sickness, because of the prospect of losing her to Lendeva.

And then he thought: why should I?

There was no need to defer to his brother. Indeed, he must not: this he knew, as though his life depended upon it. And indeed, it did, for what sort of life would he face without Chiku?

Mollel needed a plan of attack. He couldn't compete with his brother when it came to looks – or even, for that matter, guile.

But he had something in common with Chiku which she'd never shared with Lendeva: that sense of right and wrong, that love of fairness and a burning sense of justice.

Mollel was aware of the irony of using justice to inveigle himself into Chiku's affections, but he felt that it was in a noble cause. And slowly, he began to be proven right.

He would take any opportunity to steer the conversation around to topics of morality. Lendeva would scoff: he believed in what worked. And if that meant breaking rules, or heads, so be it. But he didn't see the light in Chiku's eyes when she heard Mollel speak about his beliefs. And although he did not recognise it – because he had never seen his elder brother as a threat – Lendeva began to be outpaced.

—You know, Mollel, Chiku had said one time. —I think you should join the police.

Lendeva had laughed, but she persisted: —The way you talk about right and wrong. You say you want to make a difference in this world. Why don't you do it? After all, being a policeman can't be so very different to being a warrior.

This time Lendeva butted in. —It's very different, from what I've seen. A policeman is only in it for what he can take for himself. He gets rich exploiting the fears and insecurities of the vulnerable. He's a mercenary who'll use his power, and his gun, for whoever pays the price. At best he's an extortionist, screwing them for what little they've got in the name of the law. And at worst, he's a gangster and a murderer, just like all the others. The only difference is the uniform he wears. That's the system. That's the way it is.

Chiku frowned, and Mollel thrilled at the wrinkle on her brow.

—So change it! she cried. —Don't just complain about it, *do* something about it. If the system is full of bad guys, you be the good guy!

—The system is like a sick animal, sighed Lendeva. —There's no point sparing it. It has to be destroyed.

—You don't believe that, do you, Mollel?

She turned those large, trusting eyes upon him, and Mollel knew what he had to do.

—No.

—You see! said Chiku, with delight. —That's exactly why you should be a policeman. Look, I've been reading about it. They're trying to get more of the smaller tribes into the force. They've suspended the high school certificate requirement for pastoralists. That's you, Mollel. Maasais just have to pass a basic proficiency test.

Mollel could feel himself being swept along by her enthusiasm. He'd never thought of himself as a policeman before – they'd always seemed exotic creatures to him, these powerful, confident, uniformed officers, swaggering along Nairobi's streets. But for Chiku . . . for Chiku he could do anything. He felt his self-doubt ebbing away, even as Lendeva laid siege to it.

—He can hardly read and write!

Chiku was undeterred. —I'll help him! Look, we sit around all afternoon anyway. I can coach you, Mollel. And then, when you're doing your homework, I can study for my secretarial college entrance exam.

—He can't, said Lendeva. —I'm expanding the business and I need Mollel full-time. In fact, I was going to tell you that we can't hang around here any more. We've been wasting too much time lately. We ought to get going. Come on, Mollel.

He looked surprised when Mollel refused. And then he looked from Mollel's face to Chiku's, and Mollel saw that he knew.

It was a while before Mollel saw Lendeva again. He would study with Chiku in the afternoons, then make his way to night-shift work at whichever venue Lendeva would direct him to by text message on the mobile phone he'd bought his brother with the reward from the car lot job. A mobile phone was worth a lot of money in those days, and Mollel had to wrap it tightly into the folds of his shawl whenever he was travelling around the city, because people were killed for a lot less. But it was a sign that Lendeva was doing well. Mollel also heard about it from Chiku, because she saw him occasionally.

When Mollel discovered that, he felt like a knife had gone into his heart. She was quite relaxed about it. Perhaps she didn't realise the significance when she said: —I can't see why your brother doesn't give you a night off once in a while. One of his new workers could cover your shift.

—He has new workers?

Mollel didn't even know he had taken on other employees.

—Quite a few now. All Maasai. He says he wants to create the biggest security company in Nairobi, employing no one but Maasai warriors. She giggled. —Sounds stupid. But somehow, knowing your brother, if anyone can do it, he can.

—So, you've seen him?

—We've met a few times in the evenings. He's taken me to dinner. He looks quite different these days, don't you think?

Mollel didn't reply. He hadn't seen enough of Lendeva to be able to judge.

Lendeva had always had the ability to draw people towards him, especially like-minded young men. Mollel could see why they would regard him as a leader. The kind of devotion he could instil, and the level of discipline which came from that, was truly awe-inspiring. In Nairobi's crowded security industry, he'd certainly be able to make a name for himself if he could ensure his staff were more honest than your average employee.

Mollel could understand the devotion, but could never feel it, himself. Lendeva was still the younger brother. And there was something more; Mollel could see flaws where the others only saw strength. Lendeva's was a cold kind of loyalty, and one which flowed only in one direction. Although his followers – and in time, there would be many – would go to any lengths for him, Mollel never felt that anyone could be sure of the same in return.

Chiku started giving Mollel tests—reading and writing, English and Swahili. She drilled him on the highway code and somehow even got hold of a police cadet training manual. She quizzed him on the rules about evidence, public safety, procedures for arrest. Finally, after several months, she declared that he was ready.

—You'll get into the police, and in a year or two I'll have saved enough for secretarial college. Our lives are ready to start!

She clasped his hand and he realised she was talking about them, being together. He had won.

But Lendeva remained a dark cloud on the horizon. Chiku spoke of him often, and when she did – even in neutral terms – Mollel's heart burned with jealousy. When she complimented him, it was torture.

Mollel thought he hid it well, but Chiku was astute. She might not have known the reason behind it, but she knew there was a rift between the brothers. And so one day she took it upon herself to resolve it.

It was a Sunday, and her mother was up-country visiting relatives. Chiku had taken the opportunity to skip church, and invited Mollel over. They spent a blissful day together, and as the end of it approached, Mollel drew himself reluctantly from her arms and gave her a kiss. He had to report for his night shift.

—There's no need. I had a word with your brother. He's moved things around. Tonight, I'm cooking dinner for my two favourite boys!

Sure enough, Lendeva turned up. He had changed, all right. He was wearing a suit. It was the first time Mollel had ever seen him in trousers, let alone a full suit, with a shirt and tie – and his dreadlocks were tied back in a conservative tail rather than hanging loose. He clutched a bunch of flowers, and when he looked down and saw Chiku and Mollel holding hands, the dismay was clear on his face.

They passed an awkward few hours. Lendeva and Mollel had never been chatty, especially in the presence of another, so it was unlikely Chiku noticed. She certainly managed to divide her attention – and affection – between them both. Put that way, it could sound deliberate, or manipulative. But Mollel would deny it was like that. He'd always considered her to be one of those people with enough love to go around, so why hoard it? And she certainly had come to love both of the brothers.

But every smile she cast in Lendeva's direction was agony to Mollel, every movement towards him, every brush of her hand upon his arm as she laughed. And when Mollel was the object of her attention, he would occasionally look over, and see Lendeva glaring back with murder in his eyes.

Chiku was drinking. Neither Lendeva nor Mollel drank. Their father had been a drunk, and they did not want to go down that route. But Chiku had had a few glasses of wine, just enough to lose her inhibitions.

—You know, she was telling Lendeva, —I always saw *you* as the real warrior, and Mollel as the sensible one. But now here you are, the businessman in the suit. You're really going places, Lendeva. Maybe there's more to you than I imagined.

Mollel had had enough.

He got up, and left the flat. Outside, in the courtyard, it was dark. He pounded up and down, barely noticing the rain which had begun to fall. Then he felt a rough hand upon his shoulder. He spun around.

—Hey.

It was Lendeva.

—You need to go back in there, he said. —She's crying. She needs you.

—What are you talking about?

—She's upset. Something I said. Go.

Mollel pushed back.

—You don't get to order me around, little brother.

—Oh, sure, he replied, his voice thick with sarcasm. —You don't want to be ordered around. So you're going to join the police force. What, you think they'll just let you do whatever you like when you're one of their uniformed goons, you traitor?

Traitor. That was the first time anyone had accused Mollel of such a thing.

—Go on then, he'd continued. Work for the people who keep us down. The police are always the first ones to turn up when a Maasai family is being evicted from their land. When the farmers accuse us of rustling, or the park service accuses us of poaching, who is it who comes with their guns? You want to know why they want more Maasai in their ranks? It's so they can oppress our people better. They need people like you, who can speak the language, who can spy on his own kin, and be a face for the public to prove there's no prejudice. Go ahead, Mollel. Let them use you. But don't pretend you don't know you're being used.

Lendeva had tugged at his tie and thrown it to the ground. He pulled off his jacket, and that went down, too. Mollel thought for a moment he was going to fight, but when he kicked off his shoes, Mollel realised Lendeva was pulling off his city clothes. They hung on him like a visible mark of everything he hated. Everything he had become.

Windows lit up as curtains were drawn back. Leering faces emerged.

—Lendeva, stop. People are looking!

—Let them look. They're not my people.

He got down to his underpants – Mollel was relieved to see those, as they are not normally worn under a *shuka* – and he still had his shirt on. That, it seemed, was enough, and Lendeva looked around him with wild eyes. He appeared transformed. Mollel heard someone up above gasp: *night runner*. And the windows started to black out again, as people retreated inside.

And then Lendeva was gone.

Back in the flat, Mollel found Chiku. She had been crying.

—Oh, Mollel. It was horrible. I never knew he felt that way.

Mollel was almost too fearful to ask. —What way?

She sobbed. —He said I was a slut, a mongrel, a worthless Kikuyu. That we were sell-outs, a tribe who'd forgotten their heritage and turned their back on the traditional way. He said he'd only realised it tonight, but I was the reason you had been changing, abandoning your own ideals. He even blamed me for the clothes he was wearing. He said you and I could never be together, and that I was making you into someone you're not. But I'm not, am I, Mollel? You're still you.

She buried her head in his shoulder.

—I'm still me, Mollel had whispered softly.

But he wasn't sure.

18

Darkness comes quickly in Nairobi, but dawn, while equally swift, announces its arrival. It's possible to see it coming, probably because, if you're awake and outside at such an hour – as so many people in the city are – your eyes are already attuned to the dark, so the subtle gradations in the eastern sky are more noticeable.

Greyness is just appearing on the horizon as Mollel and Kiunga make their way into Dandora. They'd snatched a few hours of sleep back at Mollel's flat, Kiunga in his often-used position on the couch, after they'd managed to flee the club. It didn't feel like enough. But they are not the only ones facing an early start. The district is stirring: those who work in the city, or other suburbs, are already appearing on the streets. Many will have left their homes around five-thirty and are embarking upon a five-mile walk to make it to their workplace in time for an eight o'clock start: the only real option when even a few shillings are better spent on food, or rent, than on the luxury of a *matatu* fare.

Kiunga has been mostly silent as they drive, but something has been playing on Mollel's mind.

—Did something strike you as strange after we left? he asks.

—It was strange before we left, if you ask me, replies Kiunga, a sneer of contempt in his voice. — I've half a mind to call my old team on the vice squad and get the whole place shut down. That final room . . .

He shudders.

—No, I meant outside. When we got back to the car. Inside the club, we'd been on the verge of being lynched because we were police officers, right? Yet outside, barely a block away, we got to our car and found it untouched. This is a marked police car, remember.

—Sure. And thank God for that. Bogani would have killed us if there was so much as a dent in his pride and joy.

Mollel is about to say something more, but is cut off by the trilling of a phone. Kiunga looks surprised, and reaches into his trouser pocket. He answers with his thumb, then holds the phone up to his ear with his left hand without taking his right off the wheel or his eyes off the road.

—Hello, yes? Oh, hello Sir!

Mollel can tell he'd like to salute. Kiunga's eyes scan the side of the road and he pulls over, parks the car and cuts the engine.

—Yes, yes he is, he says, and he glances at Mollel. —He's with me now.

And then it is *uh-huh* and *I see*, until he says: —Will do, Sir. See you shortly.

—Bogani, he says, unnecessarily. —He wants me to check something out.

Kiunga has one of those smart phones which have recently become ubiquitous in Nairobi. Mollel is stubbornly refusing to give up his trusty Nokia. It might not be beautiful, but it does the job.

Kiunga begins tapping on his phone's screen, its glow illuminating his face. His eyes suddenly widen, and he breaks into a grin.

—Why, Mollel, he says. —You old dog!

—What is it? asks Mollel, trying to get a look at the screen. Kiunga bats him away, his eyes darting from side to side as he reads. Eventually, he passes the device to Mollel with a smile.

Mollel takes it and tries to make out what he's looking at. All he can see is a blurry photograph. With dismay, he recognises the scene, and the people – the restaurant at Janet Kimathi's hotel. One of the people is Janet. The other is himself.

He scrolls down to read the text. There is a headline under the image:

JANET'S JINX OVER? CAN UNKNOWN HUNK MAKE HER HAPPY AGAIN?

Kiunga snatches the phone back and begins to read from the body of the text. *She's had her share of heartbreak. But Kenyan TV star Janet Kimathi seems to be back on track with a home-grown hero, here in Nairobi. For the former star of US TV news was spotted making a few headlines herself in one of the city's top eateries last night. Her companion: an unknown hunk who seemed to have her undivided attention.*

Kiunga sniggers. —I'm sorry, Mollel. This is priceless. *The romantic duo seemed to have little time for the menu, shocking diners with a hasty exit. The pair were last spotted heading for the elevators. Rumour has it, Miss Kimathi has installed herself in the penthouse suite.*

—This is rubbish, says Mollel. —It's just a regular suite.

Kiunga beams at him. —Mollel! he says, faking shock. —I never thought you had it in you!

Irritated, Mollel tries to get the phone back, but Kiunga evades his reach.

—What are you reading this on, anyway?

—*WhassupKenya.com.* You made the front page.

—That's a relief. I thought it was something people might actually see, like the *Daily Nation*.

Kiunga's eyes widen. —You've never heard of *whassup-Kenya*? Mollel, *everyone* reads this. If you want to *hide* news these days, you put it in the *Daily Nation*.

With dismay, Mollel wondered whether Adam might already have seen the same article. Or Faith. With them, come thoughts of home. He had been looking forward to catching up with his son. But when Kiunga puts his phone away and starts the car again, he swings it out and does a U-turn.

—Bogani told me to bring you to him, says Kiunga. —Seems he's an early riser.

Kiunga drives them to Kasarani, a short trip in the early hours – although, with the sky now a heavy, leaden grey and the traffic ramping up for the day, they are fortunate that they are travelling against the flow. Kasarani is a suburb even more outlying than Dandora, more a town in its own right, lying on the main road to Thika. It's the place that was chosen, back in the autocratic days of Daniel Arap Moi, for an ambitious project which was billed as a statement of national pride and intent. The name of the project revealed that the real purpose was more personal. The Moi International Sports Centre stands monument to that unlamented regime, although Nairobians, with their usual spirit of pragmatic rebellion, almost unanimously refuse to honour their late President by using its original name. Everyone calls it Kasarani Stadium.

It was built well; dictators have a habit of paying attention to detail when it comes to their vanity projects. The stadium, and its outlying buildings, which house the likes of a swimming pool and an indoor arena, have weathered years of neglect and the equatorial sun better than most new buildings in the city. Still, there is no disguising the broken windows and boarded-up doorways, nor the clumps of grass that now grow defiantly through the cracks in the concrete outside. The stadium has never fallen out of use – the popular local team, Mathare United, play their home games here – but, much like Moi's legacy, it is far from untarnished. Under this grey sky, the grey edifice looks particularly forbidding, as much fortress as football stadium.

—Here? asks Mollel, as they pull into the empty parking lot. Kiunga drives the car across it, straight towards one of the unboarded-up entrances. A metal door stands unlocked and open.

—This is where he said.

As they enter the structure, a smell of piss burns their nostrils. No lights are on in this dark tunnel, but at the far end of it, a square of sky grows as they step tentatively towards it. Towards the end, the light takes on a cold, metallic quality, too harsh to be natural and too bright for the time of day. As they walk on, the first sight of the stadium opens out before them. Mollel has an uncanny feeling of shrinking as he emerges from the confines of the tunnel, to find himself facing the vast, open bowl. Colours here seem intensified, like someone has turned the dial right up. The green of the football field is dazzling; the red athletics track which rings it is vibrant red, as are the seats which retreat in neat, vertiginous ranks high up into a second gallery.

The explanation for the strange quality of the light towers above them. On gantries ringed around the edge of the stadium, large white lights blaze. These are only a small proportion of the available lamps, about one in ten, but they still cast this cold, clinical brightness, overpowering the weak and watery luminescence of the early-morning sky.

This enclosed world appears to be in the service of just one man. Right now, he's little more than a fast-moving speck, a ball of energy, legs and arms like pistons. Mollel almost expects to see a dust trail rising behind him.

As he reaches the curve, the runner switches pace. His legs begin to cycle; his movements are lithe, rather than frenetic. He's still running faster than most people could sprint, but he looks utterly relaxed. As he rounds the curve and comes towards them, Mollel sees it is Bogani. No wonder they call him The Cheetah.

He glances down at a watch on his wrist as he approaches their stand. He seems satisfied, takes the pace down another notch, and bounces up to the low rail which divides the stand from the track. There, a towel and water bottle await him. He picks up the bottle and squeezes it into his mouth greedily, then onto his head and face. Then he exchanges the bottle for the towel. When he removes it, he finally looks up and sees Mollel and Kiunga. His face is flushed with exertion and pleasure.

—Twenty-two point four. Not bad for a forty-two-year-old, eh? That's not far off what I was scoring twenty years ago.

—Twenty-one point three-nine in qualifying for the World Championship in Tokyo, says Kiunga. —If you'd gone, you'd have ended up on the podium.

—And I wouldn't be here, says Bogani, lifting one leg and grabbing his foot.

—Two hundred metres, adds Kiunga, for Mollel's sake.

—We all make choices, continues Bogani, switching legs. —I don't regret mine. I made the choice that was right for me. The guy who went in my place is peeling potatoes in a hotel kitchen now. And me? Well, I have the keys to the stadium.

Beside the railing is a leather briefcase. A mobile phone sits on top of it, and an electronic tablet, a blank black square of steel and glass. That Bogani has felt comfortable enough to leave these here, exposed, while he sprints, is testament to the confidence he has in the security of this place, or his status, or his speed. Possibly all three. Beside the tablet is a set of keys which prove his point.

—Privileges of rank, he continues. —There's more to this place than meets the eye. In a time of emergency, this complex becomes a command and control centre. We've got everything we need to keep tens of thousands of people safe. Or, depending on the nature of the emergency, to keep the people here who need to be kept here.

Stadium, fortress and prison. This really was designed as a multi-purpose arena.

—Kiunga, I need to speak to Mollel alone. Could you leave us?

Kiunga raises his eyebrows and Mollel can feel his colleague's bruised pride. However, he replies, in a normal voice: —Sure, Sir. I'll wait in the car.

Bogani watches Kiunga disappear down the tunnel. Mollel glances at the sky. The daylight has reached equilibrium with the lamps, and the only noticeable effect of the artificial light now is the way it eliminates shadows, bringing a curious, flat effect to everything. Mollel wonders whether this is entirely down to the light, or to his lack of sleep. He missed his pills last night. And for that matter, he can't remember the last time he ate.

When he turns back to Bogani, the captain has his tablet in his hand. Mollel can see the photo of himself and Janet on the screen.

—Want to tell me about this?

—Not much to tell, to be honest, Sir. Janet Kimathi and I go back a long way. Now she's back in town, we met to catch up.

—And you just happened to want to get in touch with her in the middle of a sensitive case?

—No, Sir, it's not like that.

—Oh, so *she* got in touch with you?

Bogani is obviously annoyed by this liaison. Given his love for public relations, Mollel suspects his boss could be feeling undermined by an underling having a direct relationship with a member of the press, however innocent. How could Mollel explain that he had seen Janet watching him – or Kanja – outside the police station, and that he'd looked up her contact details on the car registration system, without it sounding like something *was* afoot?

He chooses not to answer at all.

—Listen, Mollel, I know exactly what happened the last time you spilled the beans to Miss Kimathi.

He hands the tablet to Mollel, picks up his briefcase, balances it on the railing, and releases the catches. He pulls out a thick manila file, the name MOLLEL written on the top-right corner. Documents, some photographs and what looks like a small cassette tape remain in the opened case. Mollel can see enough of one of the photos to recognise it as the mortuary file photo of a woman named Lucy, whose murder he had investigated some years previously.

Bogani flicks through the file. —I know what happens when you don't get your way. In this case, you went behind Otieno's back when you disagreed with how he wanted to handle it. As I heard, you got someone killed.

Mollel remains silent.

—I won't have freelancers on my team, Mollel. Why do you think I offered Kiunga a job, and not you? I only hope none of your bad habits have rubbed off on him.

Somehow this imputation of Kiunga's competence offends Mollel more than the insinuation against himself.

—Kiunga's a good policeman, Sir.

—The thing about you, Mollel, is that you could have been one, too. But you think you're above the law. Oh no, not in that corrupt sense. I know how you love to look down on any officer who's got his fingers in the pie. No, you think you're above the law because you're *better* than the law, and all those who work to uphold it. Your sense of justice is so much higher, and more refined, that it really does not matter who, or what, gets in the way. Even little things like rules, and orders. For example, when I order you to close this case . . .

—Sir! protests Mollel.

—When I order you to shut down this case, because we no longer have a dead girl, we have a missing girl, who her parents say is not even missing, and we have a dead man on a rubbish heap, probably one of the trash-pickers who die all the time . . .

—Sir!

—When I order you to shut down this case, I do not expect you to go running to your journalist girlfriend and start blabbing about corruption, or incompetence, or anything else that will put pressure on me to reopen it. You see, you can't put pressure on me, Mollel, because I'm not corrupt. I'm not incompetent. Far from it. As you'll find out, when I have an officer who directly disobeys me, I can be very competent indeed.

Mollel wonders what has brought on this change. Bogani had initially been supportive of him taking a risk with this case. Little has altered materially. Yet now, the captain obviously wants rid of it – and of Mollel.

Mollel looks again at the screen. The design is different to the way it was presented on Kiunga's phone and there is a sidebar of other stories running down the right-hand side of the text about him and Janet. One of those stories has a thumbnail image of a familiar face. It is the glowering, dark, bull-like face of his previous boss, Superintendent Otieno. He was the one Bogani had referred to, and he and Mollel had had their share of run-ins. But they'd also become firm allies, with Otieno recognising in Mollel a doggedness and unshakability which he'd found very useful on occasion. In turn, Mollel had come to admit, grudgingly, that the political machinations of his employer, while often displaying a little too much pragmatism for his liking, were at least motivated by a desire to achieve justice.

The text next to the image reads *OTIENO TO QUIT TODAY – Race to Replace Top Cop*.

So that was it. Otieno, having mastered the bull ring of Nairobi's criminal scene, had finally met his match in the political arena. The politicians, desperate for someone to blame other than themselves for falling security and rising crime, had picked him off. And for a replacement, why, there would no doubt be many choices – but they could do worse than a young, media-savvy captain with a name for efficiency and an unsullied reputation – provided he kept his name off any scurrilous websites.

Bogani takes the tablet back from Mollel, casting a quick glance at the screen. If he is following the same line of thought, he does not show it.

—You see, Mollel, you had two advantages when you went public before. Firstly, you were still a hero in the public eye. That counted for something back then. But that was thirteen years ago. The agenda's moved on. It's not Al-Qaeda any more, it's Al-Shabaab. Terror's not abnormal, it's normal. There's no heroism in confronting it, because sooner or later there will just be another attack. You're not newsworthy.

—Secondly, the people you spoke out about had a difficult job. They had something to hide, and because you were making so much noise, silencing you was not an option. So they did what needed to be done. A few minor figures lost their jobs, lower down the chain of command. Some arrests were made. A major victory was proclaimed in the battle against corruption. And they left you, Mollel, relatively untouched.

—Me, I'm different. I have no secrets. I have nothing to hide. I'm not afraid of anything coming out, because there is nothing to come out. You can blow your whistle as loud as you want, Mollel, and the worst that the world will see is a captain taking a strategic decision to deprioritise a case. I have very little to lose. Whereas you . . .

He tosses the file onto the ground at Mollel's feet. It lands on the concrete with a slap.

—You have a lot to lose, Mollel. In here are the psych evaluations, the appraisals, the assessments which have been made about you over the years. There are also the complaints filed, the memos written, the warnings issued. There is enough here to have you thrown off the Force. And if that does not concern you, you might want to consider how Child Protection might consider your fitness to have your son living with you at home.

Mollel bends to pick up the file, but he does not open it. Instead, he steps over to the rail, and places it neatly inside Bogani's open briefcase. As he does so, he looks at the other items there. The small cassette tape in its clear plastic case has a sticker on it which reads COLLINS KIUNGA, alongside some numbers.

Mollel closes the case and flicks the two latches shut. He passes the case to Bogani. He is aware of a throbbing in his temple and a cold, calm anger running through him which seldom remains contained for long. He knows he has to leave this place before he says or does something he will regret.

—Will that be all, Sir?

—I'll want your report. You can write it up while you're here. Make sure Kiunga signs off on it, too. It can be his first investigation for me.

Some investigation, thinks Mollel.

As he turns to leave, Bogani's phone rings. He picks it up with a dismissive nod to Mollel. —No, not yet, Mollel hears him say as he walks towards the tunnel. —I'm sure I'll hear soon.

—What's that? asks Kiunga, as Mollel gets into the passenger seat. Mollel, pocketing the small cassette tape which he'd lifted from Bogani's briefcase, replies: —Nothing.

—The boss give you a lecture about keeping off the gossip sites?

—Something like that. Look, you need some breakfast. There's somewhere I need to be. Can you take me back to Dandora?

—Sure you don't need me?

—Not for a couple of hours.

—I could manage some coffee and *mandazi*. Don't you worry about Bogani, Mollel. He's going places, you know. If you like, I could put in a word for you.

19

—I'm glad you called me, Mollel. I'm glad you came.

Mollel shifts in his seat and looks at the strange, wizened man who is sitting on a stool in front of him. Even though Mollel is also perched, rather more uncomfortably, upon an equally small wooden stool, he still looks down upon Kanja. But there is a calmness and serenity in the old man's gaze which seems to convey more power in the situation upon him.

—I was thinking about what you said, says Mollel. —I was hoping you could help me. As I said, this isn't about the case. That's been shut down.

Kanja smiles. —Let's put that to one side, for now, he says. —I doubt very much any case you work on is ever over until *you* decide it's over. We're very similar, you and I.

Mollel is irritated by this statement; irritated because Kanja is the opposite of everything he wants to be. He is superstitious and illogical. He is a phoney and a showman.

And yet, at least part of Mollel's irritation comes from the suspicion that Kanja might be right.

—See, continues Kanja. —I don't care *why* you're here. I only care *that* you're here. You need help, Mollel. I could see that in your eyes the first time I met you.

—You're right, sighs Mollel. —I do need help.

Help with the case, he tells himself. For that, he needs to find out more about Kanja, Fatuma and the treatment she was undergoing. He'd got nowhere before, and neither, apparently, had Bogani. But they'd both taken the official route.

Mollel has another plan now: to place himself in Kanja's care, and see what he can learn from the process. He's conducted enough interviews in his time to be confident that he can divulge enough information to maintain the charade, while remaining in full control.

—It was something you said when we met, he begins. —About looking for what works. I've been through enough conventional treatments to know that they're not working for me. It's time to try something new.

—Something *old*, Kanja corrects him, with a glint in his eye. —It's only Western culture that abandons the tried and tested in favour of the latest fad. Our ancestors were resilient and powerful, and they had faith in the traditional methods.

—It's a long time since I had any faith in anything, says Mollel.

—Of course it is. You find it hard to let go. I perceive that in you. Faith requires a certain surrender. A surrender of the self. Are you ready to give up, Mollel?

Mollel thinks: *like hell I am*.

—Yes, he says.

Faith had always been a problem for Mollel. As a detective, he had a natural affinity for evidence. But he knew, too, the value of a good hunch and he'd learned to trust his gut as much as his head. Despite himself, he feels a deep flutter of hope that this might work. This might be something that could bring him relief.

And then he quickly suppresses the flutter. He reminds himself why he is here. For Fatuma—and for the body on the tip, whoever that is.

Kanja is waiting for him to speak.

—Where do I begin? he asks.

—Begin at the beginning, replies Kanja, with a smile.

—How far back do you want me to go? replies Mollel. —All the way to Maasinta?

—Why not?

So, feeling somewhat self-conscious, Mollel begins with Maasinta, the first Maasai. Perhaps it is because they have been talking about tradition, or perhaps because Kanja, for all his theatrics, reminds Mollel of the *laibon*, the spiritual elder in the Maasai community, whose role it is to recite these tales. At first, he speaks from rote, falling back upon the stories like liturgy. But, after a while, he is surprised to find that he is drifting out of the safe lines these tales provide. He is doing something he has not done for years; he is talking about himself. And the ridiculous little man, with his sympathetic eyes and his tactful nods and encouraging murmurs, is providing something which has been equally absent: a listener.

Somewhere along the line Mollel has segued seamlessly from the *Odo Mongi* and the *Orok Kiteng,* to his own lineage, to his childhood and youth. His relationship with Lendeva. Leaving the village, and their voyage to Nairobi. The car lot, and their rift.

And then Mollel hears himself speaking about more recent events. About the reappearance of Lendeva in his life, more than a decade after he'd last seen him, pulling off his clothes outside Chiku's flat.

In the intervening years, Lendeva had restyled himself as Mbatiani, after an ancient Maasai hero. A messiah-type, who was supposed, according to legend, to be the one who would lead the Maasai back to the homeland they'd lost to colonialism, to agriculture, and to land grabbers.

Part political, part spiritual, his ideas had fallen upon receptive ears amongst the disaffected Maasai youth. And a movement, of sorts, had been born.

Mollel, one of the few Maasai in the Kenyan police service, had ultimately recognised the situation for what it was. But he'd never imagined his own brother to be the driving force behind it.

And yet, it explained so much. How Lendeva had abandoned his flourishing business and disappeared without a trace. All that energy – all that bitterness. It had to be channelled somewhere.

When Mollel had broken open the Mbatiani movement, and revealed their links to poaching, Lendeva had stepped out of the shadows. Mollel had tried to arrest him. But Lendeva would not let that happen. Even if one of them had to die.

Throughout, Kanja is the model interviewer. He occasionally speaks, but only to keep the conversation flowing: *what happened next?* or *how did you feel about that?* He is attentive, and unobtrusive.

And as Mollel talks, he is aware that he is exposing a vulnerability, which is unwise for a detective. But he's also listening to his instinct, and his instinct tells him that Kanja is astute enough to know when he is holding back. To develop a relationship here, he has to get Kanja to trust him. And that means that he has to place his trust in Kanja.

As his story develops, Mollel begins to see a pattern, of sorts. Perhaps because his latest confrontation with Bogani is still weighing on his mind, the pattern he sees is one of conflict.

—I have my own ideas about the right way, or the proper way, to do things, and it always seems like the world disagrees. Do you understand?

Kanja nods.

—I understand. In fact, I can help. The thing is, Mollel, you're projecting this conflict into the outside world as though it is caused by the people and situations you find yourself in. And yet, where it exists, it exists . . . within you.

Mollel mulls over Kanja's words. There is something to it, surely? Perhaps the old man is not such a fraud as he appears to be. Underneath all that spiritual hot air and hocus pocus, perhaps some sound psychological principles are coming into play. After all, if a headteacher with psychological accreditation like Mama Sharifa still calls upon his services to deal with her troubled girls, it could well be that there is some method behind Kanja's apparent madness.

—Yes, continues Kanja, warming to his theme. —The conflict is within you, Mollel. We won't get anywhere by trying to find its causes elsewhere. We must deal with the problem at the source. And the problem, to me, is perfectly evident. You are possessed by demons.

For a moment, Mollel thinks that the old man is talking metaphorically. He's heard people talk about their *demons* in a psychological sense, meaning their bad habits, their addictions, their hang-ups and their histories. But no, there is no metaphor at play here. He can tell from the old man's eyes that he is perfectly serious.

—I believe there are at least two demons at play, and possibly three, says Kanja. One has been with you all of your life. This is a birth demon, whose mother would have possessed your mother. Tell me, does your brother suffer as you do?

—He certainly has demons, concedes Mollel. —I wouldn't know what sort. It's a long time since we've spent any time together.

Kanja looks thoughtful. —I see, I see. And your second demon. Your second demon would have inhabited you at a time of great vulnerability. When you were under emotional and spiritual distress. Has there been any such time in your history?

Mollel lowers his eyes.

—And the third, continues Kanja, stroking his beard. —The third is a more recent apparition. The other two have reached an accommodation, of sorts, between each other and with you, their host. And yet the third has upset the balance. This third demon seeks to seize control. This third demon, Mollel – this newcomer – this is the demon which presents you with the most danger. This is the demon which could destroy you.

Mollel puts his head in his hands. When he raises it, he looks Kanja directly in the eye.

—This is hard for me, he concedes. —All my adult life, I have dismissed all this stuff as superstitious nonsense. I thought that medicine, and experts, had all the answers.

Kanja smiles and shakes his head. —They *think* they have the answers.

—I just . . . please, don't take this the wrong way. I want to believe . . .

—You *have* to believe. It can't work, if you don't believe.

—I want to. But I suppose I associate these kinds of beliefs with a level of . . . please don't be offended . . . a certain lack of education.

—I'm not offended in the slightest! says Kanja, suddenly beaming. —If, by education, you mean that western rote-learning which is designed to eliminate our African traditions, to render them powerless, quaint curiosities and objects of derision, then yes, I lack education. And I am proud of it! For I have something better than education.

—Which is?

—Learning! Did you ever stop to ponder the difference between education and learning, Mollel? *Education* is what they want to teach you. *Learning* is what you choose to be taught. Why, I have no education at all to speak of. But I'm one of the most learned people you're ever likely to meet!

They share a smile. Mollel's previous irritation with this character is slowly being replaced by something else: a kind of grudging respect. Be he a charlatan, misguided or manipulative, Kanja still possesses an insight and charm that no doubt has led to his reputation.

—Help me out, says Mollel. —If you could give me an example

of a person, someone like me, who you've helped. Someone educated, westernised, everything that goes against what you stand for—someone who had that sort of background, and still managed to believe. That might give me some confidence.

Kanja looks like he is lost in thought for a moment.

—What about that man I met who was leaving when I arrived here the other day? asks Mollel. —A very smart gentleman. I can't quite remember his name.

—Rehoboth? Yes, well he is certainly educated. And I think my intervention has brought him a relief, of sorts. But really, Mollel, his demons are very different to yours. Quite different. Now, there was a woman I was working with last year . . .

The door opens and a set of figures appear there, filling the space. Mollel and Kanja leap to their feet. The foremost of the new arrivals, wide-shouldered and bald-headed, is Nicodemus.

—I heard you were back in Dandora, he says to Mollel. —You didn't get the message clearly enough last night? You're not wanted in these parts.

—Now, now, Nicodemus, says Kanja, dancing up and down in anxiety. —This isn't police business. This is a private consultation. You let me practise here, and I'm grateful for that, but you really have no right to say who I can and can't treat. I am here to care for people, anyone who needs it. He is my patient, and I have a duty of care!

—Don't be a fool, Kanja, snarls Nicodemus. —You think this policeman is really interested in your hocus pocus? He's sniffing around where he shouldn't be, and you, of all people, should know what that means. Trouble.

—He's different, insists Kanja. —I'm no fool. I know what brought him here. But really, that's irrelevant. He thinks he's locking me out, but I have seen into his soul, Nicodemus, and I can help him. I can bring him peace.

—I can bring him peace, too. I bet no one even knows he's here.

—All right, Nicodemus, says Kanja, waving a finger of warning. —I didn't want to have to do this. But if you don't leave me and my patient alone, I'll have to intervene.

Nicodemus laughs; a deep-throated, hearty laugh which shakes his shoulders and reverberates around the room.

—Save your threats, old man. I don't believe any of your nonsense.

—*You* don't, agrees Kanja. —But *they* do.

The two heavies framing Nicodemus in the doorway look decidedly uncomfortable. They appear to be fighting two powerful, conflicting emotions: fear of their boss, and fear of something else.

—In fact, says Kanja, —all of the people around here who you rely on, believe in me, and my abilities. Most of them have been through this office at one time or another. And those that haven't, have heard about me. I may not be able to do anything to *you*, big man. But I could do plenty to *them*.

Nicodemus scoffs, but his bravado is less secure. He seems to be weighing up his options, aware that Kanja's threat, if not his magic, holds real power. Perhaps, in this case, it is not worth his while to test it.

—Consider this your last warning, Policeman, says Nicodemus. —Dandora is off limits for you from now on. If you're seen here again, there won't be any magic that can save you.

—We need to continue your treatment, Kanja tells Mollel, once they are alone again. —It's too dangerous not to. But it's too dangerous to do so here. I have a place – another place. A safe place. I will tell you how to find it, when I know you can come without being seen.

As soon as Mollel is out of Dandora – the moment he has crossed the road which marks the unofficial boundary between Dandora and the neighbouring estate of Embakasi – he calls Kiunga, who is nearby enjoying his second or third *mandazi*, and a cigarette. Then, while he is waiting to be picked up, he calls Adam.

—Dad!

—Hi, Adam. I've got another job for you. Can you use the internet to look something up for me?

20

Kiunga draws up, and Mollel can tell from his colleague's face that he's furious.

—Right after you called, I heard from Bogani. When were you going to tell me, Mollel?

Mollel gets in and closes the door.

—He told me to close the case. Well, I intend to. There's just a few things I need to clear up first. —He told you to shut it down. I'm on this case too. So that puts my neck on the line.

—I just need twenty-four hours, says Mollel. —Fatuma is still missing. And we have an unidentified body.

—An unidentified trash-picker.

—Since when did you stop caring about solving cases?

—Since you came up with cases which can't be solved, like trying to find an ID for a body which probably never had an ID even when he was alive. Or cases which aren't cases at all, like a missing girl who's only been reported missing by her baby sister.

—Do you really believe that, Kiunga?

Kiunga bites his lip.

—Or is it because your new boss is set to become Chief of Police? Do you really think you can trust him?

—Trust him? explodes Kiunga. —What about trusting you, Mollel? After all we've been through? You were told, explicitly, that we had to wrap up the case. But you didn't tell me.

Your career might be over, but there's no reason mine has to be. The risks I've taken for you, Mollel, over the years – but I took them. I never thought you'd consciously put me in harm's way.

—I'm not talking about harm's way. I'm just talking about a little leeway.

—I think I've given you enough leeway, don't you?

Mollel's phone rings.

—That was a pretty easy task you set me, Dad. Make it something more challenging next time.

—What have you found?

—There is a firm called ARC. Antony Rehoboth Communications. I looked up the director, sure enough, it's a guy called Rehoboth. There's even a photo. He fits the description you gave me. It's in an office block on Riveredge. I'll text you the address.

—Nice work. You'll make a good detective, one day.

—You think so?

Mollel had been joking, but the boy's eager response makes him think twice. It's a very mixed feeling that runs through him at the thought of his son following in his footsteps.

—There's more, Dad. That's what I found out on the internet. But I thought that, while I was at it, I'd have a look at the police records.

—Adam . . . says Mollel. Then he turns away from Kiunga and covers the speaker of the phone with his hand, not that it really provides any privacy. —You shouldn't have done that.

—You were still logged in to the system, the boy protests. —I thought I was helping you.

Mollel can hear the disappointment in his voice. —Don't you want to know what I found out?

—Go on, then.

—He has a record. Arrested in 2001. Dad, what does 'importuning' mean?

—God, Adam . . .

Mollel knows that importuning is a beloved charge of the Vice Squad. It's a useful catch-all when they fail to catch someone in the act, but have enough suspicion that something was going on. Basically it means asking for sex, or behaving in such a way that could be considered as looking for sex. That could apply to being in a certain location at a certain time, or even being dressed in a certain way. And, of course, it only ever applies to men who are looking for men.

—It's a legal thing, he blusters. Adam seems satisfied, for now, with that response.

—Quite interesting, Adam continues. —The arresting officer was Joseph Bogani.

—Bogani?

Kiunga looks across.

—He's your boss, isn't he? Adam asks.

—Not my boss. He's in charge of the case I'm working on.

—Oh, well. I thought you'd want to know.

—Thanks. But promise me, no more snooping around. If you're going to be a detective, you have to do things by the book.

Mollel feels Kiunga raise an eyebrow at this.

—I promise. Is Collins Uncle with you? Say hi to him for me!

—Adam says hi.

—Hi buddy! shouts Kiunga. —See you soon!

—It's just one more lead I need to check out, pleads Mollel, after he has ended the call.

Kiunga, still driving, takes his eyes off the road long enough to cast Mollel a scathing glance. The glance's meaning is clear – he's not doing this for Mollel. But the call from Adam has underlined the residual loyalty in this relationship.

The text message comes through. Mollel reads the address, and Kiunga swings the car around.

*

Even a city in constant flux has the ability to throw up new surprises. Mollel is presented with one when they reach Riveredge. This leafy street winds alongside the grandiosely titled Nairobi River, which for most of the year is little more than a brown trickle. People can occasionally be spotted washing there, or sometimes water trucks pull up and put their suction hoses into the murky pools, belying the words emblazoned on their sides: DRINKING WATER.

In rainy season, though, this trickle becomes a torrent. The water races over the boulders in exhilarating curves and crests. This is the time when the system is tested: if any of the myriad of pipes or ducts which run under the bridges that criss-cross this river are obstructed or blocked – and they usually are, by the detritus which is dumped into the watercourse every day – the water will back up and break the banks. Any dwelling or construction built into the sides of the steep, wooded ravines which run alongside the river will rapidly be undermined unless it has the most fortified defences.

It's not a sensible place to build. But this is Nairobi, so it is built upon. The trees whose roots shore up these cliffs are chopped down, and the green veins of nature, relics of Nairobi's past as a highland forest, have been covered with concrete and brick. Rows of townhouses run at precipitous angles down to the duct which was once a river; office blocks perch on stilts over where the water runs; and all of them carry names which evoke that which they have destroyed: Riveredge, Forest View, Waterside.

Riveredge was one of the last preserves of untouched gully near to the city centre, and perhaps, because so much of the land belonged to the university, people thought it was safe. The road ran, looping and swerving, along the bank, and while it was hardly the Maasai Mara, it brought a little bit of nature into the lives of those who drove, walked or cycled along it every day. Monkeys could often be seen in the treetops, lounging and laughing, it seemed, at those strange creatures fuming in their often-stationary cars far below.

But now it's all gone. Mollel barely recognises the road he must have travelled down only a few months before. The side of the road which was once covered in trees is now all granite and glass. RIVEREDGE BUSINESS PARK proclaims a sign. The towers soar above them. The views from the top must be spectacular, thinks Mollel: but what are they of?

Being in a marked police car, they can bypass the routine rigmarole of stop-and-search which, as this place is new, is being conducted with more diligence than usual, causing a tailback on the slip road. The security guard directs them to one of the completed blocks – many of them are still shells – and they park outside, stepping over a muddy square puddle where, apparently, the pavement should be. They've been told to go to the third floor, which is good, because there's no signage in the lobby.

Kiunga presses the lift button. There's no clunk of machinery springing into action; no light comes on; no ding of acknowledgment. They take the stairs.

The stairs are unfinished concrete, their edges beginning to crumble even now. This exclusive, upscale office development has more in common with the makeshift dwellings of Dandora or *Mji wa Huruma* than first glance would have indicated.

On the third floor, they exit the stairwell and find themselves transported, once again. Under gleaming lights, and sitting on an expanse of shiny marble, is a car. It's a small, red car, one of those little sports numbers from the 1960s. Upon closer inspection they realise it has been chopped in half, so there is only the front bonnet, wheels and the windscreen, behind which sits a receptionist, who looks up and smiles.

The theme continues around the room. There's an old-fashioned motor scooter suspended on one of the walls, and the guest waiting benches seem to have been ripped from a bus.

Behind it all is a bright, neon sign: a rainbow curving high over a small well with a bucket and handle. ARC, read the letters below it.

—Hello, and welcome to ARC, says the receptionist, pronouncing it as a word, not an acronym.

—We're here to see Mr Rehoboth, says Mollel.

—Oh. You mean Mr Antony? Do you have an appointment?

—Nairobi Police, says Kiunga, showing his ID.

Mollel would have gone for a more discreet approach, but Kiunga is still resentful at being dragged along and, Mollel suspects, has little sympathy for the man they're about to see, given the circumstances of their last meeting.

The receptionist presses a button and says a few words into her headset. Neither Mollel nor Kiunga want to sit on the bus seats, so they pace silently until a wall – or at least a door which is as nearly as wide as a wall – swings open and the man from the Electric Chair, whom they had last seen in the company of two others, greets them.

His eyes are downcast and he has none of the confidence he displayed when Mollel saw him in Kanja's clinic. He ushers them through to his office and the door / wall swings shut.

The office, like the reception area, is characterised by its unusual furnishings. Mollel and Kiunga are directed onto a long, banana-shaped couch, while Rehoboth takes a seat in a red, egg-shaped chair. Between them is a table made from the tyre of a truck.

On the wall are a number of posters, framed, displaying the now ubiquitous face of Nyambisha Karao, and emblazoned with slogans in Sheng and the logo of one of the major mobile phone companies.

—Yes, the décor, says Rehoboth, as though reading their thoughts. —Well, this is the public relations game. Image is everything. If we had gone for a bland, corporate look, what would that have said to our clients?

—I thought this was a communications company, says Mollel.

—It is.

—You said it was public relations.

—It's much the same. I called it Antony Rehoboth Communications because I thought that ARC was a better name than Rehoboth Antony Public Relations. RAPR. Can you imagine?

He smiles, but his observation falls flat.

—So your given name is Rehoboth, and your family name is Antony?

—Yes. As far as it matters. My mother told me – she believed – that my father was called Antony. Whether that was a first name or second name, I don't know, and nor, probably, did she. She wasn't much more than a teenager at the time. She didn't want me, but she was persuaded to bring me into this world by the pastor, a man whose love of word games, I later discovered, was as great as his love of scripture. It was he who decided on the name Rehoboth: an anagram, he told me, many years later, of *Oh Bother*.

—But Rehoboth is a Biblical name, says Kiunga.

—Indeed. It is the site of a well mentioned in Genesis, hence the well in my logo. But I also suspect that was another of my pastor's jokes. Rehoboth was the name of a well *for which they strove not*. My poor mother certainly didn't strive to have me.

Given that they have only been talking for a few minutes, Rehoboth is revealing his personal background remarkably quickly. Mollel detects the influence of Kanja, and his way of encouraging people to open up. On the other hand, what better way to avoid being frank than to appear overly confessional? Kiunga also seems to have tired of this approach.

—As I understand public relations, he says, —it's the art of getting people to talk about what you want them to talk about, and ignore what you want them to ignore. Well, we're in a different game, so I'll get straight to it. What were you doing in the back room of the Electric Chair last night?

Rehoboth blinks, then presses his fingers together, leans forward, and feigning innocence asks: —I don't know, Sergeant. What do you *think* I was doing?

Kiunga snarls. —Don't mess with us. This isn't Europe. You know what happens to your sort here.

Rehoboth looks away. —Unfortunately, I do.

Mollel tries to strike a more conciliatory tone.

—We're not interested in your private life. But you've turned up twice now, in close connection with the case we're working on. So I have a few questions to ask. First, I met you at Doctor Kanja's clinic. What were you doing there?

Rehoboth looks from Mollel to Kiunga. He sighs.

—I've been seeing Kanja for a while. He's helping me.

—Helping you with what?

—Helping me find a *cure*.

Neither of the policemen responds to this, so Rehoboth continues: —Do you think I want to live like this? To be threatened by police just because of who I am? To take the chance that, every time I step out of my door, I might be arrested, beaten up, or killed? To have to find low-down, dirty places like the Electric Chair, because they're the only places where my *sort*, as you put it, are tolerated? And then, even in my everyday life, I am petrified that someone will say something, pick up on something, notice some mannerism or glance or the way I cross my legs, or the way I walk, or look at someone, or wear my clothes. I'm terrified that something will give me away. Can you imagine the strain that puts on a person? Wouldn't you want to be cured?

—So Kanja has been trying to cure you? asks Mollel.

—I've tried everything else. Doctors. They gave me pills that nearly killed me. Pastors. Well, I told you about the one who named me. He identified what I was when I was very young, even before I did. And his version of spiritual relief involved punishing me for the very crimes he forced me to perform.

Kiunga is looking at the walls. Rehoboth has his head in his hands.

—How long have you been seeing him?

—Six months.

Mollel wonders how much Kanja charges. It never came up in their conversation. He's willing to bet that with a middle-class client like this – not to mention one who demands the maximum discretion – Kanja could virtually name his price. He feels a wave of revulsion for the little man who is so quick to exploit the misery of others.

—So I suppose your presence at the Electric Chair means that the cure is not working?

Rehoboth shrugs.

—Sometimes it does. Sometimes it doesn't. I wasn't even supposed to be there that night. I just went along to see Nyambisha Karao playing, and you know, one thing led to another. He's one of our names. He points with his thumb at one of the posters on the wall.

—The corporates like to reach out to the kids. But we can't do anything too obvious, you know. They're wise to that. So we work to get people like Karao seen from time to time with one of our products, drop a brand name into one of his songs here or there. It's funny. You know, the Sheng language developed as something underground, a counterculture. Now we're co-opting it. Rappers like Karao are replacing the picture of the Maasai on his mobile phone as the image of corporate Kenya. But I guess I don't have to tell you anything about cultural appropriation, do I, Sergeant?

He smiles at Mollel, but Mollel is not in the mood for a philosophical discussion. He produces the picture of Fatuma and places it on the truck-wheel table.

—This girl was also being treated by Kanja. She also happened to be a regular attendee, or perhaps more, at the Electric Chair. If we're coming after you, it's not because of persecution. It's because we want to find her, and you're the closest thing we have to a lead right now.

Rehoboth picks up the photo. —Pretty girl. But you'll understand, Sergeant, if I confess that I wouldn't necessarily remember her, even if our paths had crossed. What's happened to her?

—She's missing, says Mollel. —We're also investigating a death. Not her. A different person. The body of a male turned up at the Dandora dump.

The photograph flutters to the floor. Rehoboth closes his eyes.

—Not another, he whispers.

—Another? asks Kiunga.

Mollel remembers that Dora, back at the Electric Chair, had said much the same thing.

—What do you know of him? asks Rehoboth, quietly. —Do you have a name?

Kiunga shakes his head, but Rehoboth, eyes closed, does not see the gesture. Mollel, without thinking, takes a risk.

—Does the name Abdelahi Abdelahi mean anything to you?

Rehoboth looks up. His face is devastated. His skin is grey. He looks as though he has aged thirty years in the last thirty seconds.

—Abdelahi, he croaks.

—You knew him?

Rehoboth nods. Eyes which, seconds before, had been widened in horror, close, and tears begin to tumble down his face. Kiunga stands, approaches the egg-shaped chair, hesitates, and then reaches out and puts a hand on the man's shoulder.

—He was a friend of yours? continues Mollel. —A friend from the Electric Chair?

Again, Rehoboth nods. —I've not seen him for a couple of

weeks, he says, through his tears. —That's not unusual. People come and go. But I was . . . I was very fond of Abdelahi.

—You said *not another*. That means that others have gone missing, too?

—Yes. Not girls. This is the first girl I've heard of. But four or five young men, regulars at the club, have disappeared over the last few months. We've been worried about it. But, you know, it's not like we can go and report it to the police.

Kiunga, his hand still on Rehoboth's shoulder, looks abashed.

—Did you know Abdelahi was a teacher? He was this girl's teacher, in fact.

—Yes. He had to work night shifts. He once told me he used to sneak out when all the kids were asleep.

Mollel pictures Peter, the nightwatchman. Though deaf, he was still alert. He wondered how Abdelahi managed to get past him.

—Describe Abdelahi to me.

—He was such a sweet guy. He had to be even more cautious than the rest of us. Firstly, as a teacher – any whiff of this kind of lifestyle, and he'd be banned from working with kids. Secondly, as a Somali. They're even more down on our community than the Christians are. He once told me that if word got out amongst his family, he'd be murdered on the spot. Are you getting an idea of why we might turn to magic for a cure, officers?

Kiunga, who has taken away his hand of sympathy, but whose attitude has nonetheless softened, asks: —So Abdelahi was searching for a cure too?

—He was the one who introduced me to Kanja.

—Can you give us a physical description?

—He had wonderful sensitive eyes. Those high cheekbones that make the Somalis so beautiful.

—Tall? Short?

—Short. He was not a big man. Barely came up to my shoulder. He hardly weighed a thing.

Mollel asks: —Did he carry some sort of device, like a music player?

—Oh god, yes, says Rehoboth, with a smile both affectionate and heartbroken. —His music player. He took that thing with him everywhere.

—So now we have a whole new investigation, says Mollel, when he and Kiunga are back in the car. —Possibly. A number of men, linked to the homosexual back room at the Electric Chair, missing or worse. What I suggest we do is this . . .

Kiunga holds up his hand.

—No, Mollel. What we're going to do is *this*. We're going to drive this car back to *Mji wa Huruma* police post, where I'm going to take a note of its mileage and check it back in. Then you and I are going to write our final case report on Fatuma's disappearance, and we're going to log a possible ID on the body from the dump as Abdelahi Abdelahi. Then Bogani will assign the follow-up on these two cases to one of his own. It might well be me. But it won't be you, because he's already asked me to make sure you get back to Central.

—Look, Kiunga. We don't have to do this. You know as well as I do that this investigation won't go anywhere unless we push it. We'll just neglect to do the paperwork for a while. Ignore Bogani's calls. Once we file the report, it's dead.

—We don't have a choice.

—We always have a choice.

—You might have a choice, Mollel. I want to have a career.

Mollel falls silent. Kiunga, who is driving, glares at the road ahead. Mollel's anger with him is heightened by the knowledge that Kiunga's stance is perfectly reasonable. Wrong, but reasonable.

He should have seen it coming. When they'd first worked together, Kiunga had found a kind of mentor in the older man. Surrounded as he had been by typical Nairobi police officers

– lazy, stupid and corrupt – Mollel had given him a template for what a good detective could be. Sure, their partnership had been rocky at times. It had also been solid.

But there was only so far that anyone could go with Mollel as a role model. How could someone so lacking in control of their own life and career light a pathway for anyone else? Bogani was a much better example for Kiunga to follow. And Mollel would be better off without the burden of someone else's expectations on his shoulders.

—Do you remember what Bogani said about not going to the championships? He said everyone has a choice, and he was happy with his.

—Sure, says Kiunga.

—Well, I know what I'm going to do.

—So do I, says Kiunga. —And it's not the same as you.

21

Lendeva was always very loyal. Perhaps the most loyal person Mollel had ever known. But for Lendeva, loyalty was an indivisible unit. You couldn't share it. Split loyalties were broken loyalties.

After the row with Chiku, he walked away from the security business. He left Mollel a letter, with a list of all the names and contacts, told him he could take the business over. Chiku said it was all worthless.

—This isn't a business, Mollel. This is a set of odd jobs. Where are the accounts, the licences? What about tax, insurance, contracts? He might have been making a profit, but only because he wasn't paying any of his obligations. What if one of his guards got sick, or hurt on the job? What if the city council turned up and wanted to see the paperwork?

Mollel could have explained to her that Lendeva didn't exist in a world of rules and regulations. If one of his workers got hurt, Lendeva would have looked after him. If he'd been questioned by the authorities, he'd have dealt with the request in his own way. It wasn't a question of doing things wrong, it was just *different*. And as it happened, Mollel did not want to take on the business. He had other dreams, now, of being a policeman. Besides, he had no talent for managing people. They worked for Lendeva because he was Lendeva; Mollel knew he could never match the loyalty his brother inspired.

—You know, said Chiku one day, carelessly stroking his dreadlocks, —these will have to go.

It was a shock to Mollel to realise she was right. No police officer would ever be allowed to sport such long braids. She suggested doing it herself, but that seemed wrong. In Maasai culture, it is the role of the mother to shave her son's head when he graduates from warrior to junior elder.

The journey back to his village was difficult for Mollel. It was the first time in several years, and it felt strange not to have Lendeva beside him. Yet Mollel was glad to be moving up in his age-caste. Even with Lendeva's superior status, it would be unheard-of for a younger brother to become a junior elder first. This was one privilege Mollel could enjoy.

But he didn't enjoy it. As the locks fell onto the decorated leather hide on which he knelt, he knew that this was a farewell to more than his youth. He would undertake this ceremony, then bid farewell to Maasai life. He was becoming something else.

Some months later, a young warrior from the village turned up in Nairobi. Mollel was sure he was looking for Lendeva. He was one of those who had viewed Lendeva as a role model and always looked upon him with adoring eyes. He found Mollel by asking at the car lot and being directed to Chiku.

—I don't know where my brother is, said Mollel. —But if you're looking for a job, you're out of luck. He's not in business any more.

—It's not just him I need, the young man urged. —It's you, too. You've got to come home.

Unthinkingly, Mollel's hand rose to his prickly, shaved scalp.

—He's heard I'm an elder now, is that it? And no doubt he thinks it's his right to become one too. Well, that's up to him. But I'm not going to the ceremony.

—No, it's not that. You have to come home urgently. Your mother is sick.

*

Mollel had left a scrawled note for Chiku, grabbed some bread and some clothing, and struck out from the city. The young man had stayed behind to try to find Lendeva, but Mollel could not wait. From what the messenger had told him, time was tight.

It was late, and there was no way he could rely on getting a lift now. No one would stop for a Maasai in the darkness. He would have to go on foot.

Somewhere around the Athi River, where he struck off from the road and began the moonlit haul across the countryside, Mollel began to feel the city, and all it brought with it, slip from his shoulders.

It was about one in the morning, and the moon, though waning, was bright enough for him to make out a path. As he walked on, the orange sulphur glow leached from the sky and the stars returned. It was a long time since Mollel had seen them in all their glory.

He had been carrying his bundle on a stick over his shoulder. Now he untied it. The cloth of the bundle was a *shuka*, and within it were a pair of truck-tyre sandals, and a belt. He hadn't consciously decided to bring traditional clothing, but Mollel could not imagine returning home in anything else. He divested himself of his burdensome shoes and city clothes, and slipped into the familiar garb. Immediately, he felt connected with the soil beneath his feet and the cool air around him.

Each step away from the city was a step back into the past. Around the time the dawn began to paint the sky red, he heard a distant engine, and spotted headlights picking their way across the plain. He worked out where the vehicle would pass, and made his way to a point where he could wait beside the track. Within half an hour, just as the landscape was bathed in the first golden rays and he felt the warmth of the sun upon his back, the vehicle reached him. It was a pickup with a bullock tethered in the back, and Mollel knew the driver from the

Kajiado market. The man gave him a ride most of the rest of the way.

It was mid-afternoon by the time Mollel reached his home *manyatta.* At first he feared he was too late. The gentle keening of women reached him as he mounted the final hill. Smoke should have been rising from all of the huts at that time of day; there was none.

But as they rose to greet him, the womenfolk informed Mollel that he had arrived in time. He made his way into the familiar home – one which had been moved several times over the years, but which was nonetheless constructed, for the most part, using the same sticks and skins he'd helped to put together each time.

She, however, was changed. Barely more than a bundle of sticks and skin herself. The body before him was no more his mother than a drained gourd was milk.

When she opened her eyes, though – sensing, perhaps, his presence – he saw a glimmer of that long-remembered fire that had defined her.

He found himself unaccountably nervous, wringing his stick in his hand like a suitor.

—It's me, mother.

He stepped forward, so that he was no longer a silhouette in the doorway, and knelt beside the litter where she lay. Her hand rested on her chest, and he took it. It was as dry and light as a leaf.

For days, she drifted in and out of consciousness. Sometimes she would moan in pain, sometimes she cried out in fear. But she never seemed to recognise her son.

One morning, Mollel woke from a slumber at her side, to find her looking into his eyes with a searching, beseeching gaze.

Her lips parted. A low, rasping whisper: her final word.

—*Lendeva.*

22

—Mollel! *Bado kufa?*

—No, Mollel replies. —I'm not dead yet. How are you, Janet?

—Good. I'm glad you called. It's a little early to offer you a drink, but as I know you won't accept one anyway, I'm sure you won't mind if I have one. I was just shooting another piece to camera for my showreel.

Sure enough, the TV lamps are on and the room glows with low-angled artificial light. Janet draws the curtains back, hits a switch, and the lamps are killed, replaced by natural sunlight, which seems disappointing in comparison.

—I wonder when the rains are going to come, Janet sighs. —Growing up, we could always predict the weather. Now, you never know when the season will change. Have you noticed it, Mollel?

—I used to notice the weather more when I was young. It mattered more in those days. Now I just look out of the window to see whether I need a jacket.

—It's not just us, though. Everyone says it. Farmers don't know when to plant any more. They say it is global warming.

Global warming, like war in far-off lands, is something Mollel has heard of, and suspects is dreadful, but it doesn't seem to affect him. It's the sort of thing for reporters like Janet to go and investigate and feel bad about on behalf of everyone else.

—I love Nairobi in the rain, she says. —It cleans everything up. Not like New York. There, it just makes everything dirty. It doesn't come from the sky. It comes from the buildings, and it brings everything with it; the dirt and the soot and the trash. You think we have it bad here? You should see the trash in the streets in Manhattan. They never show it on the TV. You never get the smell either. Seriously, Mollel, here in Kenya we think we're the trash heap of the world, but it's everywhere. The more you travel, the more you realise everything's the same.

She is at the fridge, and turns to place a half-empty bottle of yellow wine on the counter. She pulls out the cork and pours a glass.

—Like corruption. We take a strange kind of pride in it here, don't we? The only league table we ever seem to top is the corruption index. It's got so that we're not even offended by it any more. You know, before I left, I was reporting on scandals involving hundreds of thousands of shillings. That procurement scam you told me about? Small beer nowadays. You've got to be raking in hundreds of *millions* for anyone to take notice. And even then, the scale of it makes them untouchable. It used to be rogue civil servants, crooked businessmen. Now it's even the *President*. Hey, we shrug. What can we do about it? We're corrupt. That's how it is.

—But then you get to America, Mollel, and you realise that even our corruption pales into insignificance compared to theirs. You walk down Park Avenue and try to figure out where the money comes from. They've elevated corruption to an art form. It's so embedded in the system they don't even call it corruption any more. They call it leveraged financing, or corporate instruments, they call kickbacks *consultancies*, *directorships* and *incentive packages*. No, when it comes to being the worst, Kenya isn't even very good at that.

—So what really brought you back? asks Mollel.

—Have you heard the expression, *big fish, small pond*? It's a big pond over there, Mollel. It's an ocean. No one cares who you are. I was flattered to get the offer from the US network. I made the front page of the *Nation*, Mollel. Do you remember?

Mollel remembers. It was, in part, his story that put her there.

—In Nairobi, people used to stop me in the street. But in New York, I was just like everyone else. When I told them I was from Kenya, they thought I'd said Canada. When I told them it was in Africa they'd say, 'Oh, sure, South Africa.'

—Even at the network, no one knew me. When I told the receptionist I'd come to start a new job, she thought I was with the cleaning crew. I soon realised that the fad for international reporters was just that, a fad. I spent a year in edit suites doing voice-overs on agency pictures of wars in Liberia, Sierra Leone, Congo. I've never even been to those places. But you know, it's Africa, so hey.

—Then there was September 11th. It was just blocks from us. I was the only one who wasn't broken by it. All of them, all of those other people, they cried, they stumbled, they stopped talking altogether. In the newsroom that day it was just me holding it together. I worked thirty-six hours solid. I was cutting packages together from the raw footage, Mollel, the videos of the people jumping. I took the horror and I made it TV. I did great work that day, Mollel, great work. Professional. And you know why? *Because I'd seen it all before.*

—Not that I got any credit for it. My colleagues thought it was distasteful that I didn't share their shock, or their anger. I didn't feel the need to lament, or to lash out. I wasn't jubilant when the video feeds showed Afghanistan being lit up, and they thought it was because I was a foreigner, or because I just didn't care.

—Anyway, Africa was now off the agenda and I was barely needed. I took my pay cheque and visited Western Union every month. It's amazing how far dollars will go here. My family said I was crazy when I told them I wanted to come back. So I stuck it out, producing other reporters' work, researching and writing and bashing the phones on the guest-booking desk. At least I could tell myself I was still doing journalism.

—But I wasn't, really. I was just processing material. I was a machine, converting raw video into something simplistic enough to be understood by viewers in Akron, Ohio. Then one day that material was from Kenya again. I had a bunch of uncut footage of a mob baying over a burning tyre. I recognised the location. It was here, outside this very hotel.

—I don't know if they even remembered I was on the payroll, but suddenly I was in demand again. I was drafted back up to the newsroom. The network wanted to show their expertise by having a Kenyan face in front of the camera, explaining why our country was falling apart. Except they didn't really want explanations. I had ninety seconds on screen. Take away the anchor's questions, and I had less than a minute to try to encapsulate decades of tribal animosity, unequal resource allocation, the residual legacy of colonialism, the impact of IMF-enforced neoliberalism. Eventually what it all boiled down to, was *these Africans are killing each other again*.

—The very reason I'd become a journalist was to try to tell a different story. Now I was blindly repeating the same old narratives. Don't you feel the same, Mollel? Don't you feel as though you are just a servant of the people you set out to fight? You used to want to change the system. But has the system changed you?

Mollel shrugs. She pours more wine, emptying the bottle. Its lip clinks against the glass, and Janet winks at him. —Sure you can't be tempted? Why don't you give in once in a while, Mollel? It's nicer than you think.

He reaches into his pocket and takes out the tape. It's a small cassette, not much bigger than a box of matches. He lays it on the counter. She looks at it, reading Kiunga's name written on the side.

—This is why I'm here, he says. —Can you play it?

She picks up the box, opens it, and looks at the cassette. —Sure. This is a fairly standard format. We can put it in my camera, here, and play it through the TV.

He doesn't know what he was expecting, but Mollel is surprised to see a blank screen. Gradually, though, he realises that the greyness is not uniform. There are spots and even a faint crack is visible. This is not an electronic emptiness, but a real one: someone has pointed the camera at the wall.

There is the sound of a door opening and closing. Voices murmur. One of them, closer to the microphone than the others, says: —Are you ready?

—Yes, replies a voice.

Kiunga's voice.

A blue blob enters the screen. The camera whirs and double-takes, automatically searching for focus. Mollel sees a stomach, a man's belly clad in a blue shirt. He recognises the shirt as one of Kiunga's favourites. The image shifts as the camera operator reframes. Kiunga's head and shoulders, now. He looks off-camera, uncomfortably. The voice close to the microphone speaks.

—Do you understand the purpose of the interview here today?

—Yes, says Kiunga. —Though I don't agree with it.

—It doesn't matter whether you agree with it. Do you understand that your presence here must remain confidential? You are not to speak about it with anyone?

—I understand.

—Please state your name and rank.

—I am Collins Kiunga, Sergeant at Central Police Post, Nairobi.

—Tell me about Mollel.

Kiunga's cheeks blow out and he lets out the air in a slow, solemn sigh.

—Where do I start?

After he has watched the video, Mollel feels like the Americans Janet described: speechless, angry, ready to lash out. Janet observes him a while before saying: —You want that drink now, Mollel?

He shakes his head.

—Well, at least you know what they think of you now. All of them, even your friend. I'm sorry, Mollel. It must have been pretty hard to hear that.

He shrugs, then stands, and walks to the window. The skyline of Nairobi shimmers with heat.

—You don't have to put up with it, you know, Janet continues. —You were offered a pretty decent payout back in 1998. You could have taken it and never had to work again. Hell, you could take it now, if you asked for it. I bet they'd still be willing to offer you something, just to be rid of you.

Mollel has no doubt that some of them – Bogani, especially – would love to see the back of him. In a way, sticking around has been a source of perverse pleasure to him all these years. The knowledge that he's been a thorn in some people's side was always satisfying. But now, even that meagre pleasure is gone.

He feels a soft pressure on his arm. Janet has joined him at the window and slipped her arm through his. She takes his hand, and to his surprise, he does not flinch; her hand is soft and small and the action feels unforced.

—You've been working so hard all these years, Mollel. Maybe it's time to think of yourself. Sure, they'd be buying your silence. But maybe it's worth it? Who do you owe any loyalty to? The Police Service? They were never loyal to you. Bogani? Definitely not. Otieno? He's gone. Kiunga?

She leaves that one unanswered. The tape said it all.

—Justice, says Mollel, quietly.

Janet gives a hollow laugh. —Oh yes, that one. That's a doozy. Like *truth* for journalists. It sounds great, until you realise that there isn't one justice, there isn't one truth. There are millions of them. As many versions as there are people. Sure, you can stay loyal to *your* idea of justice, or truth – but ultimately, you're just doing your own thing. If doing your own thing is all that matters, why not do it without the stress, on a nice fat police pension? I hear retiring to Mombasa is a very good option these days.

Mollel shakes his head.

—No one's getting any younger, Janet continues. —And then there's your son. You should enjoy his company while he's still around.

The mention of Adam makes Mollel withdraw his hand defensively. He turns to Janet, but she misinterprets his movement, and curls her body towards him, raising her chin and closing her eyes.

—What do you mean, while he's still around?

She opens her eyes.

—Well, how old is he now? Fourteen? He'll be off to college soon. That's all I meant, Mollel. What did you think I meant?

He's pulled away from her now.

—You're afraid of losing him. I understand. It's tough to face up to being alone.

He looks at her. When he had entered the room, she'd been standing with her back to the TV lights blazing in the sitting area. He hadn't properly looked at her face all this time.

She is without make-up today, and while her features are still fine, the skin is puffy around her eyes. Mollel wonders if it is the drink, or whether she had been crying before he arrived.

She reaches for his hand again.

—You don't need to be alone, Mollel. Everyone needs someone to talk to.

His eyes fall upon the TV screen, now blank, but which had been filled with Kiunga's image just moments before. Apparently Janet was right. Everyone needs someone to talk to.

His eye follows the cable which runs from the TV to the little silver camera sitting atop a tripod. There are black cables everywhere: thin ones running back from the camera to the bud microphones that are resting on the two seats, facing one another, and thicker cables running to the lights on their stands. A set-up for an interview.

—What did you say you were doing when I called?

—Oh, you know. Shooting some showreel. I've got to get it right this time, Mollel. Not too many chances for a woman in TV at my age.

—Wouldn't you need to wear make-up for that?

She flinches, and her fingers go up to her cheek. She looks hurt.

—Or perhaps you don't need to wear make-up if you're the one asking the questions. It's all about the interview for you, isn't it? You don't care about me, or anyone. Just the job.

She shakes her head.

—You've got it all wrong, Mollel.

She walks wearily over to the counter and picks up her wine glass. —I'm going to lie down. See yourself out.

She goes through to the bedroom, which is dark beyond the door.

She was right about Adam. Mollel had been avoiding facing up to the fact, but his son would soon be gone. Perhaps, in part, this accounted for his desire to find Fatuma. This thought is interrupted by his phone ringing in his pocket.

Sometimes, not very often, Mollel – the arch-sceptic – experiences a moment which seems to have a little magic in it. One of these moments happens now. Looking down at his phone screen, Mollel sees that it is Adam calling.

—Adam! I was just thinking about you.

—Hi, Dad.

The boy sounds excited.

—I've been working on the rap lyrics, he continues. —From Fatuma's journal. There's still a way to go, but I thought you'd like to hear what I've got so far.

—I would, says Mollel.

—OK. Have you got a pen and paper?

After a while, from the bedroom, comes Janet's voice.

—Mollel?

But the only answer is the click of the door as he leaves.

23

—I don't understand you policemen. We told you right from the start that our daughter was safe and well. Then, late last night, we got a call from the mortuary and one of you tells us that our daughter is dead. Can you imagine the impact that had on my wife?

Ngecha's emotion is genuine, but it is the anger of a businessman dealing with an insubordinate underling rather than that of a stepfather fretting about his missing child.

His wife is wearing a dressing gown. Her eyes are swollen from crying, and she has no eyebrows. Her un-made-up state reminds Mollel of Janet.

—She's not dead, says Mollel. He is watching the woman's eyes. They widen slightly, though she holds her face impassive, fighting to retain her composure.

—Well of course she's not, says Ngecha, unconvincingly. —As we have said, she's away with family.

—Let's stop lying, shall we? She may not be dead, but she could still be in danger.

Ngecha moves towards Mollel. He is a taller and stockier man, and Mollel readies himself for an assault. It does not come. The wife has stayed her husband's arm.

—So your team is out looking for her, right now?

My team, thinks Mollel, bitterly. Right now, his team consists of himself, and – thanks to the notes in his pocket – Adam.

—I have reason to believe she's alive, he says, cautiously. He does not mention the sighting at the school. That is too easily dismissed as childish hysteria.

—What have you got? demands Ngecha.

—This, says Mollel.

They all sit down and Mollel starts to read some of Adam's translation of the Sheng lyrics in Fatuma's notebook.

—I don't know what this is supposed to tell us, grumbles Ngecha.

Noura, next to him, hisses: —Be quiet.

The power is shifting in this room.

—*You act the big man*, Mollel reads. —*Everyone fears you. But I know your secret. I could break you.*

—This is nonsense.

—Quiet! says Noura.

—*You act so moral. So high and mighty. But do your voters know where you go nightly? You're not a family man. It's a scam. You take what you can. You talk about love, but I've seen you in the club. Love is just another thing to buy and sell. Go to hell.*

—That could mean anything, says Ngecha, quietly.

—*No!*

It's a childish shriek. Maryam has rushed into the room, her bare feet pattering across the floor as she flies at her stepfather, her arms whirling. He throws up his own arms to protect himself from her nails, which flail against his skin.

—It's you! the small girl cries. —It's you she ran away from. What did you do to her, you pig? You big, fat, dirty pig!

Noura scoops up her daughter, and the girl buries her head in her mother's gown. She is screaming with rage: the rage of being a small child in this world of adults. Noura casts a look of fury at Ngecha, and, ignoring Mollel, storms out of the room, taking Maryam with her.

Ngecha puts his head in his hands.

—So, what is it, asks Mollel. —Was she protecting you, or

blackmailing you? I've been in that club. I've seen the back room and I know what goes on there. You can tell me. Your wife's not here, and I don't care one little bit about anyone's private life.

Ngecha's shoulders heave and he gives a grim, barking laugh.

—You don't get it, policeman. You don't get it at all. I'm not one of *them*. He wouldn't have had to construct this whole elaborate ruse if I was one of *them*.

He looks back at the door through which Noura and Maryam went.

—Let's discuss this outside, he says.

The garden is neat and clipped, and as impersonal as the house. There are no children's toys scattered on the lawn, no washing on the line. It's like a hotel. But Ngecha is obviously proud of his domain.

—I suppose you've got more, he says. —She was always scribbling in that damn book of hers. Of course, that's just her side of the story.

Mollel does not intend to let Ngecha know that, as of this moment, this is all he has.

—So why don't you tell me your side?

Ngecha sighs.

—Thirty years of hard work got me here, he says. —And I'm not going to have it taken away.

—I just want to find Fatuma, says Mollel. —I have nothing against you.

—It's not you I'm worried about. The police are no threat to me. I've done nothing illegal.

He gives a bitter chuckle.

—Well, nothing *very* illegal. Nothing worth bothering you boys about. No, when it comes to Dandora, I answer to a higher authority.

Mollel remembers someone else saying very much the same thing.

—Nicodemus.

—Indeed. My position on the city council makes me very useful to him. And I appreciate what he does. Do you imagine for a moment that the place would be as peaceful as it is without his supervision? You may hate the tip, but through it, he provides employment and security.

—So every time there's a resolution to close down the tip . . .

—I ensure it fails. Yes. As I have done for years. But the pressure's growing. The tip's becoming too big to ignore. Everyone's *green* now. Even the President's said he wants it gone. I had no intention of caving in, but I guess Nicodemus wanted to be sure.

—He wanted to have something to hold over you, says Mollel.

—Yes. He uses the VIP memberships at the Electric Chair as his carrot and stick. That little card is highly coveted, you know. Whether it's boys or girls, there's something back there for everyone. That's the carrot. But he knows everything, sees everything. He's had cameras installed. That's the stick. There are not many husbands who want their wives to see what they've been up to in the dark.

—And that was it? asks Mollel. —You'd been with a girl back there, and Nicodemus was threatening to reveal it to Noura unless you continued to support him?

—If only, groans Ngecha. He casts a reproachful look back at the house. —She doesn't mind me going there. Why should she? It's where I met her. To be honest, now she's got the house and the car, I think she's relieved she can outsource one of her more burdensome obligations.

—So she used to . . . work there?

—Correct. Spare me your delicacies, Detective. You don't care about my private life, remember? Yes, Noura used to turn tricks. Nicodemus introduced us. He joked that she was his gift to me. A reward for compliance, as though she was anyone's to buy or sell. That's what made her want better for her daughters. I can't say I ever bonded with the girls, but I don't begrudge her having aspirations for them. She would always put them first. Nicodemus knew that.

A cloud drifts in front of the sun. As though in response, Ngecha shudders.

—You don't get to be as powerful as Nicodemus without being creative, he says. —What he did was borderline genius. He told me he had something special. A new girl. The only thing was, she was shy. I had to meet her in one of the private rooms, and it had to be dark.

Mollel can suddenly see where this is going.

—I was drunk. So drunk. I can hold my drink well, but he'd brought out this special Scotch, and kept pouring me glass after glass. I should have realised something was up. Nicodemus never buys anyone a drink.

—The room was as black as night. He must have had one of those night-vision cameras in there, continues Ngecha. —The moment she'd finished, he barged in and turned on the lights. That's when I saw her for the first time. She was wearing a wig, make-up. She looked different. But it was her. It was Fatuma.

—You have got to understand, says Ngecha. —I have my limits. I never knew it was her.

Mollel is reminded of something Janet said about justice, and truth. That everyone has their own idea of what those words mean. The same applies to morality, too. Ngecha had not been fazed by corruption, prostitution or exploitation. Nor had Noura. It's very hard to blackmail a person like that. But Nicodemus had come up with something that *would* drive a wedge between husband and wife, and destroy them both. Not to mention Fatuma. Presumably he had a tape. He probably wouldn't even need to use it. He could just keep it as insurance.

Disgusted as he was, Mollel cannot help but admire Nicodemus's strategic mind.

—You can't blame the girl for wanting to get away from here, says Ngecha. —She looked as disgusted as I was. I'm sure Nicodemus tricked her, just like he tricked me. She is probably afraid of both of us now. Not to mention ashamed—and petrified of her mother. I expect she wants to lie low for a while.

—So you and your wife have no idea where she is?

Ngecha shakes his head. —And to be honest, Detective, I'm perfectly happy for it to stay that way.

24

They buried her on the mountainside, overlooking the plains. It was a good spot. A place which, apparently, his mother had chosen for herself a few months previously. Mollel had stayed another day, distributing his mother's remaining livestock amongst her neighbours, and sharing out her meagre belongings. Then he had turned his back upon the village, and left.

It was several months before Mollel saw Lendeva again. After an agonising wait for news, and numerous disappointments, Mollel had got his place at the police training college. It was a residential course, but recruits were allowed to go home at the weekend. One Friday afternoon, Mollel exited the rusty gates of the college and saw a familiar figure crouching, owl-like, against the brick wall opposite.

He tensed slightly as Mollel approached, but he did not raise his head. Mollel knew that when his brother would not look him in the eye, it meant trouble.

Mollel had an urge to apologise – for what, he was not sure – but he resisted it. It was not his fault that Lendeva had not been found in time. It was not his fault that his brother had missed their mother's death.

He would not apologise. Nor could he bring himself to reveal who she had asked for in her final moments.

—I've been here for hours, Lendeva said. —I've not seen a single Maasai go in or come out, other than you.

—So?

—They said they wanted more Maasai to join the police service. Yet here you are, Mollel, the only new recruit in the whole of Nairobi who is a Maasai. Did you ever stop to think about that curious fact? Did you ever wonder why it was only you?

Lendeva always knew exactly what to say to rile his brother. With a surgeon's precision, he could find the precise nerve to hit. He did it by asking questions. He knew that when you really want to get under someone's skin, it's not the questions you ask them that are the most revealing, but the questions you make that person ask of themself.

As a matter of fact, Mollel was under no illusion about why he found himself in such a minority. Although the department had waived the requirement for a high school certificate, there were still those literacy and numeracy tests, which Chiku had been coaching him for. Mollel thought he had done fairly well. So it was a shock to him when the college had told him he had failed.

—This is *bullshit*, Chiku had said. —You *can't* have failed. It's *impossible*.

—There's always next year, Mollel had said.

—And they'll fail you next year, too. They'll always fail you, Mollel, it's tribalism. Don't you see? Whoever marked your test, or someone else along the line, decided that your name did not fit. They didn't want someone who didn't fit in with their neat little system. Well, this does not end here. Let's see how those big guys stand up when a Kikuyu girl's coming after them.

Mollel didn't want her to do anything, but he knew that she was unstoppable when she got like this. He also thought that it could do no harm. Chiku would have more luck protesting against officialdom than he would – she spoke their language, in more ways than one.

*

When she returned from Vigilance House, hours later, Chiku was strangely subdued. It took a while before Mollel could persuade her to talk.

—I was wrong, she said, eventually. —It wasn't tribalism. In some ways, that would be easier to deal with. This is corruption, pure and simple.

She explained that she had been kept waiting until the office was just about to close. The secretaries and other workers had been out of the door at four. It was only after they'd gone that she was invited in. The official didn't want any witnesses to the meeting.

—Ten thousand shillings. Ten thousand bob, Mollel. That's what it will take to get you into the police.

Mollel didn't have that sort of money. Neither did Chiku. It was more than a month's wage for her, and there was rent to pay, and her tuition at the secretarial college, plus the rest.

It looked as if all those hours of study had been in vain.

—We can't just give up, Mollel. We'll fight it. I'll go to his superiors. I'll tell the world. This is a scandal. We'll beat them, Mollel. We'll beat them, and then when you're in, you can do something about this corruption which is bringing our whole country down. You can change things.

But the next evening, Chiku had returned even more downcast than before. She'd been able to see the examiner's superior, but either he hadn't wanted to know about what his team got up to, or he hadn't believed her. There was also a third, more likely possibility: he was in on the whole scam, and took his cut of the *baksheesh* when it was paid.

Neither of them admitted it, but together, Mollel and Chiku had formed a plan, of sorts. Chiku was putting in extra hours in the evenings and at weekends. Meanwhile, Mollel was still doing security jobs. Night guarding. It would take a while, but if they were careful with their money – skip breakfast, skip lunch type of careful – they might be able to scrape together the ten thousand before this latest round of recruitment closed.

Then disaster struck. Mollel had been working for one employer down near the airport, at a warehouse where nothing ever seemed to come or go. One day the owner had told him he could have a night off, with pay. If it seemed too good to be true, it was. That night, the place burned down, and Mollel didn't have a job any more. The owner had explained that there was no business left, nothing to pay their salaries with, and the two months he owed Mollel would just have to be written off. He seemed to be asking for Mollel's sympathy as he told him the bad news. He didn't get it.

Mollel had trudged home from the burned-out warehouse, dreading having to tell Chiku, but she had squealed with delight as soon as he walked through the door.

—You got in, she told him, elated. —You passed the exam, Mollel. You're going to be a policeman.

He was stunned. —But I failed?

—I persuaded them to recheck the papers. They said there had been a mix-up, and that the original results were not yours.

Mollel asked her to explain how this had happened. She told him that she had gone, one more time, to plead with the examiner. This time, she had done something she wasn't exactly proud of.

—I never play the name game, Mollel. You know that. But this time . . .

She had told the examiner who her father was. The examiner might have been corrupt, but he was sufficiently impressed to find out that this was Harry Ngugi's daughter. A hero of the resistance – the freedom fighter who'd been imprisoned and exiled by the British.

—He pulled out your paper, realised there had been a mistake, and stamped the approval there and then, Mollel.

*

It only took a few nights at the police training camp for Mollel to realise that most of the other cadets hadn't so much as looked at the exam: they'd simply paid up their ten thousand shillings and reported for training.

—But where did you get the money? Mollel had asked one of them, a country boy who seemed to come from a background only slightly less impoverished than his own.

—I had people lining up to contribute in my village. I even had enough left over to buy my father a new suit for church.

—But won't they be expecting something in return?

He just laughed. —Of course! It's an investment, Maasai. They'll all benefit from having a friendly face in the police at some point down the line. That's the way it works. You don't get anything for nothing in this world.

When Mollel finally saw his brother again that Friday evening, Lendeva had changed. He was still wearing his Maasai garb, still had his dreadlocks. Mollel guessed that meant Lendeva hadn't been back to the village lately, otherwise he would have heard about Mollel becoming an elder. He couldn't imagine Lendeva would allow that imbalance of status to last long. But he seemed to not even notice Mollel's own cropped scalp. He was thin, twitchy. Distracted.

—There's something I have to tell you. You're not going to like it.

—You didn't look like you'd come to wish me well in my new career, replied Mollel.

Lendeva explained that he'd been contacted by their former client at the car lot. A delicate matter. Something needed investigating, and he couldn't trust his own staff to do it.

Lendeva had a bag with him. Mollel hadn't really paid any heed to it before, but now Lendeva reached in and pulled out a bundle of papers. They were account sheets. Columns and rows of figures.

—What am I supposed to do with these?

—It's all there, Mollel. Just follow the figures.

—What does this have to do with me?

—You'll see.

And his brother turned and left, with Mollel gazing baffled at a bag full of sheets of meaningless paper. After he'd gone, Mollel realised that he'd never even told Lendeva about their mother.

25

The Electric Chair is open, but it's too early to have attracted the crowd that will be thronging at its doors later. For now, the BEATS N BEER sign flashes more as a beacon of consistency in this desolate corner of Dandora, rather than as an enticement to any passing traffic.

Mollel, now, is part of that passing traffic although the Electric Chair is not his destination – he is sure that he would not be welcome there in any case.

The motorcycle taxi drives straight past. They round the next corner, Mollel leaning into the turn, and when they straighten up again, Mollel taps the driver on the elbow.

He is dropped near a doorway. It's a residential building but the street frontage has metal bars set into it, and hooks welded at regular spaces upon the bars. In the daytime, street vendors pay a peppercorn rent to the building's owners to display their wares upon these hooks. By night, the image is that of a sleeping creature, bristling with spines.

Light from the fires of the dump is reflected on the low clouds above. The air is thick, not just with the reek of the rubbish – which, Mollel realises, he must be becoming inured to – but with the heavy promise of rain. About time, too. It might wash some of this dirt away.

A voice comes from the doorway.

—Mollel. Come into the shadow. You can't be seen around here.

It is Kanja.

—There's no one to see us.

—There is always someone. This is Dandora. There are eyes everywhere.

Mollel enters the shadow.

—You didn't tell anyone you were coming here?

—Who is there to tell?

—OK. We can't go to my office. I have somewhere else though, somewhere special. Here, put this on.

He gives Mollel something in the darkness. Mollel turns it over in his hands. It is a wide-brimmed hat.

—A disguise, Kanja?

—A precaution, Mollel. Let's go.

When they step back out onto the street, Mollel can see that Kanja is wearing a hooded rain cape. The hood rises above his head in a sharp point, yet it still barely reaches Mollel's shoulders. Mollel suppresses a laugh at the ridiculous image the pair of them must present to any passer-by – and is relieved that there are none in sight.

The faint boom of the Electric Chair's bassline fades as they walk away from it. Dandora, originally planned as some kind of model suburb, had been built along a grid pattern. This makes it easy for Mollel to keep a sense of where they're headed. After a couple of blocks and a right–left zig-zag, he realises they're running out of street. There's only one place they can be headed.

—We're going to the dump?

—*Shh!* commands Kanja. —The closer we get, the more of them there are.

As though to make himself more invisible, the little man hunches his shoulders and picks up his pace. Mollel, feeling foolish, follows suit.

They turn the next corner, and there it is before them. High

– higher, surely, than before, or is it just a trick of the light, the way the orange glow from the fires below suffuses the smoke rising from within – glowering, towering. A city's worth of detritus.

A crackling noise around them, and Mollel feels spots hitting his face. For a moment he thinks it is ash. After all, this trash volcano feels as if it is about to erupt. But it is not ash. The spots are cool and wet, and putting a hand to his face, Mollel rubs the welcome rain over his skin.

—It won't make much difference here, says Kanja, as though reading Mollel's thoughts. —The fires never go out.

Kanja is right about the eyes, too. Mollel feels them on him as he approaches the trash heap. He has always had a sense of when he is being watched, and from which direction, and as he peers into the gloom, he sees what could be movement and hears what might be scurrying. That this place is rat-infested, he has no doubt. But other, more sentient eyes are watching their progress.

It's hard to say where the road ends and the heap begins, but by now, they are climbing, negotiating their way along a path worn by the pickers, in much the same way as the most reliable path through the bush is the trail left by animals – provided you don't meet one. Underfoot, the terrain is treacherous, and Mollel, who usually finds himself more sure-footed in his traditional sandals, is glad of his sturdy police-issue boots. Occasionally, a shard of glass glints in the red light. Who knows what other dangers might lurk beneath the surface.

They continue to climb, and as they approach a crest, Mollel is reminded of making his way across the highlands, and that moment when you realise that the mountain you've been labouring up is nothing but a foothill of the range that lies beyond. For before him is spread a topography of darkness, crackling with orange beacons here and there, but a void compared to the shimmering lights of the city so clearly delineated beyond.

Turning, he looks back at Dandora. The light from the colourful, flashing sign of the Electric Chair is visible, if not legible, from here. Following the line of the buildings, his eye falls upon the higher outline of Mama Sharifa's school, with its dormitory perched on top. There is a light burning there, too.

—Come on, Maasai, says Kanja.

They walk a while along the top of the ridge, a path that Mollel's better instincts scream out against, for in nature, this would present a silhouette to enemies and predators alike. Here, though, the smoke has begun to coalesce around them, and mingled with the soft rain, it shrouds them from all but the closest observer.

They have been walking for half an hour or more – Mollel's chest burning from the exertion in the polluted air – when they begin to descend into a shallow valley of sorts. The misty glow of the lights from the outside world fades then disappears. Mollel and Kanja are absorbed into the dump now.

Abdelahi might never have been found. Had word not got around that Mollel was looking for a girl, the body would just have broken down and been subsumed into the trash. Mollel wonders how many others have met the same fate here. The losers, the loners, the unwanted and the unloved. Murder victims. Suicides whose shameful death would need to be disguised. Even natural deaths, family members whose lives meant something and were grieved, could be brought here in the dead of night, stripped of any identifying features, and abandoned – why spend money on a funeral, when the necessities of life were so much more pressing? Even babies, miscarried and aborted, born and discarded, would form part of this landscape.

Pondering these morbid thoughts, Mollel almost runs into Kanja, who has drawn to a halt immediately ahead of him.

—Enjoying the walk, Maasai? Ready for a break? Want to get warm and dry?

Kanja cackles. In the dim light, Mollel can just make out

the small man stooping to pluck a heavy mat or tarpaulin from the ground. He lifts it, the diamond corner of blackness rising above his head, and then it falls with a slap.

Kanja is gone.

26

Mollel didn't want to look at the paperwork. He was no accountant. He told himself that he would not understand it anyway; or that it was irrelevant. Lendeva was probably just trying to get him to do his dirty work for him. Mollel wanted none of it.

His instinct told him to throw away that bundle of papers, or to use the sheets as firelighters. He knew that Lendeva, burning with fury and resentment, would not have given them to him unless, like a blackened log left in the ash-pit, they invisibly smouldered within.

But he didn't throw them away. He stuffed them into a plastic bag and shoved them under the sink. He did not think of them for a while.

Mollel half-expected Lendeva to turn up at his wedding. He had not told him about it – and had no way of reaching him – but these things had a way of getting around. On the day, though, amongst the blur of smiling, unknown faces, slaps upon the back and grasping handshakes, Mollel did not see his brother.

On the steps of the Catholic church, Mollel had noticed some friends of Chiku giggling with her. One patted Chiku's belly and raised an eyebrow. Chiku laughed and shook her head.

That was the first of what was to become a familiar refrain. As though, by formalising their relationship in a public place,

Mollel and Chiku had relinquished any rights to privacy over the creation of a family.

Faith, naturally, was the worst. She began dropping hints. —Did you hear that Susan Kamau's daughter is pregnant?

Such statements would inevitably be followed by a sigh, or a significant glance, at which Chiku would roll her eyes. Another favourite was: —You two have a lot of room here. Plenty of space for a little one.

But the months came and passed, and Faith remained disappointed. —I'm not going to put any pressure on you, she said, on their first anniversary. —But I'll be honest. There's no point hanging about. Neither of you is getting any younger and nor, for that matter, am I. I want to be around to see my grandchildren grow up.

Another year. Chiku told Faith she'd seen the doctor, and had been told there was nothing wrong: she was young, she still had plenty of time. But Mollel suspected she was lying: he heard her, at night, when she thought he was asleep, and he knew that she'd been crying.

Faith wasn't living with them, but she seemed always to be there. When Chiku was around, Faith faded into the background. When it was just Faith and Mollel, her silent resentment filled the place. She could barely hide her scorn for this Maasai interloper.

One day, when Faith had sent Chiku on some kind of errand, she cleared her throat, and Mollel knew she was going to speak about something to him. He did not relish the prospect.

—You know, Mollel, she said, —I'm worried about you.

If you've never seen accusation expressed as kindness, you've never met a mother-in-law.

—You work so hard. This police job is taking its toll on you. Perhaps you're not as vigorous as you used to be.

Mollel protested. He was healthier than ever. He'd even

started to gain a little weight since Chiku had begun insisting he should eat more than just meat and starch.

—I still think you should go and see a doctor.

But he had recently passed his police medical, with flying colours.

—Yes, but . . . I don't think they look at everything, do they? I mean, someone else might be able to help you out with this baby thing.

This baby thing?

Faith tried to reassure him. —Lots of couples go through this. Why, even Patricia Mungai's daughter was having trouble, until her husband went to see an *mganga*. They can do things that other doctors can't, you know. You won't even need to take your trousers down.

That night, Mollel told Chiku: —I don't want you to talk to your mother about our relationship.

Chiku sat up in bed. —Who said I talk to her about that?

—She seems to know a lot about it.

—The only person I talk to is you, Mollel. And you've been so distant lately. You work long hours, you never talk about your job . . .

—There's not much to tell, he replied.

That wasn't true. There was too much to tell: the cruelty, the corruption, the cynicism. The ugliness of policing the city. He didn't want to sully her with it.

—We tell each other everything, don't we, Mollel?

—Everything, he lied.

—Well then, there's something I need to tell you. I've seen Lendeva.

He'd asked her not to tell Mollel. He'd said it would spoil things. He said he wanted to be reconciled with his brother, but only when the time was right. But in the meantime, he said,

Chiku had been his friend, too. He had a right to see her, if she wished. Of course, she now said, she'd stop if Mollel wanted her to. Of course, Mollel said that she should not.

He had tried to put the thought out of his mind, over the years, but like the bag full of paperwork he'd hidden under the sink, it gnawed away at him. It wasn't that he didn't trust his wife, or even, for that matter, his brother. But he resented the fact that there was something between them that he was not part of.

He'd tried to forget about it, and thought that he had succeeded. Chiku's news – that after all this time, she had finally fallen pregnant – helped. For the first time, Mollel began to envisage a future for him and Chiku which did not involve other people. Lendeva, Faith: they would still be there, but on the periphery. There had been too many people inside their marriage. The same would not be true for their family. From now on, it would be just Mollel, Chiku, and their baby.

Except it wasn't. They needed Faith, and she became more present than ever. She moved in when the baby was born, changing nappies with aplomb, snatching the child from his father's arms when she thought he wasn't being held correctly, tutting at Mollel's clumsy attempts to soothe him. Adam, it seemed, was to become a pawn in a game that Mollel did not even know how to play.

Mollel was out of the flat most of the day, most days. When he got in, he was tired. He had missed his child all day, and always seemed to just miss him when he came home, too. Faith would protest: *he's just gone to bed!* And Chiku, herself exhausted, would acquiesce. *Let him rest.*

When Mollel got in very late, Faith would have to stay over. It made sense for her to take to the bed with Chiku and the baby. Mollel would pull up a chair at the kitchen table, place a pillow upon it, lower his head, and sleep there.

*

One day, he was unexpectedly released from duty early and found himself able to get home while it was still daylight; a strange, elating feeling. He pictured his son reaching out his chubby arms to his father, his mother smiling and raising him to his embrace. Faith was not in this picture.

But her face was the first thing Mollel saw when he opened the door. She was dressed differently; in a blouse and skirt, a new weave upon her head. She looked startled and she called out to Chiku. Chiku emerged from the bedroom. The baby was in her arms, but Mollel could not see him under the white blanket in which he was bundled. She smiled, but her smile was nervous.

—Mollel! We weren't expecting you. We . . . we got Adam christened today.

—It's been nearly a month, chipped in Faith, puckering herself up for an argument Mollel had shown no signs of starting. —He *had* to be christened.

—Can you leave us a moment, Mother?

—I'll put him to bed, said Faith. She shut the bedroom door behind her.

—So you didn't go to college today, Mollel asked Chiku. He thought his tone was fairly neutral, but her reply suggested it was not.

—You wouldn't have wanted to come, Mollel. It was all the things you hate. The priest, the prayers. I just did it to make *her* happy. Don't be like that.

Mollel wasn't sure what he was being like. He took a glass and filled it at the sink. Apparently the act was provocative.

—For God's sake, Mollel. You can't have it both ways. You said you didn't want him to be a Maasai. Apparently you don't want him to be a Christian either. Well, you might be happy to go through life as a nothing, but that's not good enough for our son. He has to be something, Mollel. Everybody has to be something.

*

That night Mollel could not sleep. The TV they had in those days could only pick up KBC, and after the news there was an interminable politics programme which featured people he didn't know talking about things he didn't understand. Mollel kept it on for the sound of the voices and to practise his English. When he went back to the sink for more water, he thought about the plastic bag he had shoved beneath it. The one Lendeva had given him. He pulled it out, sat at the table, and spread the papers out in front of him.

At first, it had all meant nothing to him. It was as dense and dull as the politicians pontificating on the television. But slowly, like hearing familiar words dropped into a conversation in a foreign language, things started to stand out for him. The first was Chiku's signature. It appeared regularly enough, and there was no surprise in that. Part of her duties was to sign off the salaries for the guards and small payments for tasks such as car washing and garbage removal. She also handled the petty cash.

Most of the petty cash withdrawals were for very specific sums. One hundred and sixty shillings for tea. One thousand two hundred shillings for a new desk lamp. But there was one which made no sense. Ten thousand shillings – bare, stark, ten thousand shillings – for *sundries*.

Beside it, Chiku's signature.

Mollel ran his finger along the line. He found the date. His mind ran back over the years. He was sure. It was around the time he had been admitted to police training.

Maybe she'd seen the light under the door, or had heard the droning of the TV. She came tiptoeing, in her nightshirt, and put her hand upon his shoulder. —It won't be long, Mollel, she whispered. —Soon it will just be the three of us again. Our family.

She looked at the table.

—What's this? Where did you get all this?

Mollel didn't tell her where he'd got the papers from. But he did tell her that he was going to quit the police. It had always been a source of pride to him that he had got in on his own merit. Yes, she'd helped, mentioning her father's name, but he wouldn't have been selected if he hadn't passed the test. How could he continue now, knowing that he had started his career already mired in corruption? It made everything meaningless.

Chiku had looked at him, astonished. The last vestiges of sleep had gone from her face, and her eyes were wide. She shook her head. —Surely, Mollel, you can't believe . . .

—What was it for, then? This payment, on that very day?

The baby was crying. Neither of them moved.

—Ask your brother.

—My brother? Don't drag him into this.

—Like he dragged me into it? He's the one who gave you these papers, isn't he? Ask him.

Suddenly Faith was there, bouncing the baby up and down in her arms. —He needs his mother, she pleaded.

Chiku's eyes blazed at Mollel. She scooped Adam from Faith's grasp and swept into the bedroom. Faith followed her, and the door slammed shut.

27

For a moment, Mollel is left alone, and he spins around. In this shallow depression, he feels entirely surrounded by the caldera of the volcano. He has no idea of whether he will even be able to find his way out. He feels lost, and utterly vulnerable. There could be any number of hostile figures out there. His sole comfort is that they're as unable to see him as he is them.

Suddenly his phone rings.

—*Shit!*

He pulls it out of his pocket. The little Nokia screen blazes in the darkness like a spotlight.

Mollel just has time to see the name on the incoming call: ADAM.

He hits the red button to reject the call, and turns off the phone.

—You'd better come quickly, Maasai, now you've woken the whole dump.

Mollel follows the whisper to ground level, and groping with his fingers, finds the edge of a half-inch thick rubber mat. The rainwater upon it glistens with the reflection of the clouds above. In this gloomy light, Mollel can just about make out a square of darkness below the mat, from which the echoing voice drifts up once more: —Come on!

Mollel reaches down into the darkness. His fingertips touch a square edge of brick or concrete.

—Feet first. There's a ladder.

He sits on the wet, soft ground and works his feet forward into the hole. Sure enough, the toe of his boot comes into contact with the rung of a ladder. Mollel reaches out, grasps the top of it, takes a deep breath, and begins to descend.

—Let the flap down gently after you, says Kanja.

Mollel holds it up with one hand as he takes two, three, four more rungs. Then, with the fifth, he lowers the rubber, which is heavy and slippery. It slides from his grip in the final inch and slaps down above him.

The darkness is total, but only for an instant. Mollel hears the scrape of a match, and tall, flickering shadows are cast around him. He is inside a vertical shaft made of brick, barely wider than his shoulders. The light emerges from the shaft's opening just a few more rungs below him. Mollel descends, then squeezes himself down low to work his way out of the hole, coming out backwards on his hands and knees.

He can tell from the smell of paraffin that Kanja has lit a lantern, and after it flares, then stabilises, Mollel takes a look around him.

He is in a room. The room is small and square, and has a door, and a window with curtains, and a stone fireplace through which he has just crawled. There is a table and a pair of mismatched chairs, a heap of blankets, and some boxes. There is a small charcoal stove beside the fireplace and a sack of charcoal, some pots and pans, and a large number of bottles of all sizes and colours. On the wall there is a lurid poster of Christ, his heart beaming out from his chest, and a calf's skull hanging from a wire.

—Welcome, says Kanja.

Mollel gets up and dusts off his knees and his hands. Kanja has taken a seat at the table and beckons to Mollel, who does likewise. They sit facing one another, with the lantern flickering between them.

—Have you ever seen the ocean, Mollel?

Mollel shakes his head.

—It's quite something. I only saw it myself for the first time when I was already a young man. I had travelled to Mombasa to sell some potions. I'd heard there was a demand for the stuff down there. I came across the ocean when I was crossing the causeway from the bus station to the old town. I couldn't believe it. Such an expanse. It was beautiful. Breathtaking. But then I started to think about what lay beneath it. I'm from the Rift Valley, like you are, Mollel. I'm used to standing on escarpments, watching the land roll away below me, only rising again as some blue, distant hillside on the horizon.

—I realised that under this water was another, similar landscape. There were cliffs, and plains, and valleys, all of them hidden. Those little white triangles of dhow sails were skimming the top of space. The huge cargo ships in the distance were suspended a mile high. I had never felt vertigo before, Mollel, but I felt it then. I left Mombasa the same day. I couldn't bear to be so close to that chasm. Well, this trash heap is like an ocean. It lives and it moves. Everyone sees the surface. But they seldom think about what lies below.

—This used to be someone's home. Think of that, Mollel. How this ocean of rubbish must have inundated it. The owner would have picked up a plastic wrapper from their doorstep one day without realising that this was the start, the first drop of the flood.

Mollel looks up. The ceiling is crazed with cracks, and the walls are streaked where liquid has seeped in.

—*He* was already here, continues Kanja, nodding at Jesus. —He didn't do much for the householder, but perhaps he has helped keep this place up over the years. It was found by one of the *chokora*, who tripped over the chimney one day. He told me about it, and I swore him to secrecy. This is just the sort of place I need. It's secret. It's isolated. And because it's under several feet of compacted trash, you'd better believe that there's no way anyone can hear anything that goes on inside. In a city like Nairobi, you'd pay a lot for this kind of privacy.

—Above all, this space is safe. It's hard to predict how people will react to the treatment and it's not the sort of thing you want to do in an inhabited area.

With that, Kanja lowers the flame on the lantern to a small, cherry glow and the light in the room fades to near blackness. —I'm sorry, but I need to open the chimney a crack, he explains, —and I can't risk the light being seen outside.

Kanja goes to the fireplace and lies on his back. He grasps the bottom of the ladder and pushes it up. Mollel hears it scraping against the brick. Kanja gets two bricks and places them under the ladder. This, Mollel concludes, must be pushing up the rubber flap a few inches.

Kanja comes out, then moves the stove into the chimney and places a few lumps of charcoal on it. He takes one of the bottles and shakes it. Mollel sees a shower of drops glint in the faint light. Then Kanja strikes a match and holds it to the stove. A lazy blue flame plays across the coals.

Kanja, on his haunches, blows on the flame until the coals begin to glow. When he sits back again, he says:

—I know why you are here, Mollel. You are not seeking treatment. You are seeking facts. You have ascertained that Fatuma, the missing girl, underwent treatment with me. You believe that at least one other involved with your case must have done the same. You want to find out for yourself what happened to them. I am happy to oblige.

Kanja is unrolling a packet. Mollel hears rustling as Kanja rubs something between the palms of his hands and throws it onto the stove. Immediately, a thick, treacly scent rises. It reminds Mollel of the odour of *bhangi*, but it is more subtle than the burned-rope smell that infests the Electric Chair. It is more resinous, almost like the incense he used to catch a whiff of on Chiku's clothes after church.

Kanja speaks again.

—Your plan was to play along until you found out more. But, as I believe I have said before, it does not matter *why* you are here. It only matters that you *are*. You see, Mollel, I identified something in you, right from the very start. It would be wholly inappropriate for me to let it pass. It would be like an oncologist spotting someone in the street with a particularly malignant mole. It is my duty to help you.

Mollel suddenly feels desperately tired. He's not eaten today; he's not slept for two days. With the heady atmosphere, he wants nothing more than to curl up and close his eyes.

Kanja takes a break from the stove, and pulls a blanket from the corner.

—Here, lie on this.

Mollel can feel an inner battle being fought, and lost: his instincts are telling him to remain on his guard, not to let Kanja get any advantage over him, physically or emotionally, and yet his body and his mind are sliding into a state of comfort and relaxation. He finds himself, for the second time, considering Kanja's offer of help. *Why not*, part of him is saying. After all, nothing he's tried previously – the talking, the drugs – has provided real relief. Why not give it a try?

And in some ways, this *is* the ultimate safe space. For Mollel has plausible deniability – the right to later disavow anything he may have said. He can open up, while retaining the right to claim he was just spinning a story, trying to ensnare Kanja into revealing the truth.

—Drink this, says Kanja.

It is sweet and cloying, and a warm glow suffuses Mollel's chest as he swallows. The sweetness both heightens his hunger and takes the edge off it; he holds out the gourd to Kanja for some more.

—Not yet. Tonight, Mollel, we have work to do. You are possessed by three demons. There is not much we can do about the first two, but the third must be exorcised. It is him, or you.

The room is getting hotter, the air thicker. Mollel lowers his head to the ground. He tries to keep himself tuned in to what Kanja is saying, but while he is able to catch the occasional word, the sentences evade him. He begins to give up – and somehow, when the words become noise, the noise carries more meaning. Now it is a chant, a repetitive chant, and one which seems to carry answers within its sonorous depths.

To Mollel's fevered mind, the chant sounds like *Ask Your Brother.*

Those had been Chiku's last words to him: *Ask your brother.* He never saw her again. When he woke the following morning, she had already left. She must have crept past him silently, trying to leave the flat without disturbing him. In fact, it was Faith washing the baby at the kitchen sink which woke him, an hour or more later. He must have slept deeply.

—Chiku forgot her lunch, Faith said. —Can you take it to her?

He looked at the bag of *githeri* on the kitchen counter. —I'm supposed to be reporting for training on the other side of the city, he pleaded.

Faith picked up the bag and put it in his hands. —I know my daughter. She didn't leave this by accident, Mollel. If she left it here, she left it for you to take to her. It is her way of reaching out to you. Don't refuse it.

The secretarial college was on the fifteenth floor, and as he walked down Haile Selassie Avenue Mollel looked up at the building and tried to identify which floor that was; he wanted to spot the window they had looked out of together the first day he had visited her there.

There was a strange clapping sound, which seemed to

bounce off the buildings, as though it were coming from great height. At first, a flock of birds were apparently the only ones to be disturbed by it. With all the construction work in the city, who could tell? But then louder noises came, and even those unfamiliar with the sound of gunfire – which most people were, in those days – could sense that something was amiss. Mollel began to see people turning on their heel on the pavement ahead of him and starting to walk – then break into a run – in the opposite direction. And all the time, there was this pop-pop-popping noise.

Mollel started to push forward. It felt like swimming. He had to thrust himself through the throng now, moving them aside with his arms.

He stepped onto the road to get away from the crush. The cars were backing up now too; some of the drivers had sensed trouble and were attempting U-turns; most of the buses had opened their doors and were disgorging worried-looking passengers who scurried away with their heads ducked. Mollel swung himself up onto the running board of a truck and looked down the road ahead. He could make out smoke at the gate of the US embassy: a flare, perhaps.

And then there was a roar, and he was knocked to the ground.

—Water, he croaks.

The gourd is placed in his hand and he drinks greedily. It does not slake his thirst, but it revives him a little. Kanja's voice fills his ears again.

—You have three demons, Mollel. Two have reached an accommodation, and it would be dangerous to disrupt the truce they have struck. One of these demons is Reason. Reason, one may feel, is not a demon, but in some ways, Reason may be the most deadly demon of all. For Reason may be harnessed to support the most insufferable acts. Reason can blind us to suffering and isolate us from love. Someone possessed entirely by

Reason can seldom be saved, for that salvation can only come by climbing down, at least part of the way, from the walls that Reason has built to protect itself. Reason's defences are strong within you, Mollel. But you are lucky. You have an ally.

Your second demon is Anger. Anger can take many forms, and in its most elemental, it will lead its host down a path of certain destruction. Your Anger has long been tempered by Reason. That has been of great benefit to you. Anger also allows you, on occasion, to set Reason aside. This is not the flaw that conventional wisdom would have you believe.

All the specialists you have seen, all the pharmaceuticals they've put down your throat and the mind-tricks they've taught you, have focused on managing Anger by allowing Reason to grow stronger. But that ignores the fundamental need for balance. Far too long, you have suppressed your Anger. And this has allowed the third demon to sneak in.

This third demon is Doubt. Doubt is the most insidious demon of all. It is time that we brought him out into the open.

Mollel coughs, and is aware of someone cradling his head. He feels soft fingers stroking his cheek. A cool, wet cloth passes over his forehead. He looks up. A face looks down at him. It is a woman's face, her eyes full of tender concern. It is a face he knows well.

Ask your brother. He hadn't thought of those words again for a long time. They'd been blown from his head, along with everything else. Along with the life he had known, and the one he thought he was going to have. Lendeva had disappeared as surely as Chiku had, and Mollel had not stopped to think about where he might be.

When the press made him a hero, for getting up and running into the rubble, he was just one of many. But he happened to be a cop, and that counted for a lot, especially to a department trying to save face. They'd failed, after all, to prevent the terrorists from carrying out the attack. And so they lavished attention on him, flattered him, cajoled him into staying in the force. And he felt he was honouring Chiku, too, by fulfilling her vision. His disgust at the corrupt payment which had got him into it was hidden, forgotten, filed away. He did not allow himself to consider it.

But by not considering it, neither had he questioned it. It had become a fact in his mind. And even though he could not have acknowledged it, his memory of Chiku as someone who embodied truth and honesty was in danger of crumbling.

So why didn't he question it? Why did he allow that most precious memory of her to be diminished in such a way?

He is surprised now to find himself asking this. He is even more surprised by the answer: *Because I was afraid of the deeper question*. A question which had to remain buried, and be buried deep.

Ask your brother.

Mollel has heard that drug users get moments of clarity so powerful that they are able to distinguish the patterns of the universe. He had always been sceptical. But now, he feels as though thoughts and memories, suspicions and fears, are coming together to form patterns he has resisted for too long.

The room is full of figures. Some of them talk to each other; some of them talk to Mollel. One of them is a smartly dressed man of around his own age.

—Hello, Mollel. Remember me?

—Of course! You are my son, Adam.

—That's right. Good to see you again.

—Good to see you too.

He wants to ask him more questions: is he married? Does he have children of his own? But Adam steps back into the shadows and when the light falls across his face again, it is Lendeva that Mollel sees before him.

—Chiku was right. You should have asked me, Mollel.

—I couldn't find you!

—You should have asked me straight away. When I gave you the copies of the accounts. It made no sense. Why would I, an uneducated Maasai, be asked to audit an office fraud? And one which was so simple that even you or I could solve it?

—You weren't asked, replies Mollel, flatly.

—No. I asked for them. I told the company I wanted those papers for my own records. The sheet which showed the payment to us for the night of the robbery. Our reward. Ten thousand shillings. I am sorry I never told you about it, Mollel. But it was my business, after all.

Mollel shrugs. He does not begrudge his brother his share of the money.

—I got someone at a copy shop to paint out the dates and wrote new ones in. I even cut Chiku's signature out with a razor blade and glued it into place before I made the final copy. I wanted to plant the seeds of doubt in your mind.

It all makes perfect sense to Mollel. He can see it clearly now; and for the first time, he understands how Chiku's heart must have broken when he accused her of stealing the money.

And then, combined with the remorse, he feels Anger welling up at the thought of the years he has considered himself a fraud, unworthy. Whereas, in reality, he *had* passed the test. Reason had seen him through.

He reaches out and grabs Lendeva. But the smile he sees is Kanja's.

—Cast out the Doubt, cries Kanja. —Let Reason and Anger destroy it!

Mollel is now grasping Kanja tightly by both shoulders. From behind the old man, a female face peers into Mollel's eyes with concern. It is the same woman – girl – who had so solicitously mopped his brow.

It is Fatuma.

28

—You're alive, says Mollel.

—Yes, she replies. —I was here all the time.

—But not *all* the time, says Mollel. He lets go of Kanja and slides to a sitting position against one of the walls. He is still in a dream-like, detached state – though he is sure he is no longer dreaming. This is the real Fatuma he sees before him.

—No, she agrees. —I came out once.

—You came to the school, at night. It wasn't a night runner, or a ghost, that Dorcas saw. It was you.

She nods.

—How did you get in? The place was locked up tight.

—The same way I used to get out, says Fatuma. —Behind the trunks lined up against the wall there's a concrete block where someone had worked away all the mortar. Once you know it's there, it's easy to slide the block out. Then you can get down along the rooftops, and use the drainpipe to reach the ground. You can get back in the same way, too.

—So why did you go back?

—I needed my book. It was all in there, for anyone who wanted to find it. The facts that put me in danger. The facts that killed my friend.

—Your friend?

—Abdelahi. He was the only teacher who listened to me,

really listened. I had quite a thing for him too, until I found out he was . . . well, you know.

Mollel did know.

—I used to stay awake at night, the nights when he was on duty. I knew he'd come round to do the late inspection. I just wanted to see him. I just wanted to know he was there. Then, one night, he disappeared. I couldn't work it out. He was back again in the morning. The next time it happened, I was ready. I followed him. That's how I found out about the Electric Chair.

The Electric Chair, she told him, was the place where she had first found freedom. The doormen had let her in, even though she was wearing only a black night-gown and slippers. It wasn't such an outlandish outfit, apparently. And even though she had no money, she didn't need it: within moments someone had bought her a drink.

She saw Abdelahi disappear behind the curtain, and would have followed him there, too, but at that moment something happened which changed her life. That something was Nyambisha Karao.

He came on the stage, and she was electrified. She'd memorised all his songs, gazed dreamily at the posters of him on her walls, but she'd never imagined she would see him perform live. And what a performance! No recording could ever capture the energy, the emotion, which he gave out right there and then. It was as though she was alone in the room with him. And when he came off the stage, and fell into the arms of an adoring crowd of glamorous, elegant women, she knew what she had to do to get even closer to him.

Luckily for Fatuma, she had learned enough from observing her mother to know how a hip-sway and a flick of the wrist could be used to best effect. She also managed to grab, on her next weekend home, one of Noura's long wigs, a pair of heels and a selection of make-up. Still, she had not managed to get Nyambisha's attention. The next time she had snuck out, he wasn't even there. She'd accepted drinks from a couple of leering drunks, and endured a few of the second-rate acts on the stage that night, but had snuck back into the dorm disappointed.

The next time, it was even worse. She had actually been enjoying the rapper this time – a young woman named Dora. The crowd wasn't wild for her – they all preferred male rappers – but Fatuma had found her inspiring. *If she can do it,* she thought, *maybe I can, too.*

But her fantasy had been interrupted when a large, bald-headed man sidled up to her. —I've been watching you for a while, he said. —Don't you think it's about time you started earning those free drinks I've been sending your way?

The idea, she explained, was quite simple. She'd get chatting to a customer, encourage him to buy a drink or two. Ideally, suggest to him that the *really* impressive guys – the kind of guys who attracted the kind of girls like her – were the ones who ordered bottles of champagne. And so the money was made.

She had grown up never wanting for material things. But she'd never seen any way out of the world she'd been presented with. Now, she did. People wanted her, and she could use that power to gain independence. It was frightening – and thrilling.

She must have been doing well, because after a couple of nights, she graduated to the VIP section. Here, she was told, she didn't have to do anything she was uncomfortable with. But the pressure – and temptation of wads of folded notes – was too much to withstand.

—I just closed my eyes and got on with it, she tells Mollel. —The power was addictive.

One night, she was leaving one of the private rooms, and saw a familiar face looking at her with shock. It was Abdelahi. The two fugitives had run into each other.

—I saw where he was coming from. We all knew what went on behind that curtain. Once we'd both got over the initial surprise, we realised we had a lot in common. And Abdelahi was one of the good guys. He wanted to save me.

—He told me that he knew where I was headed, because he'd lived a life of secrets and always wished he could have chosen a more conventional path. He told me Kanja – who I was already seeing at the school – was helping him too. I could trust Kanja. That's how I ended up here.

Mollel looks at Kanja, who nods. —He came to me a year ago, begging for help. He wanted, as he called it, a *normal* life. I told him there was no such thing. But if he submitted to my treatment, I might at least be able to help him control the demon that kept leading him into trouble. That demon had already got him a criminal record, which meant he couldn't get employment at any state school. Luckily, I knew a principal of an all-girls school who was looking for a new teacher. It would have been the safest place for him – if it hadn't been so close to that damned nightclub.

—Abdelahi knew he was in danger, says Fatuma. —There was one man he spoke about, a man who had a lot of power and influence. We all knew there were stories about young men going missing. Abdelahi thought this man was behind the disappearances, and was using his power to cover them up.

—He wouldn't tell me who it was. He said I was safer not knowing. But I thought I had it figured out. Who was the most powerful man in Dandora? The one who wielded the most influence? And the one who had the perfect way to dispose of anyone he wanted to?

—When Abdelahi disappeared, I knew I had to get away from Nicodemus. It wasn't that easy, of course. He knew who I was and he had eyes everywhere. He knew about me sneaking in and out of the school – the caretaker, Peter, was one of his spies. Through him, Nicodemus found out who my stepfather was. He wanted to have power over both of us, and he found a way to get it.

—Nicodemus promised me he'd let me quit if I did one last job for him. One last client. I was terrified. I didn't really have a choice, so I agreed.

Fatuma shudders, and Mollel notices that it's just like the shudder Ngecha gave.

—So you believe Nicodemus killed Abdelahi?

—At first I did. But then I remembered that Abdelahi called this guy *Duma*. You know, Cheetah?

Mollel can't imagine the heavy-set Nicodemus as a cheetah. Besides, why would he have let Mollel take the body from the tip, when he could easily have left it to be buried and remain undiscovered?

No, it must be someone else. Someone powerful and influential. Those had been Rehoboth's words, too—and his fear had been as genuine as Fatuma's. Besides Kanja, who linked Rehoboth and Abdelahi?

One person. One who had a zeal for finding those guilty of importuning and with the ruthlessness and power to use that as leverage against them.

—I've got to go, says Mollel, rising groggily to his feet.

—No, Mollel, insists Kanja. —You're too weak. Stay. We're on the verge of something, here. We're close to eliminating your demon. We've nearly defeated Doubt. We just need to talk a little more about Lendeva. About Lendeva and Chiku. And Adam.

Mollel grasps the rungs of the ladder. —I've got a job to do, he says.

29

Mollel pushes up the rubber flap and climbs out into the night air. The transition from the heat of the underground room makes him shiver. He breathes deeply without gagging, realising this means he has become accustomed to the dump, and to Dandora. He never thought this would happen. But he is a Dandoran now.

The night is dark and rain soaks his skin, but he can see silver in the sky as he starts to clamber towards the rim of the crater. He stumbles and slips; he needs light, so he pulls out his phone and presses the power button. The light from his screen should be enough to guide him.

It might be the strange drink that Kanja has given him, or the strange effect of the overheated room, but somehow he feels as though he is able to make connections that have previously eluded him. He has access to an understanding which is almost revelatory.

Equally, it could be his detective instincts kicking in. But Mollel is sure that he now knows who the killer is.

The phone screen lights up with two lines of text. *Missed Call: Adam. New Voicemail.*

Adam. Why had Kanja mentioned him? He wonders how much he had divulged while he was semi-delirious. But what had Adam to do with his demons? Crossly, Mollel tries to dismiss the thought. *I was only playing along with Kanja,* he reminds himself. *I found the girl. I'm about to find Abdelahi's killer. I don't have to think about any of that nonsense any more.*

But he can't help it.

By the green-blue light of the screen, he picks his way upwards. As he reaches the top of the rise, he sees light dawning on the horizon. But then he corrects himself: dawn is still an hour away. Just as he had previously mistaken the fires of the tip for sunset, he has now taken artificial light for the coming of day.

Some four miles away, a plume of white rises into the sky. Mollel finds himself almost transfixed, walking towards the column of cold light, drawn to it.

—Hey! Watch where you're going!

He feels movement beneath him, and hears the sound of plastic sheeting being pulled back. He looks down at the source of the voice, which now gives a strangulated cry.

—*Night runner!* it gasps.

Mollel realises that the light of the phone is shining up at his face, and casting a ghastly pall upon him. He quickly flips it over, and recognises the squirming figure at his feet.

—Kitu. It's me, Mollel.

The trash-picker blinks and pulls the plastic around him. He seems to be protecting himself from the rain, but he's also trying to hide something; Mollel knows an attempt at concealment when he sees one.

Mollel leans down and pulls the plastic away. On Kitu's feet are the pair of light-tan brogue loafers he'd been wearing when they first met.

—Not very practical footwear, Kitu.

Mollel can practically hear him cringing. —He didn't need them any more. I didn't want them just to burn.

—So you *did* see the body before it was destroyed. Any chance you saw the person who brought it there, too?

—Please don't take away my shoes, snivels Kitu.

—I'll buy you new shoes. Hell, I'll buy you a full set of clothes. Just tell me who you saw.

Kitu describes him. It's not much of a description – tall, slim and athletic – but it's enough to confirm Mollel's suspicions.

He looks up again at the glow rising from Kasarani Stadium, where Bogani is running.

Bogani. His car, parked a discreet distance away from the club, had been there often enough to get himself noticed. Was he recognised there one night? By Rehoboth, a man he'd taken in for importuning some years before? Perhaps he thought Abdelahi had confided in Fatuma. It would certainly explain why he'd wanted the case shut down once the link to the Electric Chair became clear.

Mollel has to get off this dump. But time is not the priority it once was. Fatuma is alive, and Abdelahi is still dead. Bogani does not know that Mollel is on to him. Besides, there is another thing weighing on his mind. He presses the button on his phone for voicemail.

—Hi, Dad. Sorry, I guess you're busy. I just wanted to let you know I did some more translation of Fatuma's lyrics.

Not needed any more, thinks Mollel, but he keeps listening. He enjoys hearing his son's voice.

—It was pretty tough, but there's some clever stuff in there. You've got to focus on how it all sounds, not how it's written. At the end of the verse about the big man, the one whose secret she knows, there are these lines. *Wewe ni mfale wa huruma. Mwewe wa huduma. Mwuaji. Who? Duma.*

It means . . . hold on . . . *You're the king of mercy.*

King of Mercy, thinks Mollel. Or boss of the City of Mercy. *Mji wa Huduma.*

—Betrayer of the service. Killer. Who? Duma. And *duma*, of course, is Swahili for cheetah.

So, thinks Mollel, Fatuma did suspect it was Bogani, too.

She probably didn't trust Mollel quite enough to tell him. How could she be sure that policemen would not stick together? He hardly blamed her.

—Anyway, Adam's message continues. —I thought this was pretty important, Dad. Just in case it is, I'm going to call the station and see if I can get you there.

With rising disquiet, Mollel calls home. After what seems like an unbearable number of rings, Faith answers. Her voice is thick with sleep.

—No, he's not here. He told me he was helping you with a case. When the police car came to collect him, I assumed you were in it. If he's not with you, Mollel . . . where is he?

30

Kanja's potion, fear, and the swerving of a motorcycle taxi in and out of traffic make a nauseating combination. Mollel's head swims and his stomach churns. He had instructed the *boda boda* driver, whose waist he clings on to desperately, to get him to the stadium as quickly as he could, and not worry about speeding.

Kanja had claimed he could exorcise that demon, Doubt. Instead, it is magnified. Doubt claws at every shred of Mollel's being.

Mollel's world has always been dark and dangerous, but he had always striven to keep his family insulated from the city's deadly side. Why, then, had he crossed the line between the two worlds? Why had he brought Adam into this case?

In part, it had flattered his foolish ego. He had got a kick out of seeing the boy's enthusiasm at helping out. His eagerness to play detective. And in some ways, it had served as validation of all the decisions he'd made over the years. The long days away from home, the night shifts, the overtime. For if the boy got a glimpse into what drove him – police work – perhaps he'd forgive him, when he was a man himself.

Is that why he's put the boy at risk?

For Adam *is* at risk. Grave risk. Bogani could not have known that Mollel was on to him until the boy's phone call. Mollel can piece together the next move. Bogani would have asked

Adam to come and meet him. Not at the police station – too many people around. So he sent a car . . . or did he pick him up himself? And he'd need to find somewhere secure . . .

And then, just as he'd mounted the motorcycle, there had been that other text message. Simply 'The stadium'.

Mollel is hoping that Bogani's intention is to use Adam, somehow, as leverage. Drop the accusation, or else. But it is the nature of that accusation – that Bogani had killed Abdelahi, and possibly other young men – which heightens Mollel's fear. While he has yet to ascertain Bogani's motives, it is clear that he acts on compulsion, but chooses victims who fit a certain profile.

The passage of time is excruciating. Each second is an agony. And Mollel cannot help but compound his mental anguish by revisiting his own guilt. Not only had he dragged Adam into this mess, but he had rejected his call just when the boy needed him most. He had failed him, because he was focused on the case. He could not be a detective and a father. He was barely a father at all.

Finally, they make it to the gate. Mollel crosses the car park – which is empty, save for one of Bogani's fleet of squad cars – and enters the black, forbidding fortress. The concrete walls rise above him, more imposing than in daylight. This is not a time for public events. No spotlights pick out the architecture, no streetlights illuminate the parking lot. As the *boda boda* rides away – he knew there was trouble, and wanted no part of it – the beam of his departing headlight is the last illumination. This is a place of shadows. All the light lies on the other side.

The entrance Mollel and Kiunga had used before is now blocked by a metal gate, which is padlocked on the inside.

Mollel looks around for any other way to gain access. He pulls out his phone, to use it for illumination, but the battery has gone dead.

He feels his way along the wall. His fingers find a thick pipe, and he hears rainwater gushing within. But he seems to recall barbed wire winding around the pipe further up, to stop ticket-less sports fans from gaining access. Bogani has chosen this place well.

The only way Mollel's getting in is through magic or prayer, and he believes in neither. Kanja would attempt to cast some kind of spell. Faith would get down on her knees and ask God to intervene. What about Lendeva? What would he do? Transform into a night runner?

Mollel realises that, in his panic, he is losing his objectivity. If this were any other case, he wouldn't be wondering what other people would do; he'd be attempting to get inside his adversary's head.

Mollel again pictures Bogani getting the message from Adam at the police station. Going round to the flat to pick up the boy. Adam would have become aware that they were not headed for the police station, but Bogani must have told him some convincing lie to account for the destination. Probably he'd told the boy that Mollel was waiting for them there, and Adam was so excited to be participating in this adventure that he wasn't on his guard. No doubt, to put the boy at ease, Bogani would also have mentioned his athletic prowess. Wasn't that why he had chosen this place? Aside from its excellent security, it was the scene of his previous glory.

Mollel begins to feel as though he is getting somewhere. Bogani – so inscrutable – is being laid bare as Mollel strips back the layers of his personality. The immaculate uniform. The gleaming squad cars. Mollel remembers the first time he rode with him, through the slums of *Mji wa Huruma.* The way he turned heads. The way he said: *I like to be seen.*

The stadium, the lights; this is his way of hiding in plain sight. But it is more. It is a defiance of society. *I'll play by the rules,* he seems to be saying. *I'll play by the rules, and I'll play better, and be more successful than anyone else. But I'll break them too.*

The champion runner who never went to the championships. He had chosen the police instead. And yet, here he was at the stadium. And a stadium, however impressive, was nothing without an audience.

Kiunga is a rule-follower, which was why Bogani had trusted him. But Mollel is a fellow rule-breaker, one who shares his secret. Mollel is his audience. And suddenly, he gets it. Bogani has not shut him out. He's inviting him in. But he does not want Mollel in the cheap seats. He's the VIP.

And as Mollel comes around the great curve, up ahead, almost as predicted, he sees a light. There is a wide canopy cover, so that drivers can pull up and their passengers can exit without being bothered by the rain – or the general public. This is the way guests of honour gain access to the arena.

There is a door – not a metal gate this time, but a glazed double door like a storefront. A roller shutter has been raised and light comes from inside; the foyer itself is dark, but in a corridor leading from it a bulb burns. A trail of light.

Mollel pushes one door and it opens. Cautiously, he steps inside. His soaked shoes squelch on the red carpet. He advances towards the corridor. A camera glistens in the corner. He wonders if he is being watched.

The corridor ends at a T-junction, but it's clear which way to take. Mollel follows the light. As he comes to a stairwell, it's the same story: up is illuminated, down is dark.

Mollel is still trying to get into Bogani's head. This is a show, put on for an audience of one. Mollel is sure that Bogani never wanted to be found out, but now he has been, he would want to demonstrate just how clever he is. Taking Adam was the sure way to bring Mollel to him, without the Maasai bringing backup. They both know that that is a risk no father would take.

*

Holding Adam gives Bogani two options. The first – and the best for Mollel – is that Bogani considers this a threat. *Arrest me*, he could be saying, *and your family will pay the price*. The second – and possibly more likely – option is that Bogani fears that both Mollel and Adam know too much, and he has brought them together to deal with them both. And his position, this location, and his ruthlessness suggest that he could do so with impunity.

A dark corridor, now, on an upper level. On one side there is a series of doors, but only one of them is open. Through it streams the white blaze of the stadium floodlights.

Mollel edges through the door frame. The sight ahead makes him gasp. For eyes accustomed to the dark, the bowl of the arena presents a dazzling display. Mollel finds himself in an executive box, open at the front, the three walls framing the empty fourth like a massive picture. The box must be dead centre, because the image before him is perfectly symmetrical – the football field retreating, the track ringing it, the swoop of the stands and the diamond tiara of lights.

In the centre of the field, as though ready for kick-off in a game with no teams, stands a tall figure. And at his feet, a body.

—*Mollel,* says a voice inside his head. —*You made it. I've been waiting for you.*

31

The voice is Bogani's, but it echoes with unnatural power.

—Yes, Sergeant. I see you. How's the view from up there? I wanted you to fully understand the situation, before we spoke.

The figure in the centre circle gives a laconic wave. Though tiny, the shape of a pistol in his hand can clearly be made out.

—Come, join me.

Moving forward, Mollel sees an aisle of steps leading down from the box to the edge of the field. He hops over the low rail and begins to jog down the steps. The figure at Bogani's feet does not move. Mollel reaches ground level, vaults an advertising hoarding, and crosses the track. His feet step on to the neatly trimmed, slippery grass of the football pitch.

—Take off your jacket. Arms out. I don't want any surprises.

This time, as Bogani's words ring out, Mollel understands why they sounded as though they were inside his head. He's talking through the stadium's PA. Closer now, Mollel can see that Bogani has a microphone in his left hand. And from here, though it's small, there's no doubt that it's a gun in his right.

At Mollel's feet, a dozen shadows spin out in every direction. Bogani, likewise, stands in the centre of a star of shadows. Of the figure at his feet, Mollel can make out the curve of a back, soaked shirt clinging to skin, and the nape of the neck and the side of a close-cropped head. Two hands rest behind the back, together, palms out. A glint of silver from cuffs around the wrists. This gives Mollel a little hope: why cuff someone who is already dead? But the closer he gets, the more vulnerable he feels. Bogani wants to put on a show. If he intends to kill, he will want Mollel to see fear in the victim's face, before he dispatches them both.

—I guess I don't need this any more, says Bogani, and he flicks a switch on the microphone and lets it drop to the ground. His voice is calm, level, normal. Mollel reaches the central circle.

—That's far enough.

Games, thinks Mollel. Bogani has planned this out like a sport. And this is what it is to him, even the killing. Sport.

—Well? asks Mollel. —I'm here. This is what you wanted, isn't it?

—Bogani laughs. Now he is close, Mollel can see his chest rising and falling as he takes deep breaths. He is psyched up. His eyes glint, weighing up his adversary. Mollel does not wish to play this game.

—Want, Mollel? I didn't *want* any of this. If I did what I wanted, I'd have medalled in Tokyo, gone on to the Olympics and scored myself a nice sponsorship. After retirement, maybe moved to the States, taken up a cushy coaching job somewhere sunny . . .

He holds his hands out in the silver rain. The gun points, for a moment, at Mollel, then at the prone figure.

—No, it's not about what we want. I don't need to tell you that, do I, Mollel? It's about duty.

Mollel knows Bogani wants to talk to him. He has the feeling that this is a long-held, often-rehearsed speech he's about to hear. Mollel could well be the first person it's been addressed to – unless it was the last thing Abdelahi and the other victims heard.

Even so, Bogani's first words surprise him.

—I'm not gay, you know, Mollel. I need you to know that.

Despite the danger that surrounds him, Mollel is amazed. Bogani stands virtually on the edge of admitting murder – and certainly abduction and assault – and yet his prime concern is establishing his heterosexuality. No wonder the likes of Abdelahi have to hide; their lives are worthless. Killing them is a lesser crime than *being* them.

—You've seen everything this city has to offer, Mollel. You know the toll it takes. But as I recall, you started in traffic. Nice gig, traffic. Know where I began? Vice. I was naive. I only really knew school, and running. I wanted to be a policeman because I wanted to make the world a better place.

—I know this job is seen as a path to enrichment. But that wasn't my goal. I wanted to do good, and I wanted to do it better than anyone else. That competitive streak, you see. Instead of chasing medals, I decided to chase down criminals. I figured that at least my athletic prowess would come in handy, somehow. And it did. Just not in the way I expected.

—I was flattered to be approached by the vice squad. It's not common for a newly qualified cadet to be actively sought out. But they said I was exactly what they needed. Someone young, and very fit.

—They didn't call me the Cheetah any more. They called me the Chicken. *Kuku*. Ever tie a chicken to a stake, Mollel, to try to catch a jackal? Well, that was the idea. They sent me in to the hangouts, the meet-ups, the pick-up joints. They dressed me up nice and taught me to make eyes and spot the signs and as soon as the signal was sent – the words were spoken, the hand put on my arm, the proposition made – on went the cuffs. Snap! Good work, *Kuku*.

—It was addictive. I enjoyed being good at my job. And I enjoyed feeling wanted, even if the people who wanted me made my flesh crawl. It was a performance. A competition. When you're on the track, you don't wonder who's watching. You just want to win.

—You know the worst thing about being a captain, Mollel? Don't worry. You'll never have to deal with it. The worst thing is that it gets you off the streets. You're not nabbing bad guys any more, you're pushing paper. The thrill of the chase is replaced by the slow slog of careerism. I was never a long-distance guy, Mollel. I got bored.

—I remembered my days as *Kuku*. I was older now, a little heavier. It didn't seem to matter. If anything, I was more successful. Confidence can be very attractive. And I was very sure of who I was.

He looks down. The body at his feet stirs slightly, and lets out a low groan. Mollel's heart leaps. He tries not to show that he's noticed. He is in no rush for Bogani to tire of his story and move on.

—I never intended to run them in. Far too much paperwork. Besides, how would it look? A captain freelancing as a *Kuku* on his nights off? People would make assumptions. They would draw the wrong conclusion. I couldn't take that risk. But I didn't set out wanting to kill them, either. I figured I'd just give them a scare. Whip out the cuffs, drag them to the car. Maybe drive them around a bit before letting them go. It wasn't really my fault the first one resisted so much. If only he'd behaved. I really can't be held responsible.

—Then there were a few more. It was no loss, really. No one missed them. I was cleaning up the city. But one night, at the Electric Chair, I saw Abdelahi. He recognised me. I'd arrested him during my Vice Squad days. You know that, Mollel. You'll have found that out by now. Any good detective would. I'd have taken him there and then, but there were too many people around. I had to rely on him not telling anyone – and that was the good thing about these guys. They didn't really have anyone to tell, apart from each other.

And Fatuma, thinks Mollel.

—I picked him up some time later. I found out where he was staying, visited him at his hostel. I had to play the *Kuku* card quite strongly, to get him to let his guard down and come with me. I had to make him trust me so he wouldn't make a scene. It was all part of the game. I was acting. I'm not gay, Mollel.

Of course not, thinks Mollel, remembering the sheets. If he ever gets out of here, there's the evidence he needs.

—Abdelahi knew, so I had to get rid of him. He was another loner. No one mourned him. Except, I discovered, one person. It was Kiunga who told me. He's a good detective, your protégé. Perhaps not as canny as you are, Mollel, but he follows orders. He knows his duty. He called me as soon as your interview was over.

Bogani raises his foot and places it against the shoulder of the figure on the ground. He gives it a solid push, and the person rolls over. It is not Adam. It is Rehoboth. His eyes roll in reaction to the light, but he is barely conscious. There is a large, raised bruise on his temple: a classic night-stick blow.

Mollel looks around him in sudden, disorienting panic. This empty stadium might as well have sixty thousand people in it, for all his chances of spotting Adam. Bogani chuckles. —Oh, he's here, Mollel. I want both of you to see this. I want you to see that I take no pleasure in it. It's purely necessary.

Yet he can't help a dart of his eyes at this – for all his protestations, Bogani is relishing every moment. Mollel follows his eyes to the side of the track. There, in the home team dugout. Is that the shape of a person? As though sensing Mollel's gaze, the shape seems to move. It *is* a person. This time, Mollel knows it is Adam. He's not sure *how* he knows—but he knows.

*

Rehoboth starts to mutter: —Please, please . . .

Bogani tuts and lowers the pistol so it is pointing at Rehoboth's head. —On your marks . . .

Mollel can't make it from where he is, on the line, to tackle Bogani before he pulls the trigger. He is agonisingly close – but not close enough. Bogani has planned this down to the last detail.

—Get set . . .

Suddenly there is a crackle of static and an explosion of sound. A voice echoes out.

—Captain Bogani. We have Tactical Support in the stadium. There are four snipers with you in their sights right now. Drop the weapon.

Bogani smiles. —Sergeant Kiunga, he shouts. —So the split I tried to generate between you and Mollel didn't work out. I thought Mollel would be too proud to call you.

The tape. Mollel should have known he'd not found it by accident. Bogani had ensured he saw the label, left it there where Mollel could easily palm it.

—Such loyalty! mocks Bogani. —But I'm afraid it amounts to very little. You see, I am the divisional commander for Tactical Support.

He puts his left hand in his pocket and pulls out his phone. —And they go nowhere without calling me first.

Just then, two things happen. His phone rings. And the lights go out.

Mollel leaps forward. He takes the ten yards in three bounds, throws himself at the captain, and falls with him hard onto the hard, cold ground.

There is a flash, and a bang.

32

—*Bado kufa,* Mollel?

Mollel's smiles turns into a grimace as he heaves himself up in bed.

—No, Janet. Not dead yet.

—Steady.

She rushes to his bedside and helps him settle, putting a cushion behind his back.

—Is it painful to talk? she asks.

—Yes. But that's how you know I must have something worth saying.

So he talks and she nods, and writes notes, and occasionally glances at her phone, which is counting the minutes and seconds as it records.

He talks about a city where councillors poison their constituents and drown them in rubbish because that buys them a house in the suburbs. Where trash-pickers steal a dead man's shoes while their overlords grow rich. A city where young men can be murdered because society hates them, and deems their lives worthless. And where the police service, to save face, is liable to cover up those murders, and quietly shuffle the senior captain who committed them away to some high-security mental facility. Unless a good journalist gets hold of the story.

When he's done, Janet turns off the recording, and puts down her notepad.

What about Kiunga, Mollel? I watched your face while you were watching that tape of him. You looked like your heart was breaking.

Mollel shrugs. —Bogani knew what he was doing. He meant for me to find that tape. He thought that if I didn't have Kiunga to rely on, I'd give up. It was hurtful hearing Kiunga say those things. But they were true. Unreliable, unpredictable, erratic: I can't deny it. Besides, it was very old. Did you see how slim Kiunga was? He's put on a lot of weight since then. We'd only been working together a few days. Kiunga didn't know whether he could trust me. I hardly trusted myself.

All the same, thinks Mollel, he was glad Kiunga had taken his call when he phoned him from the top of Dandora tip that morning.

—Anyway, he's making amends now. I've got him out, tying up a few loose ends for me.

—Like what?

—I reckon he owes Rehoboth a favour. So I've got Kiunga setting up a meeting between him and a talented young female rapper. With his contacts, I'm sure Rehoboth can make Dora a star. And Dora's promised to take Fatuma under her wing, too. Fatuma doesn't want to move back home, that's understandable. But she will keep an eye on her sister, Maryam, and makes sure her stepfather treats her well.

—And Nicodemus?

Mollel sighs. —Some things are too big for one detective to solve. Maybe Kanja can work his magic.

There had been a moment, Mollel thinks, when he had almost believed in that magic. He'd come close to thinking that Kanja's magic had discovered something – helped him discover something about himself. Something painful. And in confronting that pain, he might, at least, have slain that demon: doubt.

Faces flash before him. His wife, Chiku. Lendeva. His son, Adam.

Kiunga had rescued him from the dugout. He'd gone down there from the control room straight after calling Bogani's phone, to distract him, and killing the lights. The boy's wrists were chafed from where he'd been cuffed to the seat, but otherwise he was fine. He seemed undamaged by his experience. If anything, he was excited.

—I know what I want to be when I grow up, Dad, he'd said, when Mollel came round after having the bullet extracted. —I want to be a policeman.

Mollel would have laughed, but laughing hurts.

blog and newsletter